Bend for Me

Also by Jessica Yeh

Something Tragic

Bend for Me

Jessica Yeh

Desert Palm Press

Bend for Me

by Jessica Yeh

© 2019 Jessica Yeh

ISBN (trade): 9781948327312
ISBN (epub): 9781948327329
ISBN (pdf): 9781948327336

For permission requests, write to the publisher at lee@desertpalmpress.com or "Attention: Permissions Coordinator," at

Desert Palm Press
1961 Main Street, Suite 220
Watsonville, California 95076
www.desertpalmpress.com

Editor: Nat Burns

Printed in the United States of America
First Edition June 2019

Acknowledgement

I want to thank all of my readers and everyone who encouraged me to continue writing after I completed my debut novel. I am so grateful for the positive feedback and support. I never would have expected it. I always thought I was destined to be a "one-and-done" author. I'm incredibly humbled and flattered by all of the kind words I've received. I hope this next novel continues to bring a smile and a laugh to anyone who takes the to turn each page.

Thank you to Nat and Lee at Desert Palm Press for all of their work and dedication to making this book the best it can be.

And a special shout out to my loved ones, who bring me so much happiness and love on a daily basis. You know who you are.

Chapter One

EARLY ON SATURDAY, AVERY was lounging in her apartment, wearing a tattered, paint-stained tee with cheesy chip dust sprinkled across it. A pair of loose basketball shorts hung from her waist, shorts that once belonged to a random hook up whose name she couldn't remember. Orange fingers crinkled the bag as she snacked, waiting for her best friend and roommate, Emma, to get dressed.

"I can't believe you're making me do this," Avery grumbled through her final handful of chips. She tossed the bag aside and untucked herself from the couch. A few crumbs fell onto the upholstery and she looked in the direction of Emma's bedroom before brushing them onto the floor.

"I saw that. You're vacuuming when we get back," Emma called out.

Avery looked down the empty hallway. *How did she even?*

The redhead appeared from the shadows, propping herself against the wall to slip on a pair of sneakers. "Come on, we're gonna be late."

Avery grunted, tying her own shoes. "Nobody sane willingly gets up this early to exert themselves."

"Danny and I do."

Avery expelled a laugh as she grabbed her snapback from the coffee table, flipping her hair before placing it on her head. "Yeah, maybe for morning sex."

Emma rolled her eyes as she swiped the keys from the counter. "Or maybe for exercise, which you could use some of, as well."

"Calling me fat, eh?"

Emma sent her a toothy grin. "Nah, just lazy."

Avery shrugged with a chuckle. "All right, I guess that's fair."

They locked the door behind them before taking the stairs down to Emma's car. Emma had a thing against elevators and Avery hated it. She especially hated it before seven in the morning.

"Ugh," Avery shielded her eyes with the lid of her hat. "It's so bright."

Emma snorted as she gave Avery a shove in the direction of the car. Avery flopped into the front seat, not bothering to buckle her seatbelt as the engine revved to life. "So, why can't Danny go with you again? I'm not the most flexible person."

"Oh, don't I know it." The corner of Emma's lips quirked to the side.

"Fuck off," Avery shot back.

"Always so grumpy. I don't know how I tolerate you."

"Because I'm a goddamned angel. And I let you drag me to a seven-a.m. yoga class with a killer hangover. I should be getting serious brownie points for this."

Emma laughed. Her eyes still keyed on the road. "One, goddamned angel is an oxymoron, *moron*. Two, you just admitted you're losing your touch. What happened to going all night, huh, party girl? And three, you know you're willing to go just so you can see girls in yoga pants."

"Well, I definitely am a butt kinda gal."

"You're gross."

"Love you, too, Em!"

***

Iris Yoga Studio. The smell reminded Avery of a cheap discount store air freshener — the kind with an obnoxious name like Oceanside Summer or Breezy Escape. An olive-skinned woman with deep green eyes and dark wavy hair stood at the front of the room. Avery quickly zeroed in on the skimpy sports bra that accentuated a chest resting just above a tan, taut stomach. The floral leggings she wore were practically painted onto her skin.

"Nice of you to join us, Emma." The woman spoke with confidence, but her voice was gentle. The combination sent a jolt down Avery's spine.

"Sorry I'm a little late. Danny's out of town visiting his family this weekend so I brought a friend."

The instructor nodded. "And you are?"

Avery stood dumbstruck, eyes still raking across the slender frame, long legs, and toned arms.

"Ow!" She rubbed at her ribs, resisting the urge to attack Emma with a jab of her own in retaliation. "Oh, umm, I'm uhh..."

Emma raised a brow in amusement, reveling in the falter of Avery's typical nonchalant, player façade. "Miss Eloquent here is Avery."

The instructor's eyes twinkled in greeting. "Welcome, Avery. I'm Kadence. Have a seat, ladies."

Avery hesitated under the weight of judgmental eyes as they moved to the pair of open mats at the front of the room. She ran her palms across her T-shirt and baggy shorts. They probably reeked of beer and smoke. Avoiding eye contact with the rest of the class, she took her snapback off, tying her hair into a sloppy bun before wilting onto the cushiony material.

"Let's start with some sun salutations, shall we? Open your chest. Feel your spine elongate. Imagine a string tugging at your head while your tailbone sinks into the earth." As Kadence narrated, the rest of the room hung onto her every word.

How does anyone believe this mumbo jumbo?

"Breathe in," Kadence instructed. As though sensing her resistance, she hooked her gaze on Avery, who slammed her eyes shut. "Breathe out."

The room echoed with the sound of deep breaths. After a beat, Avery's eyes popped open and she observed the way Kadence's thick lashes cast shadows along the slopes of her cheek bones. *Honestly, she's not too bad looking. If only she wasn't so much of a yogi.* Shaking the thought, she released an abrupt breath through her nostrils.

"Again." The corner of Kadence's mouth twitched upward, her voice soft and smooth. "Let's try to breathe a little slower this time."

Emma snickered next to her. The comment was obviously directed at Avery. Avery squeezed her eyes shut. A water machine trickled in the corner, a flute spewed random notes on a backtrack disk, and the girl sitting behind her had a stuffy nose that whistled every time she exhaled. Instead of feeling calm, Avery felt her senses being overstimulated.

"Block out the world," Kadence repeated. "Let your chest inflate. Fill with clarity. Exhale anxiety."

Avery tried to be serious. Really, she did. But God, did this sound like a load of bull! Disregarding the exercise, Avery resorted to observing the instructor's breathing patterns, the tight fabric on her chest rising and falling.

"In. Out. In. Out." Kadence repeated the mantra. Her eyes fluttered open, meeting Avery's.

Busted.

Avery diverted her glance to the floor, cheeks tinted pink with the embarrassment.

"Good, class. I can tell that some of you were very focused."

Har. Har. Very cute.

"Now allow yourself to come back to the sound of my voice. Listen to your surroundings. Feel your consciousness shift." Kadence's eyes remained trained on Avery as the room resurrected. "Let's move to a simple stretch. Everyone lay on your stomachs. For the next movement, watch me first. I'll walk you through it, then you can modify as needed. Our first move will be the cobra. Keep your feet together, ankles touching. Press your palms into the mat and lift your upper body to the sky." Kadence arched as she dictated the movements. "You should feel a nice stretch in your stomach, especially your abdomen, and lower back. From here you have two options."

She scanned the room as her eyes settled on Avery. "The first is the locust. When you're ready, slowly reach your arms back and raise your legs. You should feel a tightness in your rear. This will help strengthen and tone your butt."

Avery couldn't help but smile, watching the teacher's muscles tense. Emma coughed a "perv" in her direction, but Avery feigned an innocent smile. After all, she was simply being a *very focused* student.

"If you'd like to challenge your flexibility instead

of strength, grab your ankles like this." Kadence curved her spine as her long, slender fingers wrapped around thin ankles, chest now fully on display. Avery's eyes widened.

Don't stare.

"If you want, you can even rock a little." Kadence demonstrated the movement and with every tilt, Avery received a full view down her bra.

Don't fucking stare.

"Okay." Kadence slowly released her limbs. "Let's all get into cobra pose and I'll come around and help you get into your next position."

"How are you doing, Avery? Feeling relaxed?" Kadence asked, transitioning from Emma to Avery.

More like dying.

Avery's arms buckled at the sultry whisper of her name.

"Looks like you're a little too relaxed." The teasing instructor lowered herself to sit cross-legged in front of the struggling klutz. She placed her hands atop Avery's ribcage, hoisting her into place. Avery felt her skin sear through her T-shirt.

"There you go. Now, locust or bow?" Kadence was so close that Avery saw the slightest ring of brown around her pupils. The honey coloring sprouted into her iris like evergreen in a forest.

"Sorry, what?" Avery stammered.

"The pose." Emerald eyes sparkled. "What would you like to do?"

Besides you?

"Uhh...bow?"

Kadence let her hands graze Avery's shoulders so she could fall forward, pulling her arms behind her. Kadence leaned in and Avery found herself at eye level with her chest.

Yep. Definitely dying.

"You're doing great. Just relax." Kadence directed Avery's hands to grasp around her ankles. "Nice job. Only hold that pose for as long as you're comfortable."

Once she seemed satisfied with Avery's position, she proceeded to the next student. Within seconds, Avery could no longer hold on. She released her grip, limbs colliding with the mat.

Damn it.

"Very smooth." Emma giggled, rocking in her bowed position.

Kadence's head shot up, craning her neck away from the student she was working with. "Everything all right?"

"Uhh, yeah. Just a little more intense than I thought it'd be." Avery sat up, legs splayed out in defeat.

"You're good at this," Emma taunted. "Very graceful."

"I hate this."

"Ya know, I don't think you do." Emma grinned, closing her eyes again, inhaling deeply. "Just wait until we do downward dog."

Avery rolled her eyes, fidgeting as she waited for the rest of the room to finish the position.

***

"How did you like your first class, Avery?" Kadence asked when the class had ended. After locking up, she and the roommates walked toward the parking lot.

Avery adjusted her snapback to the side with a

rough tug. "I thought yoga was supposed to relax you."

"It does. It just takes a while to get comfortable," Kadence said.

"Oh, trust me, Avery gets comfortable real quick," Emma chimed in.

Avery glared.

"Maybe next time you'll feel differently."

Next time?

Avery shuddered. "There might not be a next time."

Kadence frowned. "Shame. But I respect your decision. It's not for everybody. Thank you for giving it a try though. It was nice meeting you."

"Yeah, definitely." *Why is my voice so high?*

"Emma?" Kadence redirected her attention. "Lunch with Danny and Melody when he gets back?"

"Absolutely. And don't forget about Friday."

"Can't wait! Text me." Kadence nodded with a final wave, climbing into her car.

"Earth to Avery. Come back to me, Avery."

Avery jostled her head, swatting at the snapping fingers in front of her face.

"Wow. You're into her, aren't you?"

Avery scoffed. "No way. She's straight. And probably eats granola for every meal. I bet she grows her own fruit in a small box garden and has flowers placed all around her apartment, too."

Emma shook her head. "Your imagination is wild. That's just how she is in class. Kadence is pretty cool. Come to the party and you'll see."

"I wasn't invited."

Avery thought the freckles on Emma's face would fall along with her jaw. "Excuse me? When has that ever stopped you from crashing a party?"

"Touché." Avery wiggled her brows, pointing a finger gun at her roommate.

"Okay, slow down there, killer. You're losing your cool factor."

"Am not." Avery huffed as she collapsed into the passenger seat. "I'm just tired and dehydrated."

"Yeah. Your thirst was unreal. Like, you weren't just a little parched. You were in a fucking desert and Kadence was an oasis."

"Shut up."

"Suck it up." Emma nudged her in the ribs.

"Stop doing that!"

"Fine. But you do have some sucking to do — the vacuuming kind. Oh, yeah, don't think I've forgotten."

Avery let her head fall into her hands with a groan.

Chapter Two

THE WEEK FLEW BY without Avery noticing. She was swamped with completing an exhibit for her gallery showcase. Friday, she was sprawled out in the living room, tubes of paint littering the coffee table. Just as Avery swiped hair from her eyes, there was a knock at the door.

"Get that, will you?" Emma shouted from down the hall.

She opened the door to find Kadence, pink lips turned up in a smile.

"Hello, Avery. Nice to see you again."

Avery scanned Kadence, who was dressed in dark, skintight jeans. A red tank top sat under her leather jacket while her dark, silky hair cascaded on her shoulder. The tresses rested delicately on her collarbone and the entire combination rendered her unrecognizable from the woman in the yoga studio. Except her eyes. Those were pretty hard to forget.

"Uhh. Hi." Avery stood in the doorway with her hand on the doorknob, jaw agape.

"Would it be cool if I maybe came in?"

"Oh, yeah, of course. Being inside is good, ya know? Because of weather and stuff."

Wow. Real smooth, Avery.

"Emma!" Avery called over her shoulder. "Kadence's here."

Jessica Yeh

Her roommate hopped through the hall, one heel on, while she tried to hook an earring through her earlobe. "Oh, hey!"

"I brought stuff to pregame if you want." Kadence held up two brown paper bags.

"You're my hero. Go ahead and start. I'll be ready in a sec," Emma replied before scurrying off.

Kadence turned her attention to Avery. "Are you coming to the party with us?"

Avery rubbed at the back of her neck. "If that's okay." *No. Don't ask. Assert yourself!*

"Of course." Kadence grinned. "We have enough mutual friends, I would suspect. Are you gonna get ready as well?" She eyed Avery's paint-stained shirt.

Okay. Game on, you can do this. "Why? You don't like the look?" Avery answered, quirking a brow as she smoothed her hands along her curves.

Kadence shook her head. "The look is great. The paint on your face is a bit distracting though." She reached out a hand, thumb caressing Avery's cheekbone.

Shit. Fuck. Abort! "I, umm. I was kidding." Avery stumbled, backing away from the warm fingertip. "I'm going to change. Cups and shot glasses are in the cabinet, furthest one from the left. Help yourself. Be right back." She tried her best to exit gracefully, rounding the corner straight into Emma's room.

"You didn't tell me she was coming *now*," Avery hissed, closing the door behind her. "I look a mess."

"You're always a mess," Emma pointed out. "Besides, you said you weren't into her. What does it matter? You've definitely looked worse."

"Gee, thanks."

"My pleasure," Emma quipped with a grin.

"Why do I live with you again?"

"Because no one else would tolerate your bullshit."

Avery groaned, raking a hand through her hair only to get fingers caught in the tangled locks. "Ugh. You're right. I am a mess." After struggling to finally free the digits, she flopped onto the bed with a grunt.

"Come on." Emma poked her in the stomach. "Relax, Avery." She teased her, using the same breathy tone as Kadence had done. "Breathe in. Breathe out."

"I literally hate you." Avery collected the pillow by her side, giving her friend a good whack with it.

"I adore you, too." Emma brushed her off with a wave of her hand. "Now, pull yourself together. Either help me finish my makeup before Danny gets here or go keep Kadence company."

"Neither of these options sound appealing."

"Too bad. Kadence texted me the other day. Said she thought you were pretty cute."

Avery was intrigued. "Really? What did she say?"

Emma burst out laughing. "You *are* thirsty. I thought you said you didn't care."

"I mean, I...I don't." *You could at least try to sound convincing, Avery.*

"Yeah. Clearly."

Avery flipped her off as she exited toward the bathroom.

"Love you, too, darling!"

***

In the bathroom, Avery scrubbed her face with vigor, picking some dried pieces of paint from her hair. She gazed at her reflection with a sigh. She couldn't let herself get this way. Not again. It was too risky. Her hands gripped the edge of the sink until her knuckles turned white. *Breathe.*

She fumbled to her room, stepping across piles of laundry, empty paint bottles, and a random assortment of brushes. She desperately needed to clean. The gallery opening had occupied too much of her time. Throwing open the closet door, she tossed an array of shirts on the bed. Nothing seemed nice enough to wear. She let out a dramatic groan.

"You okay?" Kadence inquired from the kitchen.

"Never better," Avery replied, just in time to trip on her skateboard, head colliding with the wall. *Damn it.*

"Avery?" She heard the scraping of a barstool. The next thing she knew, Kadence was hovering above her. "Are you all right?"

"Yeah, uh, just couldn't figure out which shirt to wear."

Kadence laughed. "Well, no need to throw a fit about it." She maneuvered around the clutter, picking up a baby blue button-up. "This one. It'll look great on you."

"Oh, umm, thanks."

"No problem." Kadence's tongue wet her lips.

The moment was cut short by a shrill scream from Emma. "Danny's here. Let's drink."

"We probably shouldn't keep her waiting."

"You're probably right."

"Wait! I almost forgot. Your signature accessory." Without breaking eye contact, Kadence grabbed Avery's snapback off the hook by the door and placed it atop her blonde hair. "There. Now you're ready."

"Oh, uhh, thank you."

"It was definitely my pleasure." Kadence winked before sauntering off to join the pregame.

***

By the time they set off for the party, Emma and Danny were feeling a nice buzz. Kadence, on the other hand, was as composed as ever. Even while downing shots, her face had remained impassive, not even flinching when the one hundred fifty proof slid down her throat.

They climbed into Avery's car. On any other day, it would have had at least one old burrito wrapper and some crumpled up receipts in it. But with the gallery show occupying most of her time, she hadn't had a chance to trash it.

"Jayce is meeting us there," Danny mentioned before climbing into the backseat with Emma. Jayce was Danny's roommate and Emma's older brother. "Hopefully, he won't notice how wasted his sister is going to get, if not already there."

On cue, Emma giggled into his chest, taking his shirt between her teeth as she gnawed the fabric. Danny laughed, batting her away as he reached to buckle her seatbelt. "Anyway, he might be too distracted to notice."

They all knew what, or rather who, he was referring to. Lola and Jayce had a totally non-committal-not-together-totally-platonic relationship. At least, that's what they both insisted upon, while unable to keep their hands off one another.

Avery started the engine and pulled out of the parking lot.

Kadence raised a brow. "Shouldn't you put your

seatbelt on?"

Avery shrugged, continuing to put the car in reverse. "Nah. Wrinkles my shirt."

Kadence hardened her stare. "Let me rephrase that. Put your seatbelt on."

Taken aback by the gritting of Kadence's teeth, Avery obliged. The moment it clicked into place, Kadence relaxed again, eyes friendly and welcoming.

"Anyway." Avery tried not to think about the strange occurrence. "Who's DD tonight?"

"I'll do it," Kadence volunteered.

"What? No. I meant between Emma and me. You should drink."

"I can handle my liquor," Kadence assured her. "You'd be surprised."

"That so?"

"Kadence will be fine," Danny said. "I'd take her word for it if I were you."

"Kadence is quite the party animal," Emma added with a nod.

"I don't believe that for a second," Avery said.

Kadence grinned, cocking a single brow.

Avery decided to give in. "All right fine. You're DD on the way back."

***

"I'm sorry, what floor?" Avery gasped when they arrived at the host, Melody's, apartment complex.

"Seven." Kadence laughed. "My sister lives on the seventh floor."

"I'm going to die."

"Come on, lazy. It won't be that bad." Emma linked her arms through Avery's and Danny's as they followed Kadence up the stairs.

Avery took a moment to appreciate the toned legs up ahead. *Yeah, maybe not that bad.*

The party was in full swing when they arrived. Avery recognized Jayce making out with Lola on the couch. She wasn't that well acquainted with Emma's workout buddies, but at least a handful of guests were part of their overlapping circle of friends. Avery was surprised she hadn't met Kadence earlier. After all, she and Emma went out almost every weekend.

"Hey!" A woman with a sharp stare and even sharper cheekbones approached them, a beer cradled in the crook of her arm. Definitely the sister, Avery noted.

Better turn on the charm. "Hi, you must be Melody. I'm Avery, Emma's roommate."

Melody studied her. "Yeah. I've heard stories about you."

"Oh, have you?"

She didn't take the bait. "Yeah, so don't fuck anything up. And you." Melody pointed a finger at Kadence. "Be careful."

"I will." Kadence rolled her eyes, brushing Melody's finger from under her nose.

Avery shuffled her shoes as the two held one another's stare. Finally, the older sibling relented, leaving with Emma and Danny. *Well, that was beyond uncomfortable.*

"Hey, I'm gonna get a drink. Want one?"

Avery blinked. "Shouldn't you be drinking water?"

"You just worry about yourself." Kadence patted Avery's arm. "I'm a big girl. I can handle myself."

"Oh, really?"

"Be my partner?"

Avery choked on her own spit. *Is she U-Hauling?*

"What?"

"Drinks. One for one, all night?"

Oh! Duh. Calm down, Avery. "Deal."

***

Avery followed swaying hips into the kitchen where they were handed a beer upon arrival.

"Avery!" The voice belonged to Jayce, who beckoned her with a wave.

Avery was always amazed at how both Emma and Jayce had the same burning hair, angled chin, and fair complexion sprinkled with freckles. "Come with?" she asked. Kadence nodded, following her.

"Lola refuses to be on my team for pong. I think you should help me teach her a lesson."

Lola hid a smile behind her hand before turning to Kadence. "What's your name?"

"Kadence."

"All right, Kadence. You're on my team." Lola pulled her by the wrist, and despite knowing the situation with Jayce, Avery felt a tingling in her gut. Giving a hard yank to her hat, she smothered it.

"You're going down," Lola teased, readying the first ball.

"This early in the night?" Avery said. "That's rather forward of you." She was rewarded with Jayce's high five and a flip of the bird from Lola.

"All right, Jayce. You're sleeping on the couch when we get back."

Jayce's face fell. "Aww, babe! Come on. Avery's the one who said it."

"Yeah, well, Avery's an ass." Lola laughed. "Beloved ass, but still an ass."

"That's fair." Avery nodded. "Sorry, Jay."

"Fine but what if we win? Can I sleep in bed with you?" Jayce bargained as he pouted in Lola's direction.

His not-so-girlfriend bit her lip, deliberating. "Fine."

"What about me," Avery teased. "Do I get to join you?" She wiggled her eyebrows suggestively.

"If you win," Kadence cut in. "I'll take a body shot off you."

"Ya know, that sounds more like a reward for you than it does for me. Drink for drink." Avery reminded her with a smug grin plastered to her face.

"Never said I wouldn't return the favor."

"Oh, it's so on."

***

In the end Kadence beat her out by three whole cups.

"Body shots, as promised." The raven-haired woman grinned, taking Avery by the hand and into the kitchen. She rifled through cabinets until she found what she was looking for. With a confident smile, Kadence shook the bottle at Avery.

"Shall we?" She grabbed a few pre-sliced limes from the fridge, already knowing where they were. It was like she had planned this. And, as though there was a flashing neon sign, a hoard of people filed into the kitchen just as Kadence handed Avery the salt.

"Tequila shots!" The crowd hooted.

Avery quirked a brow at Kadence in suspicion.

"I may have texted some people while you were

busy losing at beer pong." Pink lips quirked up in amusement.

"You little—" The words died in her mouth when Kadence shrugged off her jacket and pulled her shirt off, revealing a black lacy bra.

"Well? Crowd's waiting."

Avery held the salt, baffled. "W-where should I...?"

"Wherever you want it," Kadence said with a devilish grin on her face. She placed a lime in her mouth and laid back on the counter.

She's doing this on purpose.

Avery traced the trail along her collarbone, preparing herself. She had a thing for nice collarbones, probably from the years of drawing anatomy for her art classes. And as much as she hated to admit it, Kadence's were divine. The woman cocked a brow, teasing Avery to swoop in. Avery let her tongue glide on olive skin. Despite the sheer amount of salt, Kadence's skin tasted sweet and Avery's nostrils flooded with the smell of her dizzying perfume. She downed the shot, bending to take the lime from Kadence's mouth. Avery felt herself burning as teeth scraped against her own plump lips. Her eardrums pounded as the crowd erupted with cheers and a 'Get it, Bennett.'

Kadence beamed, propping herself on her elbows before taking the shot glass from Avery's now sweating hand. "I believe I owe you something. Let's get it on, *Bennett,*" she said teasingly, following the whistles of the crowd.

Avery unfastened the top few buttons of her shirt, allowing it to hang off her shoulders. As she mounted the counter, Kadence took Avery's hat from her head, placing the accessory atop her own dark curls.

"Open." There was a glimmer in Kadence's eye as she placed the lime in Avery's mouth. Her fingers traced down her stomach, unbuttoning the shirt even farther until she was completely exposed. Kadence poured a light trail of salt along her stomach and between the valley of her breasts.

Holy. Shit.

The sultry vixen gave a wink before laying a flat tongue against simmering skin, taking her delicious time as she went. Glowing green eyes never broke their hold until the last second when Kadence threw her head back, swallowing the tequila. She latched her lips to the lime and Avery had to hold back a moan as the woman bit down, juice trailing into her own mouth. She pulled away with a confident smile and took a bow. "And that, ladies and gentlemen, is how it's done."

The spectators exploded into chaos.

"Thanks! I'll be here all night," Kadence said.

Dazed, Avery sat up to find multiple eyes glued to the two of them. In a corner, she saw Emma and Danny watching the scene pan out with a scowling Melody by their side. She hastily buttoned her shirt, before hopping off the counter and moving toward her roommate.

"Emma, I need her number. *Now*," Avery demanded, laughing and trying to reach for her roommate's phone. Emma pulled it away, spinning on her heels as she cackled.

When Avery turned, Kadence had vanished and Jayce was lying on the counter with salt on his abs, Lola staring hungrily at him.

***

By the middle of the night, Avery was starting to feel the effects of the alcohol. She wondered how Kadence managed to remain so composed. Deciding to call it a night, she headed toward the kitchen. It was probably best to sober up. To her surprise, she found Kadence pouring another drink, passing another to Avery.

"Bottoms up."

Before she could retort, an engineer named Sam slid between them, eyes drooping as he offered Kadence a sloppy grin. "Hello there, Avery, Avery's friend. I don't think we've met before. What's your name?" He placed an arm on the wall beside Kadence's head, swaying into her personal space. Knowing the drunkard was harmless, Avery let him continue.

"I'm Kadence."

"Well, Kadence," Sam slurred. "I just wanted to say that you are absolutely stunning. Wouldn't you agree, Avery?"

"Oh, yeah. Absolutely. Of course." Avery laughed at her inebriated friend.

"Miss Kadence," Sam said. "Would you allow me the honor of having your number? I would love to meet you for a drink some time."

Avery had to hand it to him. Sam was even more shameless than she was about flirting with a pretty girl.

"I think I'll have to pass. Thank you, though."

Sam shrugged as he bowed out, holding his drink up in salute before blowing a kiss. Kadence laughed, catching the imaginary gesture in her hand.

"What?" Avery said when he departed. "A stunning lady like you isn't into intoxicated boys? Sam's harmless, I promise."

"A lady like me is not into boys in general."

Kadence shrugged as if she hadn't just come out to a complete stranger.

Holy shit. She isn't straight?

"Is that a problem?"

For me, yes. "Not at all! I just didn't peg you as…"

Kadence raised a brow in challenge.

"Appearances can be deceiving."

"Yeah, I think I'm starting to realize that."

Suddenly the thudding of bass music vibrated in Avery's chest. She held out her hand. "Can you dance?"

"I think I can manage."

***

Kadence could *definitely* manage. She pulled Avery to the middle of the dance floor, turning to back her rear into Avery's front. Her hips moved in time to the beat of the steamy track. Avery's amber eyes were transfixed on the flow of the dancer. Her throat went dry. She took several gulps of her drink, mesmerized by the way Kadence controlled her body. The temptress tilted her head to the side to glance at Avery over her shoulder. She leaned farther, dipping forward before pushing her rear out as she rose, grinding against the center of Avery's shorts.

Jesus fuck!

Luckily, or rather unluckily, Emma interrupted them with a flustered Danny hot on her heels. "Kadence! I'm so glad you finally came out with us. This is so fun. You're so fun. Everyone is so fun."

Avery threw her head back with a laugh as she helped Danny pry Emma's grip from around Kadence's neck.

"Avery is the best, isn't she, Kadence?"

"Oh, most definitely." Kadence gave an exaggerated nod.

"I'm sensing sarcasm," Avery accused.

"She won't know the difference."

"What difference? Difference between what?" Emma tilted her head, swaying forward.

"Easy there. Told you." Kadence gave Avery a knowing glance before redirecting her attention to their inebriated friend. "Say, Emma, how about we get you something to eat, yeah?"

"Oh, my god," Emma squealed. "Yes."

"You okay?" Kadence asked, retrieving Avery's car keys from her pocket. "I can come back for you after if you still want..."

"Are *you* okay? You're the one who has to drive?"

Kadence nodded. "Sober as a judge."

***

They pulled into a small diner and ordered Emma a plateful of pancakes, bacon, and an omelet. Avery settled on a burger while Danny went for chicken nuggets and fries. Kadence simply sat with water in front of her, watching them.

"I don't get it. How aren't you drunk?" Avery asked, hand over her mouth as she spoke with stuffed cheeks. "You had as much as me and I'm starving."

"I'm a recovering alcoholic," Kadence deadpanned. "I've had way more in one night."

Avery gagged on her burger, coughing violently before gulping down her soda.

"Kidding." Kadence shrugged, making her tone light and airy to resemble her yoga voice. "Don't forget to breathe."

"Kadence made a funny." Emma clapped.

"Thanks, I try." She gave a small smile, but Avery sensed something was now off about the woman sitting next to her. The rest of the evening was spent scarfing down hundreds of calories, hoping not to regret them in the morning. Avery tried not to think about the strangeness of Kadence's behavior, as she squirted more mustard onto her burger.

***

After dropping Danny off at his place, the trio made their way to the apartment and tucked a sleepy Emma into bed. Exhausted, Avery took a moment to collect herself as she flopped onto the couch. Kadence joined her a moment later, albeit descending in a more controlled manner.

"Thank you for driving," Avery said with a sigh. "I'm sorry if—"

"Don't apologize. I had a great time."

"You're probably tired. Are you sure you're okay? You can always crash here." *Forward much? Shut up. I'm just being polite. Sure, Bennett. Whatever helps you sleep at night.*

Kadence shook her head. "I'm fine. I promise." She stood and allowed Avery to walk her to the door, pausing for a moment. "Tonight was fun. I'm glad I met you." She smiled, leaning to place a soft kiss on Avery's cheek.

Avery felt her ears burn as they pulled apart.

"By the way," Kadence hovered, lips ghosting on the shell of Avery's ear, "Check your pocket."

Before Avery could process what had happened, Kadence was already descending the stairwell. Avery looked down, scavenging through her shorts until she found the tiny piece of paper. A grin split across her face as she read the seven scrawled digits.

Chapter Three

KADENCE SHRUGGED OFF HER jacket, draping it on the chair before pulling her tank off. A small thud followed as Avery's snapback landed on the floor beneath her. She had forgotten she still had it. To be honest, she had been a little distracted. Avery was attractive, albeit a bit cocky. Still, Kadence didn't mind looking at her. There was no harm in just looking, right? Those honey-colored eyes and golden tresses were a welcome contrast from... She shook her head, clearing her mind of the memories. *Not tonight.*

She placed the cap on the kitchen table as a reminder to return it and finished preparing for bed. She stepped through the routine— wash face, brush hair, brush teeth, take pill, lie down, count. At seventy-four, sleep took her.

***

The morning sun spilled over the horizon as Kadence stretched her arms above her head. She rotated her wrists, waiting for the left to crack and pop back into place before she let them fall back onto the mattress. After a quick shower and a slice of toast, she grabbed a banana and her water bottle, packing them away into her bag. No surprise, Emma and Danny were missing from class, and Avery most definitely was not in attendance. Kadence couldn't say she hadn't wished that maybe, by some miracle, Avery had had a change of heart. She sighed, rolling out her yoga mat.

***

Kadence returned to her apartment and was greeted with an unlocked door. Inching it open, she found her sister waiting at the kitchen table, legs crossed and a coffee — most likely black — in hand. Kadence prepared herself for an interrogation.

"Uhh, hey, Mel. How'd you get in here?"

Melody shrugged. "I still have my key."

"I thought I said you could get rid of it."

"Well, I'm glad I didn't." The older woman narrowed her eyes. "What the fuck happened last night?"

"You mean, you don't remember?" Kadence tried to joke with a shrug. "Wow, Mel, I didn't think you got *that* drunk."

Her sister's face remained stiff. "You know what I'm talking about. The blonde."

"You're blonde." Kadence shrugged. She didn't have time for this, nor did she have the energy.

"Kadence Diane."

Kadence sighed under Melody's scrutinizing gaze. Her sister eyed the snapback on the table. "She stayed last night?"

"We're just friends." Kadence knew her sister was being overly protective, but she couldn't fault her. After all, she hadn't exactly given Melody a reason to believe she was to be fully trusted alone again. But she was trying.

"I saw you leaving with her and her friends."

"They needed a ride."

"You drove?" The boom of Melody's voice caused the hair on the back of Kadence's neck to rise.

Kadence bowed her head. "She drove us to yours, so I said I'd drive us back." She dug her toe into the floor, preparing for the woman's wrath.

"Drinking and driving is dangerous, Kadence! You know that." She slammed her coffee cup onto the table. The hot liquid sloshed over the ceramic edge, splattering onto the surface of the table and onto her hand.

"Mel." Kadence saw her sister's skin turning red from the scalding temperature, but Melody shook her head. "I...it's not a big deal. It's only a fifteen-minute drive, twenty tops."

"It is a big deal."

"It takes thirty minutes for the effects of alcohol to metabolize—"

"That's not the point and you know it."

Kadence sighed in defeat. "I know, but I've done worse."

Melody softened, coming to her side. "That's what I'm worried about."

"It's okay. See, I'm okay." She gestured to herself with a wry grin. "My tolerance is still just as high as it used to be."

Her sister gave a pointed look.

"Sorry. It's...I wasn't thinking."

"Look." The older woman pinched the bridge of her nose. "I'm glad you had a good time. I'm happy to see you finally breaking out of your shell again. After the...after it happened, I was so worried about you, Kae. And when I found out that I could have lost you, I just..."

"I know." Kadence gave her hand a squeeze. "I'm sorry, Melody."

"Please, be careful. I want you to be able to move on, but does it have to be her? I just don't trust her. You deserve better than that."

"I don't deserve anything."

"Hey, don't say that. You're lucky. You're still alive."

"At what cost?" Kadence felt her chest constrict. "Shit."

Melody's eyes widened. "Kae? You still with me?"

She felt her body collapsing in on itself. Her ears rang and her head rattled with the blare of sirens. Red and white lights flashed behind her eyelids as she clutched at her chest, struggling to breathe.

The squealing of tires. The crunch of metal. A blood-curdling scream. Her arm ached. Iris's blood splattered across the dashboard.

"Kadence!"

She looked at her girlfriend, head hanging limp, eyes closed.

"Iris?"

No response.

She flung off her seatbelt, leaning across the center console to search for injuries.

"Calm. Breathe. Come on, count with me," Melody urged, combing her fingers through Kadence's hair.

"No." She felt her hand trembling. "Please, don't do this." She prayed to whatever higher being existed. "Take me instead."

"One, two, in, out." She heard her sister's voice in the distance.

"Baby, no!" She felt for a pulse but was met with nothing but rapidly cooling skin.

"One, two, three, in out," Melody said again.

There were arms around her, pulling her away from her girlfriend's lifeless body. "Ma'am, we have to get you into the ambulance. Your friend needs immediate care."
"She's not just my friend," was all she managed to say.

"One, two, three, four, in, out." They cycled to thirteen before her vision refocused. Kadence whimpered, falling onto her sister's chest as tears tracked down her cheeks.

"Shh." Melody wiped them away. "Are you okay?"

She gave a weak nod.

"Do you want me to stay here for a few days?"

Kadence shook her head in refusal. "I don't know what happened. I was doing so well."

Melody hummed sadly. "Let me at least take you to lunch?"

Kadence simply nodded, not bothering to put up a fight.

***

After slipping on their coats, the siblings made

the way down the street, opting to walk. Melody was right. What she had done was stupid. Kadence couldn't believe she had let herself lose all sense of judgment just because of a pretty girl. She hadn't done something so reckless in a long time. When it first started, she drank to numb all the pain. She wanted to be in control again. After that horrifying image of her girlfriend's body ingrained in her brain, the only way to wash it away had been with alcohol. But then, it became the problem.

It took a while until she found a new, healthier outlet to calm her anger with the unjust world. And she thought it was working. Her nails dug into her palms, and jaw clenched as she observed the city streets. Every person walking by was consumed by their own world. They were unaware of how each life could overlap. How one action could cause a chain reaction. All of this would be accessible knowledge to them if they would look up from their damn phone. It could have changed an entire lifetime. It could have rewritten a love story, instead of ending one.

"Hey, don't beat yourself up, okay? Like you said, you're okay. Just…" Melody's voice cracking would have been undetectable to most, but Kadence knew. "Just don't do it again."

Kadence could read the silent words in Melody's shimmery gaze. *You're all I have left.*

"I want you alive."

"I am alive."

"You are, but you're not living, not all the time anyway. But I saw the old you, a happier you, last night. The Kadence that drank to have a good time, not the Kadence that drank to shut herself away from the world."

She nodded in agreement.

"I've missed that Kadence."

"I'm sorry."

"Me, too."

The conversation fell silent, the only sound between them being their footsteps against the concrete as the somber atmosphere eclipsed them.

Melody cleared her throat. "Hey, Jordan is coming home from his business trip this week. He wanted to go hiking with Danny and his girlfriend."

"She has a name, you know. We've been hanging out for months."

"Yeah, well..."

Kadence shook her head with a chuckle. Melody was never one to easily warm up to others, especially those who were close to her friends and family. It was just part of her nature. After their mother left them, Melody stepped in to fill her place. Their father was a musician and he used to spend afternoons making up songs just for his daughters. When he passed away, Melody took it especially hard, opting to cling to the only family she had left. At times, it would result in a very terrifying and overbearing Melody, but that lightened after she met Jordan.

"Fine. Emma. I guess she's all right but I still..."

"You can stand her, but only for so long?" Kadence filled in the rest with a knowing grin. With Melody, that was basically as good as it got. "You cold-hearted bitch."

"I'm highly selective," the older woman defended, tilting her nose into the air. "But I will say that she *is* better than his other ex. What was her name? Clearly she didn't make much of a lasting impression on me."

Danny was Melody's best friend and they had grown up together. When Emma first came around, Melody was extremely wary of the girl, especially after his messy break up.

"Jeanne," Kadence recalled with a grimace. "She was so fake. At least Emma lays it all out there. She's blunt. Like you."

Melody released a puff of air from her nose, the closest thing to a laugh she ever let out anymore. Kadence missed hearing Melody *really* laugh. Kadence knew that her sister was afraid Kadence would get attached to someone. She was even more scared of that someone leaving her. There was only so many times Melody could pick up a shattered glass heart before she got cut herself. Kadence needed to try harder to be better.

"Let's just forget about her. When do you wanna go hiking?"

"Saturday, after you're done teaching your class. We can all meet at the studio?"

"Works for me."

Chapter Four

AVERY YAWNED, ARMS THROWN above her head. Her throat felt dry as she licked her chapped lips. She started to extract herself from the sheets, but soon realized a weight pressed against her. An arm was draped across her waist. She gave a gentle slap to her roommate's butt. Emma swatted it away in a half-conscious state.

"Hey, Em. Wakey, wakey!"

"Your breath stinks," Emma mumbled, burrowing into the sheets.

"So does yours," Avery countered with a grin.

"Why are you in my bed?" Emma huffed while using her leg to nudge Avery out of her personal space.

"You know you're in *my* bed, right?"

Emma sat up slowly, surveying her surroundings. "Shit."

"You've always been a drunk cuddler."

"You're so loud," Emma moaned, covering her ears. "My head hurts."

"You shouldn't have drunk so much."

With great effort, the two migrated to the bathroom. Emma handed her the tube of toothpaste and Avery gave it a squirt, allowing the gel to coat her brush before shoving it into her mouth.

"I had to do something to drown out the sexual tension between you and Kadence."

Avery pointed a foamy brush in Emma's direction. "There was no sexual tension." She returned the bristles to her mouth, scrubbing a little harder.

Emma nudged her in the hip and Avery sidestepped so she could spit into the sink. "You sure? Cause I'm pretty sure I saw you eye-fucking her on multiple occasions last night."

Avery followed, turning the nozzle to wash the bubbles of toothpaste down the drain. "I'll have you know, *she* was the one who gave *me* her number."

Emma's forehead wrinkled in surprise.

"Ya, girl's still got it." Avery ruffled her hair in the mirror, winking at her own reflection. She pointed a finger at mirror-Avery before following Emma to the kitchen. As she rounded the corner, she found her roommate nursing her headache with a glass of water and pain relievers. Two boxes of cereal sat in front of her, as well as a cup of instant noodles.

"Pick."

"Ramen. No competition."

The redhead pushed the foam container across the table and Avery chuckled at the lethargy of her roommate. Pulling back the lid, Avery broke off a piece of the uncooked noodles, popping it into her mouth.

"Come on, Avery. Use water."

Avery rolled her eyes with a grin, taking the cup and placing it under the hot water dispenser. "Fine, Mom." She tapped the counter as she waited for the noodles to cook, watching Emma struggle to open the cereal box. The plastic crackled, irritating her headache, each piece of cereal clinking against the ceramic bowl.

Emma groaned and Avery snickered at her friend's theatrics, returning with her now cooked noodles.

"So, are you gonna call her then?" Emma asked after downing a spoonful of cereal.

"Call who?"

"You know who."

Avery shook her head, not wanting to give her roommate the satisfaction. "Not unless it's for a booty call." She pretended to grope at an imaginary figure.

Emma glared.

"What?" Avery shrugged. "I was kidding."

"Don't make this awkward."

"Why would it be awkward?"

"Because you can be an ass sometimes. And Kadence is my friend. If you screw around with her, you may be able to avoid her, but I won't. We do yoga together and her sister and Danny are close."

"Kadence is a big girl. She can make her own decisions."

Emma set her spoon down. "I'm serious, Avery. Kadence is different."

"I mean, she's just another girl." Avery shrugged and inhaled another mouthful of ramen.

"I mean it. Don't."

"Why are you freaking about this? I wasn't going to call her anyway. Relax."

"Why not?"

"Too easy." Avery scarfed down the last bit of noodles, ignoring the way Emma's face began to match her hair.

The redhead took her spoon and flung a soggy piece of cereal in Avery's direction. "You're such an ass! I'm trying to level with you."

Unaffected, Avery leaned back in her chair. "So, then level with me, I'm all ears."

"I don't know. Kadence is just different, okay? When we first met, she was quiet. Not shy, just…" Emma ran her tongue across her teeth, searching for the right word. "Guarded. She only talked to Melody."

Avery snorted. "So, she had a stick up her ass?"

"No." Emma massaged her temples. "She just seemed, well, I don't know...broken, I guess? I just don't think you should play around with her. If you're going to do this, you can't make it a one-night stand. You can't toy with her."

Avery tried to lighten the mood. "You're being particularly suffocating this morning."

"Damnit, Avery. It's time to grow up." Emma's spoon clanged against the tabletop. Clearly the hangover was not going well. "You can't just *use* her. She's not another girl you can just fuck and chuck. I get that Logan hurt you, I do. But you're treating her like that doesn't make you any better."

She did not just go there. "You calling me a fuckboy?" Avery glared daggers into Emma.

"No," Emma groaned. "I'm just saying Kadence doesn't deserve—"

"And I did?"

"That's not what I—"

"Save it," Avery bit out before storming away. "I'm going out."

***

She had gone to his apartment to surprise him. He wasn't supposed to be back for another day, but Avery wanted to do something special for her boyfriend. She walked in to find clothes strewn on the floor, a pair of panties that were definitely not hers atop the mix. Then she heard a grunt and an "Oh, Logan! Don't stop!" Two voices chorused into their orgasm.

Avery had never run faster in her entire life.

The next day, Logan texted that he was back from his trip. When she confronted him about what she had seen, or rather, heard, he had brushed it off with a shrug, stating that it wasn't like they were exclusive or anything. Yet, just a few weeks before, he had promised her forever.

"I just said that to get you to sleep with me. You were so pissy that week," he had reasoned. It had been the anniversary of her father's death and Logan had been the first person to make her smile that day.

***

It was then she vowed never to let herself fall in love again, never to get attached to anyone, especially anyone who could hurt her.

The first few months were hard, but a year later, Avery had transformed herself into a new person—cool, smooth, and aloof. Every once in a while, a little piece of the old her would come out, mostly with Emma or Jayce, but she would shove it back down, hidden in the shadows of the person she was now.

Avery found herself wandering until she came to the local park, settling on the swing set. She hadn't been there in quite some time but took comfort in the fact that the place hadn't changed since her last visit.

"Avery, is that you?" A scamp of a boy approached her, a basketball under his arm.

She wiped her eyes with the back of her hand and plastered on a smile. "Oh, hey Ryan. What's up?"

"I haven't seen you in a long time."

"Sorry, bud. I've been a little busy."

"Are you busy now? Do you wanna play a game with us?" Ryan held out the ball.

She recognized a few faces of the younger group. She had come to the park in the past with Logan, who was the basketball coach for the local junior team. After he moved away, she couldn't bring herself to return to a place where so many ghosts of her past still lingered.

She shook her head. "I can't today."

"Oh." Ryan's dejected expression sent a pang of guilt through her. "Soon though?"

"Sure, kiddo." Avery feigned a smile. "I'll try."

Another broken promise. She filed it away with all the others.

***

Avery eventually returned to the apartment. Her temper settled after her fuse had blown. Her eyes were burning from lack of sleep and sensitivity to the sun. Danny and Emma were cuddling on the couch, whispering intimately to one another when she walked through the door.

Emma straightened. "Avery, I want to—"

Avery held up her hand. "Already forgiven, babe. I brought Chinese. Enough for Danny, too." She placed the peace offering on the coffee table.

Danny shook his head, unraveling his arm from Emma's shoulder. "I have to head out to meet up with Melody."

"Send her my love," Emma said.

"And mine," Avery added with a wiggle of her brow. "I'm sure she'd just adore that."

"I will." He laughed as he exited the apartment.

"I really am sorry," Emma said when the door clicked shut.

"Don't worry about it." Avery brushed it off. "You

know I don't hold grudges unless you really fuck up."

"But you shouldn't hold on to those things either," Emma pointed out. "It's not healthy. Aren't you tired?"

Exhausted. "No," Avery lied as she distributed the takeout containers. "But I bet you are. What did you and Danny do while I was out?"

Emma rolled her eyes at the insinuation. "You're unbelievable."

Avery knew she was putting up walls. And Emma might not have known how to knock all of Avery's down, but she definitely knew how to get around them.

"New subject. How's the gallery prep going?"

"I want to kill myself."

"No, you don't."

"Okay, I don't, but I'm so stressed." To drive the point home, she groaned, rubbing a hand on her face. It coated orange sauce on her cheek and Emma chuckled, taking a napkin and wiping the sauce away. "Can't take me anywhere," Avery said, poking fun at herself.

"Maybe some places. As long as they're already dirty places."

"Dirty, you say?" Avery waggled her brows.

"Oh, yeah." Emma leaned in, playing along. "Real dirty. Hiking. Want to come?"

Well played. "Absolutely," Avery laughed sarcastically. "Not. That would require me to have time to do that, and also, the motivation to do so as well."

"You've got to release that anxious energy somehow."

"Oh, trust me. I know how to release energy." Avery winked.

"Avery." Emma's tone turned serious.

"Relax. I'm not going for her. Kadence is off

limits. I got your message loud and clear."

"All right. All right." Emma held up her hands in defeat. "Let's just forget it for tonight. Let's have a girl's night. We haven't had one in forever. Just you and me. No Danny and no L—"

"Losers," Avery finished for her. "Or lays for that matter."

Honestly, Avery would never bring anyone she messed around with to the apartment. It gave off the wrong message. If Avery were to sleep with someone, it would be casual and on her terms. She was always upfront about it from the start and going to the opposite party's place made it easier for her to slip out and cut ties if she ever felt that things were getting too serious.

***

By the end of the week, Avery was seven days closer to her exhibition date and eight half-completed paintings deeper into her work. The sun was just peeking over the skyline, shadows cast against the ground. It should be inspiring to see from up in her apartment— they had one of the best views of the city, but she felt nothing. She had hit a roadblock yesterday evening and hadn't slept since.

"All right, Bennett. I'm doing this for your own good." Emma stormed into the room with a spray bottle in hand.

"Em." Avery eyed the plastic container and her roommate's finger on the trigger. "What are you doing?"

"You haven't left the apartment for days. You haven't showered, and I'm pretty sure you've forgotten to eat at least half of your meals."

"Chips and salsa." Avery grabbed for her palette.

"Those aren't a proper diet. Even for you." Emma placed a hand on her hip. "At least get a burrito to go along with it."

Avery shook her head, retrieving her brush from the easel's ledge. "I'm fine. I just need to get this done. And if I stop now, I might not—"

Her words were cut off by a cold spray of water against her face.

"Emma! What the fuck? You could have ruined it!" Avery rushed to examine her painting.

"It's oil paint, Avery." Emma tossed the bottle to the ground. "It doesn't mix. Besides, it's just mist. Now, come on. Get dressed. Something comfortable," Emma commanded as she pried the brush from Avery's grip.

Avery looked back at her canvas as she was dragged away from her work. "Why? Where are we going?"

Emma pushed her into the bathroom, turning on the shower. "Yoga."

"No," Avery whined, recalling how much of a disaster her last attempt had been. "Why?"

"It'll do you some good. Now, go shower. You reek." She gave another push forward before shutting the door, holding onto the handle when Avery tried to make an escape.

Avery grumbled as she stripped off her shirt, catching a whiff of herself. *Damn*. Maybe Emma was right. She did stink.

***

They arrived at Iris Yoga Studio just as Kadence

was setting up the room, on hands and knees as she rolled out the mats. A wave of warmth flooded Avery's cheeks.

Emma beamed at the reaction. "See, told ya you could use this."

"I thought you said she was off limits," Avery hissed, sticking out her tongue.

"Real mature." Emma nudged her forward. "I'm just trying to get you to smile."

"You know, I don't understand you sometimes."

They sat in the middle of the class and Avery fumbled through the entire hour, with Kadence's slender hands skimming Avery's body to correct her posture. Avery's cheeks burned all the while as green eyes twinkled in amusement.

"Alright, well, that was fun," Avery huffed as Emma and Kadence chattered, sharing a laugh about one of the many falls Avery had during the class.

"I'm heading out of here." She was Avery Fucking Bennett, for Christ sake! She was supposed to be smooth and quick on her feet. Yet, here she was, the butt of the joke. On top of that, she had now wasted more than an hour of a day she could have spent painting or laying out a new piece. She was about to stomp away and wait by the car, when Kadence called out.

"Wait, aren't you gonna—"

Her words were cut off by a red SUV pulling into the parking lot, honking its horn. The group turned to find Melody and a tall, brusque looking man in the front seats of the vehicle.

"Move it." The older woman cupped her hands at her mouth "Sun's out and I'm impatient." When they finally pulled up next to the trio, Melody scowled.

"What's *she* doing here?"

The way the woman spoke irked Avery. "Taking a yoga class. And going hiking." Avery puffed out her chest.

"Really?" Emma raised a brow. "What about the—"

"Try and keep up," Avery cut off before marching to the car, mood soured.

***

They followed the SUV to the outskirts of the city, Avery's amber eyes trained on Kadence in the rear of the leading vehicle. The crew gathered at the base of a mountain where a small gazebo and hiking map stood. Both were weathered by the seasons, the words faded and paper yellowed by the sun.

"What trail do you guys wanna take?" Emma asked.

Kadence was chatting with who, Avery learned, was her sister's boyfriend, Jordan, while Danny unpacked a few bottles of water and an emergency first aid kit from the trunk of the car. The only person paying attention was Melody, who stood impassively at Avery's side.

"The hardest," Avery said with determination, not daring to buckle under the sharp gaze.

"Avery." Emma furrowed her brow. "I don't think now is the time..."

"The red trail." She pointed to the map, gritting through her teeth in a feigned smile she shot in Melody's direction.

Melody tilted her chin up, accentuating the chiseled angle of her cheekbones before taking the lead up the trail.

"All right, you asked for it." Emma shrugged. "Let's go, gang."

Melody and Jordan started off the hike, leading a few feet ahead with Kadence trailing behind. Danny and Emma trod in a more leisurely pace, holding hands as if they weren't hiking up the steepest *fucking* mountain Avery had ever seen. Her calves were aching as she puffed up the incline. Bugs were bombarding her face as she sweat through her clothes, chest heaving. Avery willed herself to focus on her footing, not wanting to fall too far behind, or worse, give Melody the satisfaction that she was actually dying.

"I didn't take you for the hiking type." A soft voice startled her. "Sorry. I didn't mean to scare you." Kadence giggled through her apology. Avery looked around to find that the rest of the group was out of sight. Kadence must have fallen back to make sure she wasn't lost.

Avery sighed. "I'm not..." There was no point in pretending anymore. It was rather obvious.

"So, what made you wanna come today?" Kadence's smile was genuine, and Avery's gaze faltered. She diverted her eyes from the hypnotic green.

You make me want to cum. She inwardly kicked herself. *Step up your game, Bennett.* "Just trying to appreciate one of nature's many gifts and most beautiful views." She winked at Kadence and Kadence's cheeks tinted pink. *Nailed it!*

"Hmm, I think you probably could've done that just by looking in the mirror," Kadence purred. Actually, *purred* before jogging to catch up with Danny and Emma.

How the fuck did she turn the tables on me?

Avery watched, jaw slack, as Kadence resumed her conversation with Emma as though nothing had happened.

***

By the time they decided to take a break, Avery had already downed her entire water bottle and part of Emma's, still feeling parched as hell.

"I'm so thirsty!"

"Are you now?" Emma teased with an impish grin.

"I. Fucking. Hate. You."

If it wasn't so damn hot, she probably would have gotten back at her roommate for the morning's events by pouring the rest of her water bottle on her head. But the liquid was too precious to waste at the moment. She took another swig, wiping her lips with the back of her hand.

When Emma skipped off to join Danny and Jordan by the creek to skip rocks, her attention fell to Kadence who had busied herself with some stretching. Her leg was propped against a tree as she leaned forward. She reached for her sneaker, slender fingers wrapping around the toe of her shoe. Avery felt her legs turn to jelly at her flexibility.

A harsh voice hissed in her ear causing her to yelp in surprise. "What are your intentions with my sister?"

What was with these siblings and their obsession with scaring the shit out of her?

"What are you talking about?" Avery looked up to find Melody towering above her.

"Don't play dumb with me. I know about your reputation."

"What rep?"

"Danny said you sleep around. And judging by your actions so far, I wouldn't be surprised if you did."

"Are you slut shaming me?" Avery stood and took a step forward.

"Of course not." Melody didn't waver as she pursed her lips. "I'm just stating my observations."

"I have needs," Avery stated with a shrug of indifference. "I satisfy them. I move on."

"Well, keep those needs to yourself around Kadence," the woman threatened. "She's too good for you."

"Probably. But sex requires the consent of both parties." She shouldn't be poking the bear. Avery could practically see the steam coming from Melody's ears.

"Don't play chivalrous with me."

"What you're saying would imply Kadence wants it just as much as I do."

"Why, I ought to…" Melody raised her fist and in a flash of a millisecond, Avery realized the stupidity of her mistake.

"Hey!" The two looked to find Jordan heading toward them.

My fucking savior.

"Everything okay?" he asked, coming to his girlfriend's side and wrapping an arm around her.

"Just perfect." Melody faked a sickeningly sweet grin. "Just trying to get to know Kadence's newest friend."

"Come on, babe, let's get to the trail." He shot an apologetic look over his shoulder as he escorted the temperamental older sister away.

Avery forced herself to sprint to where Kadence was now leading the pack, ducking at the brush overhanging the beaten path.

"Careful of the spiny ones," Kadence pointed out. "They can get stuck in your hair."

Avery nodded as they hiked in a comfortable silence. She occasionally stole glances at Kadence who would smile each time she caught her looking. But the woman chose not to say anything.

"Watch for the snake..." Kadence informed after a beat, pointing toward the ground beside Avery's foot.

"What?" Avery squealed, fleeing in no particular direction. She never felt so exhausted in her life and when she turned, the group was laughing, especially Emma. Kadence bit her lip, a playful smile threatening to spill. She bent to pick up the snakeskin, dangling it in the air. "Snakeskin. You didn't let me finish my sentence."

"I don't care," Avery shouted from her distance away. "That's still repulsive."

Kadence dropped the shed skin, brushing her hands on her leggings before coming to Avery's side. "Wrong time of day." Kadence pointed to the sun. "They won't be out for another two hours or so."

"Where'd you learn that from?" Avery asked, curious as to where such a random bit of knowledge came from.

Kadence sighed, a sadness filling her gaze. "A good friend taught me."

Avery wanted to ask her why she suddenly didn't have such a beautiful glimmer in her eye, but something about using a pick-up line at the moment felt wrong. Instead, she nodded, allowing the rest of the group to join them as they hiked along the trail.

***

They finally made it to the top and Avery felt like she could conquer the entire world. The view was shrouded by green treetops and open skies and the air was fresh and cool. Perching on a boulder, Avery inhaled. It was freeing and she realized she was thankful she'd decided to go along. That was, until she realized they had to go back *down* the mountain, too.

Another two and a half miles later, Avery couldn't feel her legs and she was pretty sure her lungs had disintegrated. One would think, with gravity and all that inertia, the hike down would be a little easier. It wasn't. If anything, it was harder. With the steepness of the hill, her thigh muscles were tense, struggling to keep her from falling forward or twisting her ankle. In her attempt to steady herself, she stepped into a particularly wet patch of dirt, ruining her new shoes. What made it worse was she couldn't even tell if it was mud or something else. She prayed for the first option.

At the base of the mountain, Kadence took her by the wrist, tugging her to the red SUV where she retrieved a small packet of wipes.

"You're a saint, you know that?" Avery beamed as she took Kadence's offer, kneeling down to clean her shoe.

"You just seemed upset." Kadence shrugged, crouching to join her while the rest of the group exchanged their goodbyes. She was so close that Avery spied the small freckle on Kadence's lip and the light brown ring around her pupils drew her in again.

Kadence's lips tilted to the right, breaking eye contact with Avery. "You missed a spot." She took the wipe from Avery's hand, fingers brushing against hers as she cleaned off the area Avery had been too distracted to see the first time.

"Don't indulge her," Emma said, now aware of the two hidden behind the vehicle.

"No, please do." Avery grinned. "Keep indulging."

Kadence let out the tiniest chuckle. "All clean." When she turned away, Avery glared at her roommate for interrupting.

Emma shrugged, mouthing an insincere "sorry."

Avery was about to flip her off when Kadence spun on her heel.

"Oh, Avery," Kadence said, climbing into backseat of the red vehicle, "I almost forgot. I still have your hat. I'll give it to you next time you come to yoga."

Avery willed herself to have some self-control, shaking her head. "Not happening."

"You said that last time, yet here you are."

Avery shrugged. "I guess people can change."

"All right, Avery." Kadence smiled coyly as Jordan started the engine. "Well, if you want it back, you know how to reach me." She departed with a wink and a wave, leaving Avery dumbfounded yet again.

"Two days," Emma declared as they headed toward her car.

Danny shook his head. "Three, I'd say."

"What are you two talking about?" Avery cocked a brow as the red vehicle drove away.

"Before you call her," Emma informed her.

Avery rolled her eyes, swiping the keys, but not before she heard the rest of their conversation.

"I know Avery."

"But I know Kadence."

They shook on it.

On Tuesday, Danny paid Emma twenty dollars.

Chapter Five

AVERY WAS GETTING RESTLESS. She never gave her clothes to anybody, let alone her favorite snapback. Yet Kadence had possessed it for more than a week. Preoccupied, Avery spent the majority of her time holed up her makeshift apartment studio, trying to find the proper inspiration for the big event. This mainly consisted of pacing back and forth and glaring at a large white canvas. Just as she was debating stabbing herself in the eye with a paintbrush, her phone buzzed.

Emma Walsh: Don't forget to eat!

Avery ignored it. A sliver of green later, it chimed again.

Emma Walsh: Seriously, Avery. Put down the damn brush and get some food!

She added a streak of gold to the sad excuse of a masterpiece. Less than ten minutes later, the rumble pulled her from her work yet again.

Emma Walsh: Avery Bennett! I swear to God, you better take a break and eat something!

It was accompanied by a series of red faced emojis.

With a frustrated groan, Avery picked a stopping point and set her brushes in a small glass of water. After a shower, Avery still didn't quite feel herself and she blamed a certain pair of green eyes and a missing snapback. She stomped to her desk, riffling through the drawers. Tucked away was a small sheet of paper she had saved from a few weeks ago. Grabbing her phone, she tapped the numbers and waited.

"Hello?"

"Hey, uh. It's Avery."

"I could tell. I was wondering if I'd ever hear from you again. Are you naked?"

Avery's eyes widened. "Whoa! Wh…what?" Her intention was to call Kadence and ask her for her hat back, not have phone sex. Not that she would be opposed.

"Without your snapback." She could almost hear Kadence grinning through the phone. "You feel kinda naked."

Scheming little minx.

"Kinda, yeah. So, uhh, what are you doing right now?"

"Nothing. Just in my apartment reading."

"Want to grab some lunch?"

What are you doing, Bennett? Inviting women to lunch is not what you do.

"Sure! Where should I meet you?"

"My apartment. I'll take us to a place."

"All right." Avery could hear the sound of shuffling on the other line. "I'll be there around one fifteen-ish."

"Works for me."

The second the call ended, Avery sprinted, yes, actually *sprinted* her lazy ass to her laptop, googling the healthiest eateries she could find. She thought she had the whole thing under control, but when Kadence arrived ready to return Avery's snapback, her mind betrayed her.

"Keep it on. You've had it for this long. A few

more hours won't hurt. Besides, it looks good on you."
Something about Kadence blushing while putting on the
hat was incredibly attractive. Well, Kadence in general
was pretty attractive.

"Okay. So, what were you thinking? Italian?
Mexican? Thai?"

"I've got a place."

"And that is...?"

"I think I'll keep it a surprise. Trust me?"

Kadence hesitated to reply.

"Smart." Avery laughed. "I wouldn't either."

***

Everything was going much better than the first
few times interacting, and Avery was glad to finally have
the upper hand. Until she got the menu. Aside from the
phrases 'vegan' and 'gluten free' she couldn't
understand a thing on the menu. And even then, she
wasn't even sure what being *gluten free* entailed.
Healthy, probably.

"I'm sorry about Melody, by the way." Kadence
apologized, after placing their orders. "She can be a bit
intense."

"Ehh, she doesn't scare me."

"Really?"

"I'm fearless."

"The snake would say otherwise."

"Hey, I was just thrown off. And it was just the
skin, remember?"

"I do." Kadence's lips tugged into a smile. "Hard
to forget."

"I am pretty unforgettable, aren't I?"

"Do you always talk like this?" Kadence asked.

"With lines?"

"Only to gorgeous girls like you."

Kadence simply blinked and Avery had to commend her for remaining straight-faced, despite how much it absolutely blew. "You're not afraid of *anything*? I don't believe that."

"Because I'm just so unbelievable...ly awesome."

Kadence shook her head, rolling her eyes. "That was terrible."

"Hey, I'm trying here."

Normally, Avery would find her inability to flirt frustrating, but hearing Kadence throw her head back, releasing an airy laugh made it somewhat tolerable. She didn't mind the fumbling as much.

When their food arrived, Avery scarfed down her salad but even when her plate was empty, she felt as though she hadn't eaten at all.

"How was it?" Kadence asked, finishing up her last bit of kale chips, which Avery learned were not chips at all, but roasted leaf looking things. So misleading.

"Oh, it was amazing," Avery lied, rubbing her belly for effect. "I'm stuffed. I don't think I could eat..." Her stomach voiced its disagreement with a growl.

"Stuffed, huh?" Kadence cocked a brow. "Come on, I've got the perfect place for a second lunch."

***

"Five Guys?"

"The only men I need in my life," Kadence said as she opened the door. The smell of burgers filled Avery's nostrils and she thanked the gods for the gift of grease and meat.

"And here I thought you were one of those typical health nuts."

"I warned you appearances can be deceiving."

"You did."

"So, what'll it be? Little cheeseburger? Bacon cheeseburger?" Avery's mouth watered as Kadence read off the menu. The narrator herself was pretty mouthwatering as well.

"Hello." The cashier greeted the pair. "What can I get for you?"

Kadence stepped up to the counter. "A cheeseburger with everything on it, medium fries, and a drink." She stepped aside.

He leaned in, directing his attention to Avery. "And you?"

As Avery pondered her order, she felt a hand at her waist. The scent of coconut perfume overpowered the smell of grease and fries. She stared at Kadence's hand, cheeks burning.

"Baby," Kadence purred into her ear. "Just get a burger. You can share my drink and fries." She brushed her nose against Avery's cheek.

Fuck me. What is going on? "Kadence, what are you doing?" Avery barely squeaked out her question.

"I just can't wait to eat." Kadence raked her nails up Avery's arm. She turned to the cashier. "She'll get the same. Cheeseburger, everything on it."

Avery couldn't breathe.

The cashier cleared his throat and quickly punched in the order before handing her the receipt.

Kadence shot him a feigned smile, pulling Avery by the waist and escorting her to a table.

"Sorry about that," Kadence apologized once they settled. "He was eyeing you and not in a good way."

"Oh? Are you jealous?" To be honest, Avery hadn't even noticed the cashier's behavior.

"No."

Ouch. That hurt.

"I just hate when women are objectified. He should have been respectful of you, especially if he wanted it to get him somewhere," Kadence grumbled. "I had to do something to get him to stop."

"My hero." Avery batted her eyes with a grin, hoping to lighten the mood.

"I'm not a hero," Kadence muttered with a frown.

Avery studied her, unsure how the conversation had taken such a drastic turn. Maybe a different topic. "Call me crazy," Avery said, taking a fry from their shared stash.

"Crazy," Kadence said, bouncing back with sass.

"Okay, you. Anyway, like I was saying, call me crazy, but you're pretty chill. Not what I expected, but it's good."

Kadence shared a small smile. "I enjoy your company as well."

"Hey." Avery pointed a fry at the woman. "I never said anything about that."

"Maybe. But your eyes did."

"Oh, so you've been looking into my eyes." Avery lifted her eyebrows.

"Better than you, looking at my chest." Kadence called her out. Avery realized she had just been berated, especially after Kadence's reaction to their cashier.

"I...sorry. It's just...I'm an artist. Sometimes I forget that staring at anatomy is considered creepy."

"Are you? What do you usually paint?"

Heat pooled to her cheeks as she answered

sheepishly. "Nudes."

"Oh."

"Does that make you uncomfortable?" Avery wrung her hands. She could be confident, and even cocky about her body, but when it came to her art, she was the complete opposite. It was her safe space to be herself. In the rawest, truest, and most honest shades.

"Not at all." Kadence offered an easy smile. "I think it's awesome."

Avery grinned. The rest of the meal was spent in easy conversation until Kadence had to leave to teach. Avery watched her retreating figure, longing to be able to prolong their time together. It wasn't until she returned to her apartment that she realized she was so enraptured by Kadence she had forgotten all about her snapback. Again.

Chapter Six

"YOU WORK TOO HARD," her girlfriend lectured, hands on her hips. *"You're going to tire yourself out."*

"I have to get this done, Iris," Kadence responded from her hunched position.

"The document will still be there when we get back. Come on, Kae. It's just for a few hours. You need to take a break. You should at least eat something."

Kadence shook her head with a frown, turning her attention to the computer, fingers banging the keys. *"I have to get this report to the director of marketing before the end of the day. And then there's the contractor for the room. And the paints. Oh, shit! I forgot to pick up the paint."*

"Hey, hey! Kadence, love, calm down." Iris's fingertips soothed down her spine. *"It's fine. We can get them tomorrow. What do you say we take a trip to the studio for a little? They just put in the flooring."*

"No, I have to get our lives together. How are we going to get by if—" She stopped when her girlfriend interrupted her with a chuckle.

"We deserve better than just trying to get by, Kae." Iris circled her arms around Kadence, tugging her out of the chair. Kadence stiffened her body, weighing herself down as her girlfriend wriggled around her.

"Babyyy," Iris whined, jutting her lower lip out in the biggest pout she could muster. It only took a tremble

of her lip for Kadence to crack.
"Okay. Let me change."

Avery was nothing like Iris. She was brash and cocky, yet everything about her seemed to intrigue Kadence. She was strangely deflective and forcibly happy at all times. But there was something about those doe eyes that made Kadence wonder if the flirty behavior Avery projected was just a defense mechanism, similar to the one Kadence used when things got too serious. Maybe Avery was just trying to get through each day, the same as Kadence.

***

"What's that still doing here?" Melody jut her chin toward the snapback that had reappeared at its initial spot on the kitchen table. "I thought you said you were going to return it."

"I did."

"And yet, it's still here."

"You don't like her, do you?" Kadence had an inkling that Melody wasn't Avery's biggest fan after the way she had sized her up during their hiking trip. It was almost comical how intensely Melody had stared daggers into the back of Avery's head. If it were possible, she probably would have killed her.

"She's a pig." Melody folded her arms. "In every sense of the word."

"Always so quick to judge."

Melody glowered, frowning so deep Kadence thought she'd break her jaw.

"She's not that bad. I think there's more to her than she let on."

"You're defending her. You're so innocent sometimes," Melody said with a mix of endearment and annoyance. "Always so trusting. Seeing the good in people. While I, well, let's be real here. I'm a cynical cunt."

"There's good in everybody. Iris taught me that," Kadence mumbled. The name of her ex-girlfriend still tasted bittersweet on her tongue. Iris had taught her a lot of things. She was incredibly kind and patient, wise and intelligent. Honestly, she was more than Kadence deserved. Maybe that's why the universe took her away from her.

Her sister softened, placing a hand upon her knee. "Yet, you don't see it in yourself."

Kadence tensed.

Melody sighed. "I just don't want you to get hurt."

"I won't get hurt. We're just friends."

"For now. But I know you. You said the same thing about Iris, too, and then, *bam*, one day you realized you were in love with her. Next thing you know, you're moving in together."

"Yeah, but you liked Iris."

"Because she was nothing like Avery."

"No." Kadence sighed. "She wasn't." The mood grew somber.

Melody cleared her throat. "Look, let's not talk about the past. Whatever makes you happy, okay? Just promise me you'll be careful?"

Kadence nodded. She wanted to argue that there was nothing going on between her and Avery but now, she wasn't so sure.

"So, are you gonna see her again?"

Kadence shrugged, trying to divert her attention

elsewhere, rather than look her sister in the eye. "I'm not sure. Would it be that bad if I did?"

Her sister remained silent, a small smile on her lips. "Disastrous."

"Of course. Totally reckless." Kadence laughed in agreement, ignoring the strange tug at her heart. "I told her to come to yoga and I'd give it to her then." She gestured at the beaten accessory, worn from many adventures that Kadence wished Avery would tell her about. Kadence wondered if she should be this curious about just a friend. "But I'll probably end up giving it to Emma to pass along. Avery doesn't seem like the yoga type."

"Neither did you."

"I guess that's true."

Iris had initially gotten her into the activity, insisting it could be a nice couple's activity. Kadence went every once in a while, mostly when her girlfriend had an empty spot in class. But the majority of the time, yoga was Iris's thing. After her passing, Kadence found that going to the studio made her feel a little closer to her lost lover, and much less angry with her situation. She had worked so hard, saved up so much money, and for what? None of it mattered when Iris died. She quit her job, finished opening the studio, and named it in honor of the woman. And she buried every scrap that was left of her heart and soul in it.

Melody cleared her throat. No doubt aware of what her sister was thinking of, or more so, who. "Come to my house tonight. I'm hosting a movie night with Jordan, Danny, and Emma. Sometimes I regret introducing my best friend to my boyfriend."

Kadence gave a knowing look. "You want me to mediate between you and Emma?"

"I just don't trust her," Melody said for the second time that day.

"You don't trust anybody."

"I trust you," Melody said with a wave of her hand.

***

"So." Emma leaned forward with rapt interest as they waited for the rest of the group to arrive. "I heard you hung out with my roommate today."

"I did," Kadence confirmed with a nonchalant nod. "I was trying to return her hat."

"And then you ended up leaving with it." Emma hooted with laughter.

"I should have thought to bring it tonight. You could have given it to her."

"Oh, no." Emma held up a hand. "I'm glad you didn't. I love it."

A knock on the door cut the conversation short.

"I'll get it," Emma said, hopping up from her seat. She returned with a bouquet of flowers in her arms, thrusting them in Melody's direction.

"They're for you."

Kadence grinned. Jordan had texted her after her yoga class to clue her in on the evening's events.

"There's something else at the door, but I can't lift it by myself. Melody will you help me?" Emma asked as sweetly as she could, batting her eyes.

Melody clenched her jaw as she rose. Kadence took that as her cue to take out her phone to start recording. Through the doorway, a mountain of flowers emerged, overflowing in Danny's arms. Finally, a smiling Jordan stepped across the threshold wearing the half grin, half smirk he always had on his face when Melody was around.

"Jordan." Melody's tone was guarded. "What the fuck is this?" She glared at the bouquets, placing her hands on her hips.

Jordan's grin widened, unfazed by Melody's hostility. "Mel, I know you hate surprises and grand gestures, but I hope you'll make an exception just this once."

"Jordan Hanson." Melody grimaced. "I swear to God, if you—"

"Let the man speak," Kadence cut her off. Only then did Melody realize the camera and a horrified expression crossed her face. When she turned to her boyfriend, he was already on one knee.

"Oh, no!" Melody shook her head. "No way. This is not happening."

Jordan smiled at her overreaction. "Melody Cooper, I know you don't need anyone in your life to make you happy. We both know that you're independent and strong enough to take care of yourself."

Everyone in the room chuckled.

"But I want to do it for you, if you'll let me. You make me happy. And I want to return the favor. Every minute of every day," Jordan said. "You're strong and sometimes a bit stubborn. But that's probably my favorite things about you. And best of all, you know that I'm stubborn too. When I want something, there's no turning back. And Mel, let me tell you, I want *you*. So, Melody Cooper, will you marry me?"

"I...I..."

The camera shook as Kadence stifled a giggle. Not many people could fluster her sister, but Jordan wasn't just anyone. He and Melody had been together since college when she shoved him out of the way in the campus bookstore because he was taking too long to pick out a notebook. The next day, Melody found out he was her TA. The two spent the first semester making one another's lives absolute hell. And the two spent the second semester making out and raising hell. A love-hate relationship was just so very Melody. And Jordan had just the personality to complement her sister's.

Melody's eyes grew wider by the second. She clenched her fists, opening and closing them at her sides as Jordan opened the ring box.

"I...I'm sorry." Melody rushed past the group and out the door.

"Mel, wait!" Kadence dashed after her as she exited the building. Outside, the cool spring air swirled around her, wind blowing her hair in every direction. She hooked her fingers around the wild strands as she searched for any sign of her sister. Going with her gut, Kadence veered left. Around the corner, on one of the bus benches, sat her sister, slumped over.

Kadence shoved her hands into her back pocket as she approached. "Hey. You aren't trying to run away, are you?" She tilted her head at the bus schedule. Instead of a snarky comment, Melody looked up with teary eyes, sending Kadence into a fit of alarm. Her sister rarely ever cried. In fact, Kadence had only seen her cry three times. Once when each of their parents died, and the other when Kadence almost did.

Melody didn't cry the day she broke her arm, or when a five-year-old Kadence accidentally dropped a heavy weight on her foot. Melody Cooper didn't cry from pain. She did though, cry from loss. And Kadence hoped that this wasn't the case this time.

Kadence knelt in front of her, placing both hands on her sister's knees. "Do you wanna talk about it?"

Melody averted her eyes, training her gaze on a very domestic couple walking their dog.

Kadence understood. She took a seat to the older woman's side and waited. She waited for the tension to leave her body bit by bit. She waited until Melody's locked glassy eyes returned to the present and her shoulders deflated.

The cool night wind nipped around them. It was getting to a point when the mornings and afternoons were reasonably warm, comfortable enough to enjoy the sun, but the nights, dark and alone, were less forgiving.

"I saw it coming." Melody finally spoke, shivering.

"Well, yeah. You've been together what, five years now?"

"Six." Melody's voice was flat.

"Yes, so six years. You've been together for six years. It was bound to happen. Unless you—"

"I don't want to leave," Melody interjected.

Kadence chuckled. "Then don't leave him. All you have to do is say 'yes.'"

"No, that's not..." Melody groaned, rubbing her face. When she removed her hands, her eyes were wet, cheeks tear streaked again.

A wave of concern rushed through Kadence's veins.

"Mel, please, tell me what's wrong?"

"Jordan got a job offer. He's being promoted."

Kadence blinked, worries decreasing in severity. "But isn't that good? He deserves it. They're always sending him out for business trips and—"

"It's in Iceland."

Her heart stopped.

"He wants me to go with him."

She pushed past the way her stomach dropped, plastering on her bravest face. "And you should."

Melody's jaw was set in stone. "I can't just leave…you." The whispered word was lost in the bustle of traffic, but the sentiment lingered in her eyes.

"I'll be all right." Kadence tried to assure her, burying the guilty feeling in her heart. Melody had always put her younger sister before herself. She was guarded and careful, because she saw what investing your heart into someone could do. What it did to Kadence when that someone was suddenly taken away.

Melody's bottom lip disappeared between her teeth as she struggled to voice her concerns. Kadence still understood though.

"When does he have to decide?" Kadence asked.

"End of the month." Melody sniffed, wiping away her tears in anger.

Kadence swallowed. "And the move?"

"In three."

A silence fell. As much as she loved her sister, it would be selfish to have Melody stay here just because she didn't think Kadence could take care of herself. She needed to prove to her sister she was okay without her. Jordan was good to her, and good for her. She hoped she wouldn't let fear dictate her relationship or cause her to let go of something that could be perfect for her.

"You don't have to take care of me, Mel. You deserve to be happy, too." Kadence said it like it was the most truthful statement she had ever spoken, the most important of words ever to leave her lips. She wanted happiness for Melody. That was all she ever wanted.

"I am happy."

Kadence detected Melody's honesty as a peaceful air fell across her sister. She knew Melody was thinking about Jordan. "Then say yes."

***

"So, the other day was uhh...interesting," Emma said Saturday morning after yoga class.

"Yeah." Kadence nodded in agreement.

"Is she okay?"

"I think so. She's just a little hesitant to get so dependent on someone else."

"I think we all know someone like that. But what about you? Are you okay? You seem a bit...off."

Kadence feigned a smile. "I'm good."

Emma raised an eyebrow. "You can tell me, you know. We're friends. I'm here if you need someone to talk to."

"Thanks, Em."

Kadence knew Emma was being genuine, but she only felt comfortable talking to Melody about certain things. This time it was a little more complicated since Melody was the reason for her conflict in the first place. She had a sister, a confidant, a support system, all placed dangerously in one person. *What is going to happen when that person leaves? Hopefully not the same thing as last time.* Emma had said they were friends, something she hadn't allowed herself to have in a long time. But lately, she'd found herself befriending quite a few new people.

"Do you maybe wanna hang out later? Get your mind off things? Avery has been asking about you."

"Yeah?"

The game she and Avery had been playing the last few days had been quite comical. Even amongst the chaos of Melody's proposal meltdown, the texts Avery had been sending her always managed to take her mind off things. Kadence found herself wishing for more of them, especially the horrendously attempted pick-up lines. Kadence would giggle rereading them before typing back a witty response.

"Well, mainly she's been asking about her hat. But same difference."

Kadence laughed. "It's in my car. Do you wanna just give it to her?"

Emma shook her head. "Nah, maybe later tonight. For now, it'll at least give her something else to obsess about instead of just the one. She could use the distraction."

"Her art show still stressing her out?"

"You have no idea." Emma rolled her eyes. "She always gets like this around this time of the year, but it's even worse with the show added on top of it."

Kadence wanted to ask what she meant by 'this time of year' but resisted the urge to pry. If Avery wanted to share, she would let her do so on her own time. That's what Kadence would want for herself, anyway. Besides, they had only ever hung out a few times and texted a few conversations. That most likely didn't constitute as the "pour your heart out and let me into your soul" point just yet. Things between her and Avery were light and easy. Kadence wanted to keep it that way.

"Maybe you should invite Avery to hang out with us." So much for light and easy.

Chapter Seven

AVERY HADN'T MOVED SINCE Emma left that morning. In fact, she probably hadn't moved since a few days ago. Her stomach was literally eating itself, but she couldn't do much other than snack on a handful of chips, washing the saltiness down with a dangerous mix of coffee and energy drink.

Occasionally, she would attempt to convince Kadence for her hat back, but even those attempts were half-hearted. Her mind was enslaved by the gallery exhibition and everything else came second. She tried compliments and pick-up lines, her usual go-to, but those didn't quite seem to charm the woman the way Avery had hoped. She refused to beg, but she did come pretty close this morning. Almost, but not quite. She couldn't bend just yet.

From her small corner of the apartment, Avery busied herself in the studio. She vaguely detected the sound of jingling car keys, signaling her roommate's return. She pivoted on her heels, palette still in hand, as she used her free hand to lock the door. She was going to be in for an earful if Emma found out she had skipped yet another meal.

"Avery! Hey, yo, blondie. I know you're in there." The rap of knuckles sounded on the door.

Avery tiptoed to her canvas.

A jiggle of the knob followed another set of harsh

knocks.

"Don't make me go in there. Avery Ass-wipe Bennett, come out."

"It's Aselin. And I already did. Four years ago."

"This is not a closet." She could practically hear her roommate rolling her eyes. "And if it was, it would probably be easier than having to pick this lock again."

The click of the latch followed, and the door swung open with a bang. Avery's shoulders tensed at the disturbing sound. She turned to her roommate in defeat. Avery knew she was a mess, paint streaked through her hair and across various parts of her body. The circles under her eyes were so dark it was a wonder she was still standing on her own.

"Avery," Emma cooed, pulling open the blinds.

Avery squinted, shielding her eyes. She blinked a few times as her dry eyes, now watering from sensitivity and lack of sleep, adjusted to the new atmosphere. She eyed her canvas, immediately regretting her decision when the white reflection seared into her retinas.

"Damnit, Em. Now the lighting's all off."

"You can deal with contrast later. Food. Now." Emma grasped her by the wrist. Emma was being a good friend, but Avery just wanted to focus on getting her paintings done, no matter how much of a roadblock she was having in the creativity department. If she focused on this, it would keep her mind from drifting back to Logan.

Avery shook her head. "I'm not hungry."

"Fine. We don't need to get food. But you still need to get out of the apartment. You're practically molting." She emphasized her point by picking a strand of oily hair between her fingers, rubbing the grease on her shirt. "Go shower and let's get you some fresh air."

"Nooooo," Avery whined, stomping her foot. She was being stubborn and downright childish, but she was frustrated and angry and hurt. All of these emotions were hindering her from creating something beautiful. All of these emotions were preventing her from seeing lights and colors. All of these fucking emotions because of one *fucking fuckboy*.

Emma pointed in the direction of the bathroom. "March."

Avery chided herself for letting Logan get under her skin yet again. This week marked the anniversary of her getting her heart broken. Twice in one week. First with her father's death. Second, with the end of her only serious relationship. She had the right to be in a sour mood.

Emma shook her head as she looked through the unfinished works scattered across the floor. At least she was willing to give Avery a few more minutes to wrap up at a stopping point. Instead, Avery spent the allotted minutes wringing her hands as her roommate surveyed her progress.

"These are gonna be great, Avery," Emma encouraged with a gentle smile. "But don't you think maybe you should step away from them for a little? Come back in a bit and look at them from a new perspective."

It was something her father used to tell her when she got hung up on certain concepts she couldn't perfect. This was why they were best friends. Even at her worst, Emma still knew what to say to get Avery to clear her mind.

"What do you say? Wanna take a break?"

Avery nodded, setting down her brush. "Just for tonight. Then it's back to work."

Emma nodded in agreement. "Then it's back to work."

They worked together to clean the brushes, capping the tubes of paint before closing the studio door and heading toward the bathroom.

"Thanks, Em." Avery pulled Emma into a tight squeeze. "Really."

"All right, Bennett. Don't get mushy on me now."

***

Avery expected hiking. She expected kayaking. Hell, she even expected skydiving when it came to Emma. What she did not expect was Kadence Cooper sitting in her living room with her snapback in her lap, fingers laced as they rested beside the cap. Her hair was tussled on her shoulder, a simple white top and black skinny jeans adorned her curves, fitting her delicate frame. Even with the monochromatic tones, all Avery saw was color. Specifically, forest green. Like fresh grass and towering trees. Like the earth and clarity. She swallowed. She shouldn't be thinking this much about an outfit. Avery equated the lack of sanity to paint fumes and being trapped in the studio for too long. It was just Kadence. *Just another girl.* She stood straighter as she approached.

"Hey, gorgeous. Did you miss me?"

Kadence beamed at her with sparkling green eyes. "Hello, Avery. Emma invited me to hang out."

"I'm glad she did." Avery shot her a sultry grin.

"You look nice," Kadence complimented, offering Avery her snapback.

As Avery accepted it, her fingers brushed against Kadence's, eyes still locked on green. A shiver skyrocketed up her spine. *That's not good.* "Is this your way of saying I don't look like a drunken mess for once?" Avery tugged the accessory onto her blonde waves with a wink.

Kadence chuckled. "No. Just, you look nice."

No banter, just a straightforward compliment. Avery's heart pounded. *That is definitely not good.*

She rubbed at the back of her neck. "Well, thanks."

"You're welcome." Kadence brushed her hair across her shoulder, giving Avery a whiff of dizzying perfume.

Avery's stomach did a dance. *What's happening to you, Bennett? You need to get laid.*

"So, what are you thinking?"

Shit. So many things. Most of them inappropriate. "Uhh...what do you mean?" As Avery cocked her head, a blonde tress fell across her eyes. She curled her lip, blowing it in place with a puff of breath. Kadence gave a look of, well, Avery couldn't quite place it. But in a flash, it was gone.

"What would you like to *do*? Emma said you could pick the activity for the evening."

Avery's mind immediately went to the gutter.

"Nothing sexual," Kadence reprimanded, already reading Avery's mind.

"Life's too short." Avery shrugged, trying to make light of the situation.

"It really is."

Something about the way she spoke the three words made Avery wonder if Kadence understood. If she had seen loss, too. Avery tried to not imagine a frown on that breathtaking—*Whoa, now. Settle down. Kadence is hot but calling her breathtaking is not okay.*

She pushed the thoughts aside, crediting it to Kadence's aesthetics. *Yeah, that's it. I'm an artist. Kadence is aesthetic. That's. All.*

"So, what's the plan, ladies?" A third voice broke the two out of the staring contest Avery hadn't realized they were having until she blinked.

Avery shrugged. "Whatever you guys want to do, I guess?"

"Aww come on, Avery. That's not fun," Emma booed. "The sun's shining. We have a whole afternoon and evening to us." She opened her arms, gesturing at the windows. "We could go hiking."

"No." Avery shot down while noticing Kadence grinning in her peripheral vision.

"Bikes?" Her roommate suggested.

Avery shook her head.

"Fishing?" Emma supplied.

Avery was pretty sure that one was just to annoy her. She scrunched up her nose, earning a laugh from Emma and a stifled giggle from Kadence.

"Well, for fuck's sake, Avery, then you come up with something," her roommate said with a teasing groan.

She was about to object when Kadence stepped in, interrupting their bickering with a sly grin. "I think I might know something we can all do."

Emma grabbed the keys, tossing them to Kadence. "Lead the way, Cooper."

***

The Arkade. Avery mentally cringed at the horrendous choice of typeface and uneven kerning. Neither Avery nor Emma had ever heard of the establishment, but Kadence seemed intent on strolling straight through the doors of the shady-looking complex. It looked like the remnants of a deserted warehouse.

When the doors parted, Avery's jaw dropped. Despite its outward appearance, the game hall was quite impressive. There were multiple bars lining the walls, vintage arcade games, casino slots, bowling alley, trampolines, air hockey and pool tables, a rock-climbing wall, and even a giant chess board with three-feet-tall pieces.

Avery gave an impressed whistle. Amongst the zing and buzz of multi-colored lights, Kadence stood in her black and white outfit, contrasting against the bright colors. Avery had never seen anything like it.

"So, where should we start?"

Before she could answer, Avery and Kadence's wrists were being tugged by a zealous Emma.

"Well, rock climbing it is, I guess." Kadence laughed and Avery found herself laughing, too.

They donned harnesses and started climbing. After half an hour, Avery was winded and excused herself to the bar. She downed her drink, enjoying the cold liquid making its way down her throat.

"She's a firecracker, isn't she?" An airy voice said at her side. Kadence stood to her left, rolling her wrist, wincing as she massaged the joint.

"Emma? Yeah. But I love her anyway." She smiled as they watched Emma ring a bell hanging from the ceiling, giving a hoot of accomplishment. "Don't tell her I said that though."

Kadence winked. "Your secrets are safe with me."

They were standing unnecessarily close. Kadence's eyes flew to Avery's lips, brow raised in challenge. It was a silent game of chicken Avery refused to lose until she noticed Kadence was still cradling her wrist.

"You all right?" Avery nodded at the wrist.

Kadence gave a muted smile. "Of course."

Avery didn't quite believe it.

"Just haven't had to use my wrist like that in a while. I guess I'm out of practice." Kadence stuck her tongue between her teeth, snickering as if she'd made a sexual reference.

"Anyway…" Avery looked around for a distraction. "Wanna play chess?"

Chess? What am I doing? She hadn't played chess in years. Before he died, she and her father used to play a game every evening before dinner. Why would she want to bring up something that would remind her of her father? Maybe being with Kadence made it more bearable. Or maybe it was the small bit of alcohol and the lack of sleep clouding her judgment.

Kadence looked astonished at the suggestion. Sure, Avery Bennett could be a real idiot sometimes, but she was *not* a dumb blonde. And she was going to prove to Kadence she was more than what she seemed.

After ordering a light ale for Kadence, the two set up the pieces on the giant chess mat. With their size, it reminded Avery of a miniature version of Harry Potter's wizard's chess.

"You're a wizard, Harry," Avery said in her most posh British accent before she could stop herself. *The hell, Bennett? That was so lame.*

Kadence raised a brow and Avery blushed.

"I mean, wanna see me work some magic?" Avery added with a wiggle of her brow.

Kadence chuckled, shaking her head as her lips

tilted to the side.

Nice save, Avery.

"So, white or black?" Kadence waved her hand at the prepared board.

Avery looked at the other girl's outfit. *She looks good in monochrome.*

"Avery?"

"Oh, right." She shook her head. "You pick. Ladies first." She gave her opponent an exaggerated up and down. "And you are most definitely a lady."

Kadence rolled her eyes with a light-hearted smile, walking across the room to take her place across the board from Avery. She gestured at Avery and her rows of pieces. "White goes first."

Avery lost the first two rounds. To be fair though, she *was* rusty. And the loss during the second round was caused by Kadence and her stupidly perfect face. The way her eyes would narrow, lip stuck between her teeth as she thought through each move was infuriatingly distracting. *Snap out of it, Bennett.*

Somehow through the night, Avery's goal of winning was trumped by a new objective—to try to make Kadence smile as many times as possible. She didn't know how it happened, but the way that those green eyes illuminated, though most of the time suppressing her amusement, did funny things to Avery. Funny, dangerous, and fucking wonderful things.

"Where did you find this place, anyway?" Avery asked after their third game. Emma still hadn't returned, and Avery wondered if she had purposely left them alone or if she was that excited about the trampolines. Honestly, with Emma, it was a pretty even split.

"Melody and I used to come here a lot with

my...friend." Her voice had a robotic tone and sounded rehearsed.

Avery tried to picture Melody in such an upbeat place but instead, the only image she could imagine was the woman scowling at the bright colors and grumbling at the blinking slot machine lights. Kadence's comments were difficult to believe. Though, to be fair, Avery didn't know much about Melody. Or either of the Cooper sisters.

"So, what's your story, Kadence Cooper?"

"I'm just me. What about you?" Kadence deflected before Avery could ask any further questions. "What's Avery Bennett's story?"

She had almost forgotten. She had been so distracted by Kadence she forgot what week it was, both scarring events pushed to the back of her mind. And she was smiling, she realized. *A lot.*

"My story is a bit of a long one. It might need some editing as well." Avery wasn't ready to share everything with Kadence, regardless of how welcoming and attentive she seemed.

"I like long stories. Let me get the next round of drinks." Kadence nodded at Emma who was in her own world doing flips on the trampolines. "I think we pretty much have all night. Just start with chapter one."

Chapter Eight

"YOU'VE GOT TO STOP working these late hours." Iris stalked toward her, a scowl across her face and a stern look.

Kadence blinked, realizing she had dozed off waiting for her report to run and was still at the office. She tapped her phone. Eleven forty-eight at night. She had multiple missed calls and texts from her girlfriend. She had skipped dinner and Iris had likely come looking for her after her lack of response.

"I'm sorry.

"Kae, a normal workday is nine to five. Eight to six if you have to. But this is just ridiculous." Iris's voice was filled more with concern than anger.

"I'm sorry, Iris. I just lost track of time."

Iris stood across from her desk with her arms crossed. Even though Kadence was the one sitting in the office chair, it felt more like Iris was in charge at the moment.

"I just have so much to do." Kadence's gaze fell to piles of paperwork on the glossy surface of her desk. It seemed as though her To Do pile never stopped growing but her Done pile never changed.

"I know you do." Iris's eyes softened as she let her arms fall to her sides with a sigh. "And I appreciate how hard you work, everybody does, but this isn't healthy.

Come on, we can't have you falling asleep at your desk anymore." She tugged Kadence to her feet before pressing the button to turn off her monitor. "Let me drive you home."

"But my car…" Kadence realized when they stepped outside, that a small dusting of white had coated the metal of her vehicle.

"I'll drive you back in the morning."

Kadence knew how much Iris hated driving in the snow. "I can drive myself if—"

Iris shook her head. "No. You're too tired. And I just want to get home. All these late nights and early mornings have been cutting into our cuddle time." Her smile was playful, but there was a hint of sadness in her words.

"I'm sorry, love." Kadence apologized, taking her girlfriend's hand in hers as she kissed the back of her knuckles. "I will be better."

"It's okay," Iris assured her, as they pulled out of the parking lot. "You can make it up to me later." She massaged her thumb against Kadence's, allowing Kadence's guilt to subside. Her eyes drifted closed again as she dozed off.

She awoke when her body was thrust forward, brakes squealing as the metal caved in around her. Her arm shot out instinctively as she tried to safeguard her girlfriend from flying forward. The airbag collided against her face and chest, knocking the wind out of her as the other vehicle slammed into them. Her wrist throbbed, falling into Iris's lap.

"Iris?" She asked, shaking her girlfriend's limp body. Kadence's heart, her head, her wrist… everything ached.

***

Kadence rolled out of bed the following morning with sleep in her eyes and a dull throbbing in her wrist. She rubbed at both, brushing the fragments away with a yawn before rotating the irritated joint. It cracked with a small pop. Usually that was enough to alleviate the soreness, but after straining it on the rock wall, it was still causing her minor discomfort. With a sigh, she retrieved an ice pack from the freezer and, wrapping it in a plush cloth, placed it against the tender spot.

Last night was interesting to say the least. She had expected to spend the majority of her time feeling like a third wheel between the two roommates, but instead, found herself spending almost the entire night with Avery, while Emma ran off. She was grateful to find that Avery was quite good company when she wasn't relying on obvious pick-up lines or ridiculous tactics. She liked when Avery acted as herself, not the cool, aloof image she tried so hard to portray.

Her thoughts were interrupted when the door jiggled open and Melody barreled through the front door.

"Melody?" She sat up. "What are you doing here?"

"I texted that I was coming." Her sister waved a hand.

"Oh."

"You always were shit at texting."

"Regardless, I'm glad to see you." Kadence smiled at her sister. "How've you been?"

"Good," Melody replied with a smile before noticing that Kadence was icing her wrist. Kadence tried to hide it, ineffectively stuffing her injured limb under a couch pillow. Melody continued to eye the cushion until Kadence sighed, forcing her wrist out into the open again.

"What happened?"

"I...uhh...I went to The Arkade."

Melody's eyes were like saucers. "What? With who?"

"Emma and Avery."

"Wow." Melody sunk into the couch and Kadence watched as the memories flashed behind her brown eyes. Iris was the one who had introduced the sisters to the establishment in the first place. Her free spirit had taken them on a detoured adventure after a night out at dinner.

"Go left here," Iris instructed from the passenger seat.

"Do you even know where we're going?" Kadence asked, one eye watching her sister in the backseat. Melody was sitting with her arms crossed, glaring out the window at the unfamiliar surroundings.

"Do you trust me?"

"Of course."

Melody made a gagging sound from behind them.

"Maybe take a right," her girlfriend deliberated. "Let's say two more lights?"

"Maybe?" Melody commented on the vague detail. *"What do you mean by 'maybe?' Where are we going?"*

"I don't know." Iris offered Melody a sheepish grin through the rearview mirror. *"But it's kind of fun, right?"*

"Iris!" Kadence jerked on the brake. She had to side with her sister on this one. This was crazy.

"Oh," Iris squeezed Kadence's knee. "Stop! Pull in there." *She pointed her free hand down the block at a rundown-looking warehouse. The words 'The Arkade' flashed on a dizzying sign.*

"Iris..." Kadence hesitated, tugging Iris by the wrist as she tried to climb out of the car.

"Trust me, Kae."

"Okay."

"We would have invited you, too, but..."

"It's okay. I've been a little MIA."

"You don't have to apologize. It's not like I haven't done the same thing to you."

"True," Melody agreed with reluctance in her tone.

"So, you're okay now?"

"Yeah."

"And Jordan?"

"Still my boyfriend. My fiancé, actually." Melody's face split into the widest of grins.

"I'm so happy for you!" Kadence propelled herself at her sister for a huge hug, irritated wrist forgotten. Melody laughed, wrapping her arms around her in return as Kadence squeezed tighter.

"Okay. okay." Her sister grumbled after having had enough physical contact. "Get off."

After being pried off, the realization finally set in. "Oh, my god. You're getting married. My sister is getting married!"

"I know. It's why I came here. It's gonna be crazy and a major fucking time crunch, but...Kae, will you be my maid of honor?"

"Yes! Of course." Kadence was elated. She almost went in for another hug, but Melody clenched her jaw.

Instead, Kadence cuddled a couch pillow to her chest, squeezing to expend the joy bubbling in her chest. "This calls for a celebration. Let me take you to lunch."

"You sure your wrist is okay?"

"Forget my wrist. I'm running on adrenaline right now. Let me just change and grab my phone."

She raced to the bedroom, tossing on a pair of shorts and pulling on an oversized tee. When she went to find her phone, she realized she had two text messages. One from Melody, as expected, but she was surprised to also find one from Avery.

Avery Bennett: Em told me it was your idea to invite me to your girl's night. You didn't have to do that.

She tapped back a reply.

Kadence Cooper: No prob. Thanks for coming with.

Avery Bennett: I should be thanking YOU. I think I finally got the perfect idea for the gallery. You'll have to come by and see it.

Avery Bennett: Be my date to the show?

Kadence froze, retreating to the kitchen to find Melody sitting in a daze. A dopey smile adorned her face as she eyed the ring on her hand with affection. Kadence took her phone out, snapping a picture of the rare sight before recalling the text message.

"What's with that face?" Melody asked, pointing at Kadence's conflicted expression.

Kadence hesitated before reading the series of texts out loud. Melody's expression was unreadable.

"Say yes," Melody finally said.

"Wait. Really?"

"Why not?" Apparently, Jordan's influence on the usual cynical Melody was more powerful than Kadence thought.

"Okay." She smiled down at her phone. "I will."

Chapter Nine

HAVING THE ABILITY TO manage her own schedule did have its perks. After getting past her roadblock and completing her paintings, Avery found herself having more free time—free time she was now spending with Kadence.

After the first few times they hung out, Avery realized she had been trying too hard. But she was getting better at it, if Kadence's laughter was any indication. As a result, Avery had let herself go a bit more, too.

The two were lounging in Avery's bedroom chatting. Avery was still getting around to cleaning the place up, but it was definitely a step up from the last time Kadence had witnessed the room when it had looked like a tornado blew through it.

"I originally wanted to go into international business marketing." Kadence had slowly begun to reveal little bits and pieces of herself and Avery, like a sponge, soaked up every word.

"Then what?" Avery prompted as she took a bite of her cold canned spaghetti. Kadence grimaced at her strange eating habits. Avery egged her on, grinning as she offered an outstretched spoonful.

"I think I'm going to pass." Kadence laughed.

Avery was getting addicted to the sound of Kadence's laughter. She knew what was going on with *those* feelings. And she kept trying to stop them. But with every smile, every teasing grin, every bat of those long lashes, it was harder to escape from the dangerous rabbit hole. *You're so fucked, Bennett.* "Good. More for me."

Kadence rolled her eyes before clearing her throat. "Let's get out of here. I'm starting to get stir crazy. Wanna go for a ride?" Kadence smiled devilishly and when Avery finally registered the innuendo, she flushed a flaming red. Kadence threw her head back, bursting into laughter.

Avery groaned. That was another thing she found herself doing a lot. Kadence Cooper had game, Avery could admit that much. What she didn't want to admit was Kadence was also good at embarrassing the shit out of her.

"I've got a place we could go. Lemme change first."

Kadence simply sat in place, waiting with a grin. Avery failed at trying to hide her embarrassment. Kadence continued giggling at her.

"Get outta here." Avery tossed her hat at Kadence who skittered out of the room, laughter trailing down the hallway.

***

"I'm surprised you wanted to walk." Kadence's comment was one of surprise.

"Hey, I'm not that lazy."

Kadence's lips just tilted to the side. She didn't need to voice her opinion. The twinkle in her eye gave it away.

Avery gasped in fake offense.

They arrived at the community park. Avery led them through the trees that lined the area. As the view cleared, a secluded playground, old and forgotten, appeared. It had become abandoned after the township decided to expand the property and the new equipment took precedent. But Avery appreciated it. It had its own unique character.

"I find it's usually pretty quiet here," Avery divulged as she took a seat on the swing, spinning in place until the tension of the chains by her hands was nice and taut. "It's a good place to clear your head."

She released her grip, allowing the coils to unwind as the world whirled around her. When she finally came to a halt, Avery leaned forward. In the midst of her descent, her shoe got caught on a rock, sending her to the ground.

"Oops. I fell for you." Avery grinned slyly, lying on her back. Her hair tangled with the tan bark groundcover as she stared up at the sky.

With a chuckle, Kadence joined her on the ground, head resting on the palm of her hands.

"You have a nice laugh," Avery blurted. *Oops.*

Kadence turned to face her, eyes boring into Avery's gaze before breaking into a grin. "Wow. You're looking at my eyes instead of my chest for once."

"Hey, I only look at your tits because your eyes are too distracting."

Kadence snorted. "Says you. You're the one with distracting eyes."

Now it was Avery's turn to be taken aback. When did their light-hearted banter become genuine flirting?

"I really am sorry. Women deserve to be respected and treated fairly. They shouldn't be objectified or only regarded for their bodies." Avery knew she was about to go on a rant. "I partially blame the media. Sex sells. And women are put on display to help sell products. In a way, it's artistic. But it also gets to the point where you don't even remember what they're trying to sell you. You just remember the girls. Especially if they look like you."

Kadence bit her lip. "Avery."

Why can't I shut up? Her mouth kept going. "Seriously, Kae. You're gorgeous. Like the female body in general is just…breathtaking. That's why I love painting them. They're softer and so curved. They just look so gentle and nice to touch, not in a creepy way, of course. They're just different from men, you know? They're hard and tough and sometimes even a little scary. But women, they're safe, like a lover." *Someone shut me up!*

"Avery?"

"Shit. That was too much, wasn't it?" *Yeah, like a hundred words too much.*

Kadence shook her head. "I like it when you're genuine. And you have a beautiful mind. Just as beautiful as your smile."

It had been a while since her fall from the swing, but Avery still felt that dizzying sensation for the rest of afternoon.

***

When Avery returned to the apartment, Emma was wrapped in a blanket, an overflowing bowl of popcorn in her lap. She tilted her head in greeting as Emma patted the space beside her, wiggling to give Avery room to join her.

"Where'd you go? Were you out with Kadence?

Again?" She lifted a brow as she offered the bowl of popcorn.

"Maybe."

"How's that going?"

Avery took her time chewing a handful of the snack before responding. "I asked her to be my date to the gallery showcase."

Emma beamed in excitement. "Wow! That's awesome."

Avery shrugged, trying to play it cool. "I mean, she's pretty chill."

"You sure that's it?" Emma nudged her in the side, elbow hitting the spot that caused her insides to bubble. She laughed and Avery wasn't sure if it was because her sides were so stupidly sensitive, or because she had made Avery flush stupidly red. Probably both, but mostly the latter.

"We're just friends. Per *your* request."

"I never said that. I just said don't fuck with her."

"And I'm not. We're just friends who happen to hang out at one another's places."

"Damn. U-hauling already? And I thought Kadence was the lesbian."

"I hate you." Avery took an entire fistful of popcorn, tossing it at Emma.

Emma managed to catch a few in her mouth. "That doesn't answer my question."

"No, Emma! I'm not U-hauling!"

Emma doubled in laughter, tears forming in the corner of her eyes.

"Oh, screw you."

"No thanks. I'll pass. I'm very much straight." Emma's tears sparkled on her cheeks as she tossed a handful of popcorn at Avery in retaliation. They landed in Avery's tousled blonde waves.

Avery picked a piece out of her hair and popped it into her mouth before flicking a second back at Emma. "The only straight you are is the straight-up worst."

Chapter Ten

THE NIGHT OF THE art show, Kadence arrived to find Avery's apartment in a state of absolute chaos.

"Oh, thank God!" Emma flung the door open. "She's in there."

Kadence followed the direction of Emma's thumb to find Avery hopping on one foot with a belt in her mouth as tried to pull her pants on.

"Avery, your girlfriend is here."

The increase in volume caused Avery to lose her balance, falling to the ground with a thud as a slew of profanities fell from her lips.

"Umm, we're not actually girlfriends," Kadence corrected with pink seeping into her cheeks.

"I know," Emma said. "I just like messing with her. Anyway, she's all yours. Fair warning, she's a mess right now."

"If you would have come as my date, I wouldn't be like this."

"It's not like I'm not gonna be there. I just have my own date this year," Emma objected as she ran her palms across her skirt. "And besides, your date is standing *right there*, Avery. Don't be rude."

"Oh, shit!" Avery's entire face brightened. "Kae! I didn't mean it like that. I just—"

"It's all right, Avery." After spending almost every day together for two weeks, she was much more accustomed to Avery's mannerisms, poor communication skills included. "Come on, let's get you fixed up."

Despite being confident ninety-nine percent of the time, Avery's face said it all. She was nervous. Extremely nervous. Kadence watched her pace before halting Avery in her movement.

"Let me." She gently coaxed Avery toward her with a tug of her belt loops. Slender fingers shrugged her pants up whilst tucking her shirt in and fastening the belt. "What happened to calm, collected Avery with lots of swagger?"

"She died, apparently," Avery deadpanned with a groan.

Kadence froze, blinking.

"Kadence?"

Kadence's eyes grew distant as she fought to calm her breathing.

"Earth to Kae?"

"Sorry. Just remembered something." Kadence sidetracked to the closet, pausing before grabbing a silk black tie. After collecting herself, she looped the fabric around Avery's neck. "You look great."

"Thanks." Avery's gaze dropped to survey Kadence's dress, tracing the deep vee with her eyes. "Wow, Kadence. You look—"

"Don't go soft on me now, Bennett. You coming?" Kadence moved to the doorway.

"I will be," Avery mumbled under her breath.

***

It wasn't the biggest gallery, but the space was decent enough to host at least fifty or so attendees. The clean, white walls were adorned with canvases of all styles and sizes. To the side of the entryway stood a row of sculptures, spaced evenly along the wall. Avery had Kadence at her side, a hand resting on Kadence's lower back as they greeted prospective buyers.

"Are you Avery Bennett? You did an amazing job."
"I love the green theme you managed to sprinkle in throughout each piece. What inspired you?"
"Brilliant execution and brushwork."
"Spot on blending techniques."

Kadence loved that none of the compliments seemed to go to Avery's head. She took each one with complete and genuine consideration. After an hour of networking, the artist removed her nametag, stuffing it into her pocket.

"I think it's time I focus on being present."

They each ordered a glass of wine before heading toward the back. The area was sectioned off from the rest, a small sign that read "Featured Artist: Avery Bennett" captioned the exhibit.

Kadence stepped into the space, surrounding herself in the room of green, studying each piece with precision. She passed Avery's interpretation of Mother Nature, a painting of naked trees in the form of female figures, the illusion of branches holding onto children, entwined silhouettes of people kissing, dancing, and the rebirth of a child. Everything was beautiful.

"So, uhh, what do you think?"

"Wow," Kadence breathed out.

"Good wow, or bad wow?" Avery fidgeted with the nametag in her pocket.

"Incredible wow."

"Tell me about this one." Kadence pointed to a towering painting that stood alone along the back wall. The piece was seven feet tall and five feet wide. Featured in the center of the piece was a dark-haired woman with gold flowers in her hair. Her back was to the audience, and she was adorned in both black and white. She stood on a black and white chess board, surrounded by colorful pieces. The chess king had fallen on its side with the queen, sword in hand, looking off into the distance.

She read the small plaque aloud. "Life is a battle, but you are a queen."

"Uhh, it doesn't fit the theme of the rest of the pieces, but it's my favorite. I was inspired by our night at The Arkade. I've always loved the idea of strong women not taking shit from men. I had my..." Avery shook her head. Before Kadence could ask, Avery changed to a different tangent.

"So, I usually paint nudes, but I felt like this just needed to have a woman in armor. Even though the background is all colors, your eyes are still drawn the strength of the queen. It took me a long time to get the lighting to work just right. It tricks your eyes to look at the monochromatic colors and shows that women can be beautiful, brave, and powerful all at once. I guess you could say it's one of my more feminist pieces," Avery explained in almost one single breath.

Kadence was in awe. She liked peeling back different layers of Avery every time they were together. Each time, Avery would accidentally reveal a little more depth to her character. And each time, despite herself, Kadence would be rendered speechless with admiration.

"Kadence?" Avery gulped. "I hate when you do

that."

Kadence blinked. "Do what?"

"Just...I don't know, stare and not say anything." She toyed with the ended of her tie.

"Sorry, I just...I'm at a loss for words. It's amazing."

"Oh." Avery flushed red.

"Do you take commissions?"

"Uhh, I guess. I haven't ever had a request made."

"Well, you should consider it. I'd love for you to paint me something."

"I..." Avery's gaze fell to Kadence's lips until a movement from behind Kadence caught her eye, breaking the trance. Within microseconds, her entire demeanor changed. Her amber eyes ignited, and her brows narrowed. Avery's nostrils flared.

"Excuse me for a second."

Before Kadence could register the situation, Avery was already stomping toward a man who stood in the doorway. Kadence couldn't hear the conversation, but she saw the vein protruding from Avery's neck. The man appeared to be relatively calm. He ran his hand over his hair as he shrugged. Whatever he said set Avery off. She rolled her eyes, turning her back to him before marching back to Kadence, lips pursed and mood soured.

"Is everything okay?"

"Fine," Avery snapped, rushing toward the bar. "Get a drink with me?"

"Uh, okay."

By the time she caught up with Avery, the artist had already slammed down an old fashioned, wincing at the sweetness. Kadence chewed her lip, watching wide-eyed as Avery ordered a bourbon, downing it in record time. She washed it down with a straight shot of Irish whiskey.

"Slow down, Avery. We have all night." She placed her hand on Avery's wrist, halting her from ordering another drink. Avery's skin was on fire.

"You're right. We do." Avery threw down two twenties before tugging Kadence with her.

"Avery? What...where are we going?"

Avery ignored her inquires, unlocking the back door of her exhibit to what appeared to be a storage room.

"Avery, I'm not sure if—"

Avery cut her off by pressing her lips desperately to Kadence's. Had it been any other circumstance, Kadence might have kissed Avery back. But everything about this felt wrong. Kadence pulled away.

"Avery, wait."

Avery's arms were wrapped around her waist and she leaned forward again and latched onto her neck, biting at the skin.

"Avery!" Kadence gasped, pushing against her shoulders. "Avery, stop." Kadence gave a forceful shove, causing Avery to stumble back into a pile of canvases. They toppled with a clatter that echoed off the walls. The loud bang seemed to snap Avery out of her trance, chest heaving and eyes dark.

"Damn it, Kadence. You're such a fucking tease. Am I just a toy to you? Someone you can flirt with for fun? Or do you think I won't be able to satisfy you? Am I not good enough? Are you not ready?"

Kadence didn't understand what was happening. This was not the same woman who spent the afternoon at the park passionately emphasizing the importance of respect toward women. This was a complete one-eighty from the woman who preached about female empowerment. This Avery didn't have that same playful smile on her face that made Kadence's eyes draw toward the line of her lips. The Avery Kadence took as her date had been so endearingly clumsy up until that point. This was not the Avery Kadence had felt herself growing comfortable with.

"What are you talking about? I'm not doing this because I'm not ready." Kadence shook her head. "I'm doing it because you aren't. And it's even clearer now, based on your reaction."

"You know what? Fuck this." Avery glared, throwing her hands up in the air. "Fuck Logan! Fuck everything. Fuck *you.*"

Before she knew it, her hand was colliding with the flesh of Avery's cheek. They both blinked, dumbstruck at the other's actions. It was Kadence who made the first move, fleeing the room, bursting through the doors into the cool night air. Hot tears raced down her face as she flagged a yellow taxi waiting down the street. Avery's behavior had terrified her. And Kadence Cooper was only scared of two things—love and losing control. Neither of which she had felt in a long time.

***

Kadence's knuckles jackhammered on the door. After a moment, it flew open and Jordan towered above her. It was late. He probably thought she was a threat.

"Sorry." Kadence immediately flushed, taking a step backward. "I didn't know you would be here. I'll just go—"

Her sister stepped from around the corner,

wrapped in a blanket. "Kae? What are you doing here?" Melody asked, brow knit in confusion. Her brown eyes softened when she took in the state of her baby sister cowering in the doorway. "Hey. Come here."

Melody ushered her inside, pushing past Jordan. Kadence bit down hard on her inner lip, swallowing back tears. She didn't want to cry in front of Jordan, but her resolve was fading.

"Jordan?" Melody gave him a silent look.

"Of course." He nodded. "I'll be in the bedroom if you need me." He placed a hand on Kadence's shoulder, giving her a comforting squeeze. She couldn't help but flinch and Melody studied her reaction with her eyebrows creased.

"I thought you were supposed to be at the gallery."

The statement triggered another round of tears. "I...I was."

"Kadence?" Melody scooted closer. "Hey, what happened?"

Kadence's lip trembled but she couldn't bring herself to speak any words.

"Did she hurt you?" Melody's fingers found the mark on Kadence's neck, stroking the tender skin.

"You...you were right. Avery is a pig. She doesn't respect women and she...she..." Kadence couldn't even finish her sentence.

"Oh, Kae, that's not something I want to be right about." Melody sighed, combing a hand through Kadence's hair. Kadence buried her face into Melody's shoulder, falling into the safety of her sister's hold.

"I don't know why it hurts so much," Kadence said, hiccupping. "It's not like you didn't tell me she was a player. You told me to be careful. I should have listened to you."

She knew Melody was angry — with her, with herself, and definitely with Avery. But her expression was more disappointed than anything. "It hurts because it mattered. I was hoping you'd prove me wrong because I saw the way you looked at her."

Kadence tilted her head in confusion.

"The way your eyes lit up. I saw the old you, a carefree you. She made you happy, even if you didn't realize it. Your eyes have always been your tell."

The truth hit Kadence hard and fast. For a moment, she sat numb. How didn't she realize it? She had started falling for Avery. But Avery wasn't going to be there to catch her. Somehow, Kadence had broken both of her rules. She let herself lose control *and* fall in love.

"What's going on in your head right now?" Melody took Kadence's hand in her own as she rubbed her thumb against Kadence's wrist in soothing circles.

"I don't know what happened. Everything was fine. Avery was being so sweet one minute, telling me all these incredible things about her art, and then she went to talk to some guy. When she came back it was like she became a different person. She tried to make a move on me, but all I saw was anger and pain in her eyes. So, I told her it was wrong, and she wasn't in the right state of mind. She called me a tease when I finally pushed her off me. Then I came straight here."

"I'm going to kill her," Melody snarled. "I'm going to fucking beat the shit out of that—"

"Mel, don't." As angry as she was herself, something inside her told her this wasn't just Avery. It just didn't fit the woman she had spent the past few weeks getting to know.

"You're going to defend her?"

"No, but I just...I feel like there's something else. I'm sorry for her?" She was angry at Avery, too, but maybe not to the point of wanting to physically inflict pain onto her like her sister wanted to. Maybe it was because she already got her turn and judging by the sound, it was a damn good slap, too.

"She's the one who should be feeling sorry!" Melody was seething. "You did nothing wrong."

"I know. But there was something about the way she looked when she first saw that guy. She looked so scared and so small and—"

"Just like you do," Melody pressed. "Right now."

"I..."

Kadence's phone started ringing and Avery's caller ID popped on the screen. Melody lunged for it, pressing the reject button before typing in Iris's birthday, shooting off a text to Avery. Kadence sat defeated, allowing her sister to send whatever biting message she wanted.

"I don't want you hanging out with her anymore," Melody said, passing back the phone. Kadence stared at the device in her lap, clenching her jaw. "Kae, I'm serious. Promise me you will stay away from Avery Bennett."

"I..."

"Kadence."

Kadence sighed, no longer wanting to put up any more of a fight. "Okay."

"Stay here tonight, okay?" Melody's voice softened now that Kadence had agreed. "I'm proud of you for coming here instead of—"

"Yeah." She didn't want to talk about *that*. Nor did she want to resort to it.

"I'm going to grab some blankets and pillows and meet you out here, all right?"

Once Melody was out of sight, Kadence unlocked her phone reading the messages.

Kadence Cooper: *Go fuck yourself! Stay away from me. I never want to see you again.*

She sighed, tossing it back onto the coffee table. She spent the night cramped on the couch, Melody's arm holding her defeated frame.

Chapter Eleven

AVERY HATED HOW MUCH of an ass she had been. She was no better than her fuckboy ex, and the realization made her sick. She crumpled into herself, hiding in the storage area until she could gather enough sanity to slip out unnoticed. By then, Kadence was long gone. When Avery tried to call her, wanting desperately to explain and apologize, Kadence had sent her another slap in the face.

Avery Bennett: *I'm so sorry. I don't know what came over me.*

She did though. Logan Davidson. That's what. And she let him win. *Again*. She spent the rest of her night sitting on the couch with her phone clasped in one hand, the remote in the other.

***

"Hey." Emma greeted her the next morning as she strolled through the doorway glowing, Danny in tow. He pecked her on the cheek, nodded to Avery and left.

"Have a good night?" Avery asked dryly once the door closed.

"Yeah." Emma grinned, still dreamily facing the doorway. "You and Kadence left early, too." She grinned, eyeing the bedroom.

"She's not in there," Avery said flatly.

"Just checking." Emma's tone was teasing, but Avery was far from in the mood.

"Don't worry. I won't be seeing her anymore."

"What do you mean you won't be seeing her again?" Emma placed her hands on her hips.

Avery's tired eyes fell to the carpet.

"What did you do, Avery?"

"I fucked up, Em. I fucked up big time."

A knock on the door prevented her from continuing. She sighed as her roommate turned to answer.

"Danny," Emma said expectantly as she went to answer the door. "Did you forget some...Davidson?" Emma stiffened, shifting in front of the door to block him from entering the apartment. Avery shrunk into the cushions of the couch, bile churning in the back of her throat.

"What the hell are you doing here?" Emma growled.

"I wanted to talk to Avery, if that's okay," Logan said, rubbing at the back of his neck.

"No. In what fucking universe would that *ever* be okay?" Emma hissed before slamming the door. She locked it in seconds, leaning her back against the door with a groan. "Did you know he was in town?"

"Yeah," Avery whispered, eyes glassy. "Found out last night when he came to the gallery. Surprise, right?" She laughed dryly.

"Oh, no..." Emma looked at her with concern, putting the pieces together. "Please tell me you didn't?"

Avery trained her gaze to the ground.

"You took it out on Kadence?"

"In the worst way possible." Avery ran her hands across her face with a groan. "I tried to get her to sleep with me."

"Avery..." Emma looked at her with a mixture of disappointment, frustration, but mostly pity.

"I'm an ass."

"Yeah. Obviously. Part of me kinda wants to beat you up right now."

"I wouldn't blame you."

"But another part of me knows you're probably already beating yourself up for it."

Avery grunted, throwing her face into a pillow as she pressed forward, trying to suffocate herself.

"Stop that." Emma tugged the back of her shirt. "Do you want me to say something?"

Avery shook her head in dejection. "I fucked up. It's my own fault."

"Okay. Let me know how I can help."

"I'll figure something out."

***

Something turned out to be a tall glass of blonde in the bathroom of a local bar. She was pretty enough. Ordinary looking but did well to help numb the pain for the moment.

"More," Avery demanded and the woman eagerly obliged.

"Tessa, by the way." The taller blonde panted when they'd finished. "My name is Tessa."

"Avery."

Avery returned to the apartment smelling of

alcohol and smoke, snapback sideways on her disheveled hair. She wobbled to the bathroom, washing her face with an exasperated moan.

"What are you doing?" From the doorway, Emma narrowed her eyes in disappointment.

I don't know. But I can't fix it. Avery scowled at her own image in the mirror. Emma's eyes met hers through the reflection.

"Have you spoken to Kadence?"

Avery shook her head. The alcohol was making the room spin. She let it swirl around her, distracting her from her guilt and grief. "Have you?"

Emma shook her head. "She canceled yoga."

Everything is so fucked up. "Fuck. Fucked. Fucking. Fuck." Avery repeated it until the word itself sounded comical. She giggled and teetered on her feet as Emma rushed to her side to steady her.

"Come on," Emma said, sighing. "To bed with you." She shoved Avery in the direction of her bedroom. Avery brushed the shirts from her bed onto the ground, kicking her shoes off into the closet. She couldn't stand the pitying look Emma gave her as she flopped onto the sheets. When the door closed, she pulled out her phone.

She crawled up her bed, reaching into the drawer of the nightstand. *Thank the gods for drunk food.* She grabbed two large pieces of jerky from the bag as she stared at the phone, scrolled through her contacts. She could call her again, but there were risks. Kadence could hang up on her. She could just not answer her at all. After all, she had told Avery to, as she so eloquently put it, fuck off.

She took a rather aggressive bite of the dried meat, tearing it with a tug of her teeth. *Screw it.*

Kadence's line rang with no signs of ending. Avery hung up with a sigh. She sent her another text. After no response, almost three hours later, she tried again. No answer. No response.

***

Avery's attempt the next day yielded the same results. And the next. And the next. And the next. By the fifth day, Avery had lost all hope. It didn't make any sense to her. Why did she care so much? She shouldn't be letting this rejection get to her. After all, she wasn't supposed to get attached. She flipped onto her stomach, burying her face in the pillow as she released a pent-up scream.

If Kadence didn't want to give her the chance at an apology, fine. The only way to get past someone was to get under someone else. She scrolled through her contacts, skimming the names until she hovered on a certain name. She hit the call button.

Here goes nothing.

It rang once.

Maybe this isn't such a good idea.

It rang a second time.

No, fuck it. You need this.

It rang a third time.

Who cares? It's not like you were even dating. If Kadence doesn't want you, it's her problem.

It rang a fourth time.

It's not your problem. This is all Logan's fault anyway.

It rang a fifth time.

It's fine. It's just going to be another no-strings attached fling.

It rang a sixth time. *Stop. This is so wrong.*

Just as Avery was about to pull the phone away from her ear, she heard a hesitant hello on the other end. *Well, shit.* She took a breath, collecting herself. "Hey, it's Avery."

"Oh," the voice said in recognition. "I was wondering if I was going to hear from you again."

"I've been busy." *Busy getting my phone calls rejected.* "So," Avery said in a low voice. "What are you doing tonight, beautiful?"

"You." Tessa's reply held no hint of hesitation.

Avery cracked a smile. "I knew I liked you for a reason."

There was a soft laugh on the other end. "Nine thirty. I'll text you my address."

***

Emma pounced on her the second she unlocked the entryway. "Sit down."

"Nice to see you, too, Em. My day was fine." Avery rolled her eyes as she kicked the door shut. She toed off her sneakers before tossing her keys into the bowl on the counter. They swirled against the rim before sliding down with a soft clink.

Emma crossed her arms. "This has to stop."

"What does?" Avery feigned innocence.

"You *know* what."

"She doesn't want to see me, Em. I tried. What do you want me to do?"

"Try harder." Emma bit back. "You can't keep doing this. I get that Logan hurt you. And for a while, I understood why you were acting the way you were. But it's been more than a year. You need to get it together.

This isn't you." She gestured up and down Avery. "None of this is who you are."

Avery tilted her chin in defiance, rolling her eyes.

"Avery!" Emma whacked her hard with one of the couch cushions. "Stop running from your problems. You can't just push people away and lash out when things don't work out."

"I don't have any problems."

"Yeah, you clearly do. You feel guilty about what you did and you're coping with it in an unhealthy way, just like you did with Logan."

"I'm nothing like Logan."

Emma groaned in frustration. Avery knew she was being bullheaded, but hey, no one likes being called out on their shit.

"I'm not saying you're *like* Logan. I'm saying that you aren't *handling* this the right way. You know that. This isn't you. Doesn't it feel wrong to you?"

Yes. "People change." Avery shrugged. "They grow up."

"Yeah, they do. So, when will *you*?"

***

For every day Kadence ignored her calls, Avery made Tessa cum twice. She had to hand it to Tessa, her stamina was pretty good. Probably not as good as Kadence's, she guessed, but still. She mentally berated herself for thinking of Kadence while hooking up with another person, pressing her fingers deeper into the squirming blonde as her tongue worked overtime to bring her to the edge yet again. Tessa's body arched, shaking until she had to tug Avery away by her hair, chest heaving. Avery felt sick to her stomach.

"Fuck, Avery. As much as I love when you do that, I need a break."

"Okay." Avery's voice cracked as she rolled off the woman, shuffling to the other side of the bed.

Tessa watched her tentatively.

They sat in silence.

"So, uhh, that was a new record, I think," Tessa said with a chuckle. "I'm surprised I haven't blacked out yet." The joke fell flat and she frowned. "Do you wanna tell me what's bothering you?"

"No."

"Look, Avery, I love a good hook-up as much as anyone else, but even you know this doesn't feel right." Avery hated the pitiful expression Tessa was currently giving her. She didn't need emotions involved in this. She didn't *want* them. Emotions only meant the risk of getting hurt.

"This is supposed to be a no-strings-attached sorta thing. And you're attached. To something or someone and—"

"Can you stop talking?" Avery clenched her fists.

Tessa balled the sheets between her fingers.

"I'm just going to go."

Tessa merely nodded, scooping Avery's shirt from the ground. She handed it to her before picking up her own scattered clothing from where they had haphazardly been tossed the previous night. The memories made Avery's stomach churn. They dressed in silence, engulfed in a somberness neither wanted to address.

"Whatever happens. I hope everything works out for you."

Avery could only nod before closing the door behind her.

***

Avery found herself, longboard under her feet, careening through the streets to the park. She settled onto the bench, watching a world of childhood simplicity pace by.

"Avery!" An excited, high-pitched voice called out. A blur of red hair barreled toward her, almost causing her to tumble with the force of the little boy.

"Hey, little dude." She greeted him with a smile that couldn't reach her eyes. Ryan didn't seem to notice. "What's up?"

"We're just about to start a game. Do you have time to play? You promised." Avery's stomach filled with even more guilt.

"I don't know, Rye. I'm not —"

"Please, Avery!" He clasped his hands together, bouncing on the balls of his feet. "I miss you. We all do."

"All right." She caved, following the boy to the group of young teenagers who had been tossing the basketball amongst themselves.

"Guys! Look. Avery's here." Ryan's announcement was met with a chorus of cheers.

"I want her on our team," the smallest of the boys, Evan, declared.

"No way." Ryan crossed his arms.

"I called her first."

"But *I'm* the one who asked her."

"Avery!" A matching pair of pouting lips turned to Avery.

It made her heart swell. These kids didn't know about the horrible week she had, or the horrible things she had done. They simply wanted her. They enjoyed her company. They missed her. And to have them fight over her, even if it was such a trivial matter, had Avery fighting back tears.

"Let's compromise. We can play two games. I'll play the first one with you." Avery gestured to Evan. "And then the next with you."

Ryan beamed, rushing to wrap his arms around her stomach, giving her the tightest squeeze. Avery ruffled his hair before he ran off to join the rest of his team.

Ball in hand, she coursed down the court with a parade of kids, all a foot shorter than her, chasing after her for control. Her heart pounded in her chest as she worked the pavement. Each pat of the ball against the cement bounced a little piece of her troubles away. Surrounded by youthful innocence, she let herself go.

Just as she was about to make another basket, she grabbed Evan, handing him the ball. Mustering all her might, she hoisted him into the air to make the final shot. The swift swooshing sound of the basket paired with the look on his face made all the aching she knew she was going to feel the next morning entirely worth it.

***

After the final game, she collapsed onto the grass, chest heaving. She closed her eyes, a wave of nostalgia rolling across her. Distant cheers floated in and out of her ears as she transported herself to a peaceful place.

"You're the best, Avery. Logan never plays with us," a voice said beside her.

Amber eyes fluttered open. Avery didn't have a response for the little one who praised her. She didn't want to defend him, but she also felt terrible for knowing he never would. Aside from his unwelcome visit a few weeks ago, he wasn't coming back. He was merely in town for a business trip, hoping to get laid while he had some downtime. Logan had gotten a new job a few months after their breakup and Avery couldn't be happier about his departure. She did feel bad for Ryan though. He had always liked playing ball with her ex-boyfriend. And at the time, she had enjoyed watching them and even joining them as well.

"You're better than him. At least you stop by sometimes."

The pit of her stomach dropped. Ryan continued, naively unaware of the weight his words held. "Do you wanna get ice cream with us? It's gonna be dark soon. The park is gonna be closing."

She shook her head. "I should probably head home. Thank you, though."

"Okay." Ryan pushed himself off the grass before brushing his hands on his shorts. "Thanks again for hanging out with us."

"Anytime, kiddo." She offered Ryan and the rest of the boys a wave, ensuring they safely crossed the street before going their separate ways.

Once out of sight, Avery retreated. Not ready to return to the real world, she sought out sanctuary at the playground's abandoned swing set. The seat squeezed against her hips and she wished she could stay cradled in her own little bubble.

You're better than him. Tears spilled from her eyes. Longing, loss, and despair all mixing into one salty cascade down her cheeks. She hated him, but she hated herself. *She* did this. Yes, he was a catalyst, but she was the one who dug her own hole. Now she was in so deep, she wasn't sure she'd ever be able to get herself up to the ledge again.

Just a few minutes ago, she had been at peace, at ease. And with a flip of a switch, she was in hysterics. Maybe this was the universe's way of sending her a sign, punishing her for the shitty person she had become. She cried until her choking sobs morphed into gasps for air, dissolving into the darkness of the night.

She should leave. No need to get arrested for trespassing. She dislodged herself from the seat her thighs had molded to and proceeded to the park exit. As she rounded the corner, Avery caught sight of a body lying on the ground. Her first instinct was the call the police, thinking it was a corpse.

Come on, Avery. You know that's extremely illogical. But when she stepped closer, all sense of logic flew out the window. *Okay, universe. You got what you wanted. Please stop with the torture. That's enough for one day.*

Sprawled on the grass lay Kadence, hair splayed out. Her eyes were shut, chest rising and falling. Avery felt like an absolute creep for staring, but she was unable to move. She hadn't seen the woman for almost two weeks and now Kadence was *here.* Before she could stop herself, she settled beside the raven-haired dreamer. She kept her eyes glued forward, afraid to speak and scare Kadence away again.

Chapter Twelve

KADENCE HAD GOTTEN NOTHING but silence from Avery for the past two days. She didn't know if she should feel relieved or worried. It wasn't like her to ice someone out like this. Avery had overstepped, but with the number of calls and texts she had been sending, Kadence *knew* she was sorry. And from what she did read of a few of the texts, Avery was more than genuine about her apology. Even Emma had mentioned it once or twice. But Kadence still felt conflicted about the entire situation.

To try to get her mind off the haunted amber eyes, Kadence agreed to attend a party with Melody and some of her friends. The problem was, Melody refused to release the iron grip she had on her bicep. Emma was cautiously present. Danny was playing the role of mediator between his best friend and his girlfriend. And Jordan had been trying to get Melody to relax enough to not cement herself to Kadence's side, but his efforts were in vain.

"I'm not going to drink, Mel. You can let go."

"That's not why I'm holding on." Melody eyed the room with suspicion.

Kadence appreciated how guarded her sister could be, but right now it was beyond suffocating. "I need some air."

She made her way outside, declining when

Melody offered to accompany her. Instead of returning to her empty apartment, she veered from her normal path, finding herself in front of Avery's secret park. She didn't know why her subconscious brought her here. Maybe to face her demons.

Finding a decent patch of grass, Kadence flopped onto her back and let her eyes close. She could hear Avery's husky voice as amber orbs glowed on the inside of her eyelids.

Women deserve to be respected and treated fairly.

It almost felt too real, as if Avery's presence was nearby. When she opened her eyes, Kadence startled. A figure with blonde hair was illuminated in the moonlight. She knew immediately who it was. She just didn't know how Avery had found her. She was about to run off when Avery spoke.

"Please stay." It was the crack in her voice that made Kadence's breath catch in both a terrifying and heart-racing manner. That, and the fact that Avery looked exhausted. The normal playfulness in her eyes had dwindled to nothing. Her features, normally bright and soft were sunken in, with bags hanging under her eyes. So maybe ignoring her had done more of a number on Avery than Kadence thought. No wonder Emma had approached her. Kadence felt ashamed. She had never been this cruel to anybody before.

"How did you know I was here?"

"Fate?" Avery sniffed, wiping her eyes with the back of her hand. She forced a smile, but Kadence gave a pointed look, not ready or willing to deal with Avery's typical banter.

"Honestly?" Avery sighed. "I didn't. I'm just as surprised as you are."

Kadence snorted. "Surprised? *You* want to tell me about being surprised?"

Avery's head fell. "Okay. I deserved that."

"Yeah. You did." Kadence ran her hands across her face, forcing down her emotions. *Why do you still let this woman get to you?*

"And you didn't." Avery whispered the words. The more the conversation progressed, the more Avery seemed to shrivel. Before she could stop herself, Kadence shifted closer. She didn't want to be angry anymore, but she wasn't sure if she could trust Avery either. They remained suspended as Avery's throat moved convulsively.

"H...his name is Logan."

Kadence blinked.

"The guy at the gallery, his name is Logan. He's my ex."

Kadence waited as Avery gripped her fingers through the grass, speaking with gritted teeth.

"I thought I was in love with him, but then I caught him cheating on me. In our bed with someone else."

Kadence felt sick.

"He was back in town and asked me to hook up. When I saw him again, I just...I got so crazy and all those feelings...the anger, the pain, the disappointment, the betrayal...just bubbled up. I tried *so hard* to push them away. To forget about him. But I couldn't. I took them out on you, and it was wrong."

Avery looked her in the eyes. "*I* was wrong. And when you rejected me, even when you teasingly shot me down, I just lost it. I felt unwanted. You have every right to be mad at me. But I just want you to know that I am sorry. I'm *so* sorry, Kadence."

Kadence took a moment to process the new information. When she failed to reply, Avery shook her head with a sigh. "Maybe I should go."

"I lost someone, too." The words she blurted caused Avery to pause. She couldn't figure out why she was confiding this information to Avery of all people. Maybe it was because Avery was willing to be vulnerable and honest with her.

"Her name was Iris." More painful words escaped from her lips. "You know they say everything happens for a reason and I just…" She shook her head, eyes darting to the swing rocking in the soft, spring breeze. Avery remained silent, allowing Kadence a moment. She didn't ask her to elaborate, which Kadence appreciated. Instead, she reached out to grasp Kadence's wrist, rubbing her thumb on the joint. She didn't know how Avery knew the exact spot to calm her, but she did.

"We don't have to talk about it."

Kadence nodded, an unspoken blanket of understanding falling over them. "I'm sorry I slapped you."

Avery scoffed. "I'm not. You had every right to."

Kadence nodded.

Another pause.

"I wish you would have told me about Logan."

"It wasn't something I wanted to share."

"Understandable."

"I'm sorry."

"I know. Me, too."

Avery tilted her head. "You have nothing to be sorry for. You didn't do anything wrong."

"I gave you the wrong impression. I hadn't meant to lead you on or be a 'tease' as you called it." Kadence made air quotes.

Avery's expression fell. "I'm sorry about calling you that, too. I just, I don't know what I'm doing. You just...I like...I act like a complete dumbass around you and I don't know why. Especially since..." she trailed off, capturing her lips between her teeth.

"Avery?"

"Since, uhh..." Avery rubbed the back of her neck. "Since I *did* want to sleep with you. But not like that." Avery scrunched her nose, shaking her head. "I mean, I think you're so attractive. And you're smart. And, well, I kinda like you. Shit. Not kinda, I do. Like you, that is. Goddamnit. This is not how I wanted to..." Avery groaned, hands flying up to cover her face in frustration and embarrassment.

Kadence watched Avery struggle out loud with herself, finding the moments of clumsy-Avery much more pleasant than the one who always tried to play it cool. Deciding Avery had tortured herself enough, Kadence cut her off. "Let's just take this slow, okay? Friends first."

"Really? You'd still want to be friends with me?" Bold brows shot up.

"Are you going to give me another reason not to?"

Avery shook her head frantically from side to side.

"If we're going to start again, no pretending, okay? I want to know the *real* you this time."

"Deal." Avery extended her hand. "Hello, Kadence. I'm Avery Bennett, part time artist, full time idiot. I'm working on being better though."

"Kadence." She chuckled, accepting the handshake. "Part time idiot, full time yoga instructor. I'm working on being better though."

Avery shook her head in objection, a small smile playing on her face. Kadence returned her own smile, feeling lighter than she had all week.

***

Kadence woke to incessant buzzing. She buried her face in her pillow, wrapping herself even tighter in the sheets. The sound finally stopped, only to chime a moment later. Peeping one eye open, she snatched her phone.

Reminder: *Meet Wedding Planner at 10:00 am with Mel.*

The notification had her sprinting to the bathroom to get ready.

"What's got you so giddy?" Melody raised a brow at the smile that had snuck onto Kadence's features.

"I don't know. I just feel good."

"Yeah? Where did you go last night, anyway?"

"The park."

"Yeah, you said as much. But what were you doing there?"

"Sitting."

Melody rolled her eyes. "Sitting?"

Kadence avoided her gaze.

"You wanna tell me the *real* answer?"

Kadence bit her lip. "I ran into Avery."

Melody stopped in her tracks.

"It's not what you think. She apologized. Like a lot."

"She damn well should have. But that doesn't

mean you have to forgive her. You should've continued ignoring her."

"Mel," Kadence said with a sigh. "It's not my place to tell, but we didn't know the whole story. We all have issues."

"Yeah, and mine is gonna be surviving this planning session."

For once, Kadence was thankful for the change of subject, rather than constant babying from her older sibling.

"Aww, come on, Mel. It'll be fun."

"Stressful."

"Fine, stressful, but fun."

When they arrived at the planner's office, Melody looked like a deer in headlights. The hallway was framed with an overwhelming amount of lace décor, soft pastels, and cursive quotes scrawled on the walls that highlighted the beauty of life-long marriage and commitment. Melody's face twisted into a mix of bafflement and scorn.

"Hello, ladies. I'm April." A woman extended a hand toward Kadence. "You must be the bride-to-be. You have that glow about you!"

Kadence giggled before correcting her. "Actually, I'm Kadence, maid of honor. My sister, Mel." She gestured toward Melody. "She's the one getting married."

The woman tilted her head, shifting her weight to her hip as she laced her hands in front of her. "My apologies. Nice to meet you, Mel."

Melody simply pursed her lips with a nod.

We're clearly off to a great start.

They started with a list— catering, flowers, a small venue, and an officiant and moved through the morning to compile a short, intimate guest list. The Cooper side was rather tiny, not having much family to invite. Jordan's parents, a group of small friends, and a few plus ones like Emma and Danny, made up the majority of the list. The total was less than fifty people.

"Do you want me to count a plus one for you, too?" April asked, pointing a finger to the page in front of her. The seat next to Kadence on the table arrangement was currently empty.

Kadence chewed the inside of her lip. "I…"

Sensing her sister's hesitance, Melody stepped in. "TBD. We can figure it out later." Kadence shot her a grateful look before returning her attention to the wedding planner.

April nodded, setting the layout aside before pulling out another set of papers. "Now, colors and themes." She crossed her legs with poise, hooking one ankle around the other. "Do you have anything in mind?"

Melody shrugged. "Whatever's easiest. And doesn't cost an arm or a leg."

Kadence knew Melody was starting to grow frustrated, overwhelmed, and incredibly restless. Things like this were never her forte. Emotions and feelings, it seemed, were never Cooper women's strengths.

"Seafoam green is quite popular amongst the young couples these days," the planner suggested with a teasing smile.

"Seafoam…" Melody grunted. "A fancy way to say whale piss."

Kadence gave the woman an apologetic look. Melody tended to shut down during stressful or high-pressure situations. Additionally, Melody never liked drawing attention to herself, so to have to plan an entire wedding, centered around herself and her fiancé wasn't exactly bringing out her most redeeming qualities.

April seemed unfazed. In fact, she seemed almost amused as she studied the eldest sister. After a suspended silence, Melody's shoulders shrunk back. It was almost comical to see her sister being beat at her own game. The planner broke into a patient smile.

"You know, something tells me you don't care too much for pastels...or color in general."

Kadence couldn't help but grin, stifling a giggle when Melody kicked her in the shin under the table.

"What do you think of a classic black and white wedding with a simple gold accent?" April pushed her chair back, shuffling to the bookshelf to dig through the collection.

With April's back turned, Melody shot her sister a glare. Kadence did her best to remain impassive as April cleared her throat, returning with a new book. Unlike the worn catalogues around them, this book was clean, the pages crisp and corners sharp.

"What's your opinion on doing something like this?" April's manicured finger pointed to a spread of very formal, yet elegant table arrangements.

Melody's jaw twitched, lips pressed together in a thin line. She clamped down the suppressed smile but Kadence, having years of practice of reading her stealthy ticks could detect her excitement.

"She loves it."

"You sure?" April lowered her glasses, locking her gaze with Melody. The room fell silent as a sort of blissful air swirled around them.

Melody's eyes softened and her lips tilted a few millimeters. "I do."

***

It was late afternoon by the time the two siblings left April's office, a stack of papers and color pallet samples in hand. Their next stop was to the flower shop, the same flower shop Kadence had been avoiding. The last time she'd made a purchase there, she plummeted into a panic attack, still in disbelief that the petals would be laid across a grave, rather than a bed.

Melody grasped Kadence's hand, stopping her. They stood in the parking lot of the shopping complex. Kadence half-willed God to just send a car around the corner to knock her out of her misery. "You sure about this?"

"Positive." The lie felt like shards of glass in her throat. "It...it's the best shop in the area."

"Kae." Melody's voice was patient. "I can come back another time. I understand if you don't want to be here."

Kadence took a moment to calm her nerves, eyes fluttering shut as she inhaled, exhaling with a hiss through her teeth. Melody waited.

"Okay." Kadence squared her shoulders as she took a step forward. "Let's go."

When the bell above the door rang, Kadence's stomach curled. She clenched her jaw. As Melody and the shopkeeper discussed the need for a simple white flower, Kadence felt the walls of the shop caving around her. Just before her breathing started to grow ragged, she darted through the door. The faint sound of Melody apologizing to the elderly woman whisked through her ears as she braced her weight against the car.

"Hey." Melody was already at her side. "Talk to

me."

Kadence shook her head. "I thought I could handle it."

"One day, you'll be able to walk in there again. Regardless, I'm proud of you." Melody placed a kiss on her forehead.

***

After spending the appointment hiding in the car doing breathing exercises, Kadence and Melody's final destination was the bridal parlor. Kadence sat on the plush white leather sofa, sipping on a sample of champagne while Melody grumbled from behind the curtain.

"You okay in there?" Kadence chuckled.

Melody grunted. "Zipper's stuck."

"I'm coming in."

"No, no! I've got it."

"Too late." Kadence set down her glass before stepping inside the dressing room. Melody's fingers were trembling as she fidgeted with the zipper along her back. Their eyes met in the mirror and Kadence saw her sister's eyes brimming with tears.

"This is really happening." Melody's voice was shaky as she averted her gaze. Melody had been steeling herself the entire day, but even the strongest of people had to break sometime. "Stupid zipper."

"Mel." Kadence placed her hand on her sister's. "It's okay. Nothing's going to change. You're still my big sister. You'll always have me, and I'll always need you."

Melody threw her arms around her sister, burying her face into the crook of her neck as her resolve fell away.

"I love you, Mel."

"I love you, too, Kae."

Kadence rubbed her sister's back, scratching at the base of her spine the way she remembered their mother doing.

"This dress," Kadence said when her tears subsided. "It's beautiful."

"I think..." Melody paused, straightening in the mirror. Her fingers floated along the embroidered fabric, tracing the hemline of the delicate lace accents. "I think this is the one."

Chapter Thirteen

AVERY WOKE THE NEXT morning to find an aluminum can of her favorite canned spaghetti sitting on the kitchen table. A sticky note with a bold A written in her roommate's handwriting sat next to it. Even through her anger, Emma still cared enough to lay out something for her to eat, probably knowing Avery wasn't doing a very good job of feeding herself. For the past few days, Avery had been spending more time consuming guilt than real nourishment.

She pulled her phone from her back pocket, typing a text of gratitude. She and Emma were both fiery in nature, but Emma had always been her rock, steadfast and never fleeting. No matter how many arguments they had gotten into while growing up, Emma always had her back.

With a sigh, Avery busted the seal and swallowed a spoonful of the pasta and tomato sauce. The microwave clock read eleven eleven. Something, maybe childish belief, flipped a switch in her. She dashed to the bedroom, tripping herself on a pile of old magazines. With a mumbled curse, her gaze narrowed at the offending literature. Her stomach rolled. She used to view them as inspiration for her nude portraits, but now they just made her feel dirty. She tore off the cover, crumpling the page before pitching the wad and the entire stack of nudie magazines into the wastebasket.

She grimaced at the appearance of the desk as well, covered in paint-stained cloths, papers, pencils, and old candy wrappers. It was disastrous.

Time for a cleanse. For the rest of the day, Avery occupied herself with cleaning the mess she had created during the past year. She emptied her desk of scraps of papers with phone numbers of hookups she had encountered. Most of which she didn't even remember the names of. Her blunt nails scratched the dried paint from the surface of the desk, trying not to damage the finish of the wood. After removing the acrylic blemishes, she sorted through the empty paint tubes, crusty flecks breaking off as she tossed them over her shoulder and into the trash.

She tackled the clothing in her drawers, flinging strangers' sweatpants and T-shirts into a pile by the door. She collected the unwanted articles in a black trash bag, lugging it to the front door. She cleared out the fridge, ridding it of the mountains of leftovers, pizza crusts, expiring salsa, and other preserved foods that were bound to increase Avery's risk of cancer, should her eating habits continue. Finally spent, she collapsed on the couch, amber eyes eventually drooping closed.

***

Avery woke to the sound of jingling keys and the click of a latch at the front door. She rolled with a groan.

"Hey." Emma wedged herself between Avery's legs and the armrest. "What've you been doing all day?"

Avery yawned. "Cleaning."

Emma's eyes were the size of a golf ball. "Really? Are you feeling okay?" A palm immediately went to

Avery's forehead.

"I'm fine." Avery chuckled. "Em, can I be honest for a second?"

Her roommate narrowed her brows. "Uh oh. What's up?"

Avery sat up, rubbing at the back of her neck. "I just wanted to say that I'm sorry. And to thank you for always being there for me, even when I don't deserve it. I don't know what I'd do without you."

There was a pause between them.

"You know I love you. You're my best friend. And I hate watching you destroy yourself." Emma's sad, vulnerable eyes hit Avery with a huge wave of guilt. Her hurting wasn't just affecting her, but everyone she loved and cared about.

"I...I'm sorry."

"I know." Emma shrugged. "But you shouldn't be telling me that. Kadence's the one..."

"I know. And we're working on it. Well...I'm working on it. I'll explain that later. But I need you to know just how sorry I am for everything I put you through, too. Ever since everything happened with Logan, I've been a real ass, and you've been nothing but patient with me. And I've been a shitty friend in return."

"Not really shitty. Just, uhh, kinda shitty."

Avery garnered a small smile.

"Look, I know it's been hard for you," Emma said with a sigh. "Especially recently."

"But it's not an excuse. Can you ever forgive me?"

"You know you're already forgiven."

"I know but I still want to make it up to you. Can I make you dinner? We could do one of those huge meals with everyone. We haven't done that in a long time."

"Since Logan..." Emma trailed off as Avery nodded.

"I want to bring back the old Avery and our old traditions. Would you wanna come? I mean, would you do me the honors?"

"So formal." Emma scrunched up her nose. "It's weird."

"I'm trying to be more of a gentlewoman and less of an ass. You know, classy?"

Emma chuckled. "This is a little too classy. Find a happy medium."

"Working on it."

"And Kadence?"

Avery chewed her lip. "I...I really like her. And it scares me, Em. I don't know what to do. I...Kadence is just...I don't want to be scared. But I am. I messed up. We're taking it slow, starting again. But I don't know if we'll ever be able to get to being friends. I want to. But I don't know...maybe that's a good thing if we don't. Because..." Avery swallowed the lump in her throat. "She could *break* me."

Emma placed a hand on her knee. "Kadence isn't Logan."

"What if I can't fix things with her?"

Emma looked her square in the eye. "Do you remember when you were seven and some kid decided it would be a good idea to push you off the swing set at recess?"

Avery raised a brow. "Where are you going with this?"

Emma's smile only widened as she squirmed. "You pushed her off the swings the very next day and got beat up by her brother for it. You ended up wiping your bloody nose on your hand, and then smeared it on their shirts. But you still fixed things in the end. And look at us now. Best friends; you, me, and Jayce."

Avery broke into a smile.

"You can repair bridges. You're good at it. And Avery Bennett has always been a fighter. That will never change. Even when you're beaten down."

"That was elementary school. Things aren't that simple. We're different now."

"Sometimes people change. And sometimes it's for the better."

"I..." Avery's eyes welled up as the words sunk in. *Damn. I have been doing a lot of crying lately.*

"You should invite Kae to our dinner."

"What?" Her jaw dropped. "I can't do that. That is so not platonic."

Emma dispelled her apprehension with a wave of her hand. "I'll invite Mel. It'll be a group thing."

"I don't know..."

"You can fix this, Avery. You're a good person. You can't let a few mistakes make you believe otherwise about yourself."

Avery's tears finally erupted, racing down her cheeks.

"Eww. Stop it!" Emma wrapped her in a hug despite Avery's sniffling. "Come on, where's your phone? Let's send some texts, shall we?"

***

On the evening of Avery's dinner party, the hostess fell into a fit of anxiety.

"Have you seen my snapback?" She barreled through the apartment, practically colliding into Emma.

"Which one."

"The one my dad gave me?"

"Not since you had it this morning."

"Fuck! This is a bad sign. What if she changed her mind?"

"Calm down, Bennett. Kae was fine at yoga when you came up in conversation. Everything's gonna be fine." Emma attempted to assure her. It had the opposite effect.

Avery barely avoided slicing her finger open while attempting to divide the cured meats into bite-sized pieces on the cutting board. "You talked about me?"

"Just about tonight." Emma took the knife from her hands, urging her in the direction of the cheese platter. "Geez, Avery. Breathe will ya? You're gonna give yourself an aneurysm."

Avery fidgeted with the hem of her collar before setting onto the next task. "I just don't want to screw this up again."

"You probably still will."

Avery shot her roommate a defensive glower.

"But in an endearing way," Emma said, recovering with a laugh.

"Wow. Thanks for your support," Avery replied flatly, busying her nervous hands with arranging the cheese cubes and Swiss slices.

"No problem." Emma winked, swiping a slice and ruining Avery's hard work before popping it into her mouth.

"Emma, come on!"

***

Lola and Jayce arrived together, as expected, with Danny in tow. He made his way to Emma, greeting her with a kiss. The group opened a bottle of wine, settling onto the couch. A moment later, the doorbell rang.

"What if it's her?" Avery hissed under her breath.

Emma released a belly-rolling laugh. "Considering everyone else is already here, I'd say there's a pretty good chance it is."

Shit. I'm not ready.

"Welcome!" Danny opened the door to a breathtaking figure. Kadence stepped inside with an aura that drew Avery's amber eyes to her. The rest of the room fell away.

Bennett, you are so fucked. Avery attempted a wave, cheeks burning as Kadence gave her a polite smile before turning to Danny and Emma. Avery watched with rapt attention as Kadence spoke with her hands, elegant knuckles flexing as her wrists rolled with her words. Her green eyes glowed.

A clearing of a throat and a jab to her ribs drew Avery out of her trance, hitting her at the perfect angle to cause her to yelp. Kadence's head turned in her direction and Melody scowled. *Shit!*

"What?" Avery drew her gaze away, glaring at Jayce.

He responded with a boyish grin and a wink. "You wanna offer your new guests a drink?"

Oh! "Yeah. Good idea." She fumbled to the kitchen, pouring with shaking hands. A glass of white wine for Kadence, Avery recalled her preference from the art show, and a glass of red for Melody. She felt her knees knocking together as she approached the group.

"Hi, Avery," Kadence's smile was radiant.

"Avery." Melody tilted her chin up with a grunt. Avery gazed between the two siblings as Kadence pinched her older sister's forearm. Melody tried again, this time with a peppier tone. "I mean, hey, how are you?"

"Uhh. I'm good." She gulped under Melody's guarded eyes. "Uhh, thank you for coming."

The conversation stalled in the doorway.

"Thank you for inviting us." Kadence came to her rescue. "Whatcha got there?"

"Oh," Avery held out the glasses in her hand. "These are for you. I know you like whites," she said as she passed the chardonnay to Kadence. "And I took a guess with you, Melody." She held the merlot to Melody.

"Thank you, Avery." Kadence smiled.

Avery nodded, shuffling her weight as Melody eyed her glass. "Uhh, I guess I'm gonna go check on the food now. Make yourselves comfortable," she said before scurrying off toward the kitchen.

You're sinking worse than the Titanic, Bennett. You're a fucking Bitanic.

Chapter Fourteen

KADENCE WATCHED AVERY'S RETREATING figure with curiosity. She had witnessed Avery nervous and bashful before, but this was just plain *awkward*. Before she had more time to ponder it, Melody took her by the wrist to the couch. Just as she was about to take the first sip of her drink, Melody snatched her glass from her grasp. She took a tentative sip of Kadence's drink, smacking her lips before pursing them. Kadence resisted the urge to roll her eyes.

"Okay." Melody nodded after a moment. "You can have it now."

"Was that necessary?"

"Yes."

"Don't you think you're being a bit much?"

"Absolutely not."

Kadence sighed in frustration. "I thought you were going to behave."

"I will, but how do I know if she will?" Melody leaned toward Kadence, narrowing her eyes in a dark, dangerous glare.

"Quit threatening." Kadence gave her sister a nudge with her knee. "Look at her. She already looks like she's going to pee herself."

"Good."

"Nothing's going to happen. Knock it off."

"I know how you get with pretty girls. I'm not

stupid. I have eyes. Avery's an ass, but she's still hot. And you love blondes. How do I know she won't try to pull a fast one on you again? Try to seduce you into her room." Melody's black fingernail pointed around the corner.

"That's Emma's room."

Melody gave a pointed look.

"You have absolutely no faith in me." The words held a double meaning and Melody's shoulders fell at the accusation.

"Kae, I didn't..."

"I appreciate that you're trying to look out for me." Kadence watched the wine in her glass as she swirled it. "But you have to let me live a little. Be my own person. You won't be here forever, and I've got to learn to stand on my own two feet once you're gone."

Melody remained silent, entwining their fingers with a squeeze of hesitant agreement.

***

Their meal consisted of a slow-roasted lamb shoulder with a blueberry wine reduction, potato gratin, and a side of steamed vegetables. Kadence was impressed to say the least. She was even more impressed to learn Avery had been the master chef behind it. She eyed the canned spaghetti loving woman with interest, but Avery barely looked up from pushing her vegetables across her plate. Despite the playful bickering between Emma and Danny or the riveting conversation between Melody, Jayce, and Lola, Avery remained quiet. Kadence managed to catch her glancing in her direction once, but Avery quickly averted her gaze.

By the end of dinner, Melody seemed to have tamed herself, sipping casually on her wine as she leaned back in her chair. Avery, in contrast, looked desperate to escape.

"I'm gonna get started on the dishes." Avery stood abruptly, pushing her chair from the table in haste.

Kadence took her chance. "I'll help."

She rushed after Avery only to find the woman cowering in the kitchen by the sink. Avery's eyes were glued to the dish in her hand, wide and frightened. She repeated wringing the sponge in her hand as the faucet continued to run water.

"Hey." Kadence inched forward.

Avery's spine stiffened. "H...hey, Kadence."

"Everything okay?"

"Yeah." Avery's reply was two octaves above normal. "Dandy. Just dandy."

"Dandy?" Kadence quirked a brow. "Avery, are you sure you're okay?"

"Yup." Avery squeaked the response, chewing the inside of her lip.

Kadence crossed her arms. She could be patient. Yoga had taught her that.

After a moment, Avery sighed. "Melody hates me."

"Give her time."

"I'm really *am* sorry."

"I know." Kadence nodded. "She does, too. It'll just take a little longer with her. She likes to hold grudges. It's not healthy."

"You don't hold onto anything?"

Kadence hesitated.

"Sorry. That isn't my business. You can tell me

when…" Avery shook her head. "If you ever trust me again."

Kadence appreciated Avery handling the situation with such maturity. But her amber eyes still kept darting to Kadence, then to the dishes in her hand. She looked like she was going to burst.

"Avery, you look like you're going to explode," Kadence said gently. "Just say it."

"S…say what?"

"Whatever it is that you've been holding in all night."

Avery swallowed so hard Kadence heard it.

"You, umm, you…I just…you look beautiful tonight." Avery tensed, squeezing her eyes shut. Her hands flew to shield her face.

Kadence blinked for a moment, processing the compliment before breaking into a smile. That smile turned into a quiet giggle. And that giggle bubbled into laughter. "That's it?"

Avery turned crimson.

"No!" Kadence reached out to place her hand on Avery's forearm. "I'm not laughing at you. It's just…well, *that's* what you've been holding in all night?"

"You mean, you're not mad?"

"No, that was…" She paused to find the right words to voice her endearment. "That was sweet."

"I didn't want to overstep."

Kadence tilted her head as she observed Avery's fidgeting. This insecure version of her was new. Kadence wasn't sure how she felt about it.

"I just didn't want you to think that I was trying to just get in your pants or something. I want us to be friends, but I don't know where to draw the line. Or where you've drawn the line, I guess. But I —"

"Avery." Kadence cut her off. "Stop overthinking everything. You're doing just fine. I'm not saying that I trust you, but I know you're trying. It's going to take some time. I don't think you're a bad person, Avery. I just think you made a bad decision."

"Okay. That's fair."

"We're okay, Avery. I already know you're sorry."

Avery nodded.

Kadence turned her attention to the sponge still clasped in Avery's hand. "So, do you wanna wash or dry?"

"I'll wash."

They settled into an easy rhythm. The sound of running water splashed around them while the murmur of conversation in the dining area buzzed through the doorway.

"Do you remember when I said I wasn't scared of anything?" Avery shut off the sink. Kadence nodded. "I was lying. Everyone's scared of something."

"So, what *are* you scared of?"

Amber eyes searched hers before answering in a whisper. "You."

"Me?"

"You scare me, Kadence. I don't want to hurt you and I'm so scared of messing up again and ruining our friendship."

Avery was standing in front of her with her heart on her sleeve. The same Avery Bennett that was multi-faceted and complexly layered. The same Avery Bennett that Kadence found annoyingly cocky at times, secretly clumsy, stupidly endearing, and so fascinatingly vulnerable.

"You scare me, too."

Their eyes met and something quiet fell.

"I do?" Avery's timid query floated between them.

You could matter.

Before she got to answer, Lola walked in with the remaining dishes piled in her arms, Jayce following on her heels.

"Leftovers!" Lola announced before glancing between the two with an apologetic smile. "Uhh, did I interrupt something?"

Kadence shook her head as the two additions busied themselves with putting containers into the fridge.

"Uhh, hey, Avery." Jayce's low voice was heard from behind the refrigerator door. "Is there a reason John's hat is in here?" He pulled out the familiar snapback Kadence had stolen quite a few times.

Avery's face turned beat red as she made a dash for the snapback.

"Do you always leave your hat in the fridge?" Kadence chuckled.

Avery scrunched up her nose as she stuck out her tongue. The air felt lighter. Kadence sprinted to her side, snatching the cap before dashing out of the kitchen with Avery hot on her heels. But in a small apartment, she quickly caught her just as she rounded the hall toward Avery's room.

"So." Kadence handed her the accessory. "Who's John?"

"Uhh." Avery cleared her throat as she adjusted the brim of the hat, returning it to its rightful place on her head. "My dad. He passed away."

Kadence's eyes widened. "I'm so sorry. I wasn't—"

Avery shook her head. "It's fine. You didn't

146

know."

"Still…" Kadence sighed longingly. "It's unfair losing the people we love."

"Terrifying," Avery agreed with a shudder. "Can I show you something?" Avery nodded toward the studio.

It took Kadence by surprise. Despite her visits, she had never been inside the studio. She followed Avery to her workspace, stepping across the tarp and maneuvering around canvases. Avery stopped at the closet, gesturing Kadence to her side. Kadence's breath caught. Stowed away in the back of the closet was an old painting— a man with amber eyes and dusty blond hair. He had the same wrinkles by his eyes as Avery and a kind smile that tilted to one side.

"You look like him. He seems like a great man."

"He was," Avery agreed.

Kadence shook her head. "Is."

"What do you mean?"

Kadence offered her a gentle smile as she pointed to Avery's hat. "He's still around. You carry him with you to this day."

"Thank you." Avery's voice cracked.

Kadence hummed, turning her attention back to the art. "It's amazing how well you capture people. You should consider doing commissions."

"I don't know anyone who needs one."

It sparked an idea in Kadence. "I do."

"You…you do?"

"This." Kadence reached for her phone. She swiped through a few apps before revealing an image of her sister gazing at her hand, admiring the ring around her finger.

"You want me to paint…Melody?"

"You don't have to. I just thought it would be a sentimental wedding gift," Kadence explained before frowning with a sigh. "Maybe it's stupid. Never mind."

"No!" Avery placed a hand on her forearm. It made Kadence's skin sear. Avery must have felt the spark, too, because she quickly withdrew it and cleared her throat. "I mean, no. It's sweet and thoughtful. I'll do it."

"Really?" Kadence beamed. "Thank you."

Before she could contain her excitement, Kadence's arms were around her shoulders. She felt Avery tense under her. Kadence squeezed a little harder.

"Thank you," she whispered in Avery's ear. Avery barely managed to wrap her hands around her waist before Kadence straightened again.

"So, how much do you charge?"

"I guess it kinda depends on the style and the size of the canvas."

"The style?" Kadence tilted her head to the side.

"Watercolor, oil, etcetera."

"Can you show me?"

Avery nodded, retrieving her laptop from her room before returning to the studio. It started up with a gentle whir and they settled with their backs against the wall, legs splayed out.

"So, watercolors are softer, while oils are typically bolder, and the colors are louder." Avery began searching for images to accompany her explanation. "I think you would typically like watercolors if you were to paint. They're easier to handle. They dry fast and are light enough that any mistake can be covered up relatively easily or blended so that they don't show as much anymore."

Kadence admired the soft pastel colors on the screen. "Those are nice."

"They are. But I like acrylics and oils." She started typing again before clicking the search button. The screen filled with bright still-life paintings of captured moments.

"Oils are a slower process. It takes longer for each coat to dry and should be done in layers. It's pretty difficult, I'll be honest. But in the end, it's worth it. You just have to be patient with it. They make things livelier and brighter. Plus, the colors last for lifetimes while watercolors fade."

Kadence wasn't sure that Avery noticed her habit of speaking faster when she was excited about something. Her amber eyes would also glow in response. Kadence liked it.

"I guess I overlooked those in the past. I typically would go for watercolors, something safe."

"And now?" Avery asked, thumb tapping against the space bar.

"Now." Kadence paused, searching in Avery's gaze. "Now, I think an oil portrait would be a nice change."

Chapter Fifteen

THEY SLOWLY BEGAN MENDING their friendship with easy conversations. 'How are you?' and 'hope your day is going well' texts were exchanged daily. They discussed how Kadence's classes were going, and the different artists Avery admired. Surface-level things. It was a comfortable pace and most importantly, a safe pace. Avery was still hesitant to push their boundaries, but the wariness slowly disappeared.

Two weeks after the dinner, Avery was working in the studio, the layout of Melody's portrait sketched upon her canvas. She was having trouble getting the details of the portrait just right, her phone zoomed into the specific angle of Melody's jutted features. She knew why, groaning at the blatant references of Kadence that reflected on the canvas. The bristles of her brush were just about to key into the cut of her jaw and the rise of her cheekbones when her phone rang.

With a sigh, she rubbed her paint-colored palms against her jeans. But her frustration dissipated when she read the caller ID—Kadence Cooper. "Hey," Avery greeted, jamming the phone between her shoulder and cheek. *Why is your voice so high?* She cleared her throat, trying to collect the nerves that were running amuck. "What's up?"

A breathless, frazzled Kadence was on the other side of the line. "I hate to bother you, but I have no one else to call right now. Mel's at work and Emma and Danny are on the other side of town. I know you don't have set working hours but—"

"Whoa, Kadence. Calm down. Start from the beginning. What's going on?"

"Oh." The line went quiet for a moment, the only sound Avery could detect was a slow exhale.

"My car." Kadence's voice was level once again. "I think, well, I don't know what's wrong with it, but I think I need a jump. I don't mean to interrupt your day—"

"I'm on it. Where are you?"

"About five minutes from your place, off Rivers and Chestnut."

"I'll be there in four." Avery was already swiping the keys from the counter.

"Avery, wait." Kadence's panicked tone stopped her from sprinting out the door.

"What's wrong?"

"Don't speed." The strain laced in her words led Avery to believe it was more than just a casual warning. There was a hesitant pause. "Please drive carefully."

Avery blinked at the phone before placing it back against her cheek, lips against the speaker. "Okay. Be there in six, maybe seven."

"Thank you, Avery. I owe you."

"No problem."

***

Unfortunately, it *was* a problem. They tried to jump start the car three times, each attempt failing.

Avery frowned. "I think you're going to need to get it towed."

"Shit." Kadence ripped her hands through her dark hair.

Kadence never swore. It was rare for Avery to see her so raw and, well, frustrated. It was kind of a turn-on. She shook her head, desperate to be a friend and not a horn-dog. Kadence stepped away to call the towing company, pinching the bridge of her nose.

"Yes, Chestnut and Rivers. I will. Thank you. Goodbye." After the line went dead, Kadence collapsed onto the curb, toe kicking her car's tire for good measure.

Avery settled next to the distraught woman. "Don't worry, Kae. It's going to be all right."

Kadence buried her face in hands with a sigh. "I hate to do this to you."

Avery was pretty sure that if Kadence asked her to cut off her own limbs, she would. How could she say no to those eyes?

"Do you think you could give me a ride to the nearest subway station? Maybe I can catch the next one and will only be a few minutes late for class."

Come on, Bennett. Be her hero. "I'll do you one better." Avery gave a lopsided grin. "I'll drive you."

Kadence shook head. "I can't ask you to do that."

"You're not. I'm offering. I *want* to."

Kadence blinked, but Avery held her gaze. "I insist."

Later, after the tow truck left with Kadence's car, they climbed into Avery's car, and Avery placed the keys in the ignition, twisting her wrist. It groaned to life. She caught Kadence eyeing her expectantly before recalling Kadence's insistence on wearing a seatbelt. Avery clicked the safety buckle, giving it a tap before flashing a bashful grin in Kadence's direction. Once it clicked,

Kadence's shoulders deflated. A flash of sadness crossed her green eyes, disappearing so quickly that Avery wondered if she had imagined it.

A mile into the trip, Kadence began jiggling her knee. Avery tried to ignore it, but the movement soon became compulsive bouncing.

"Hey, don't worry. Your car will be fine."

Kadence remained quiet. It took another mile before it finally made sense. Once she realized, Avery pulled to the side, withdrawing the keys from the ignition. She set them in Kadence's lap with a tender smile. "It's not the car, is it? You…you feel more comfortable if you're the one driving."

Kadence's mouth opened and closed. Avery saw the gears turning as she tried to come up with something to say. Avery shook her head. She couldn't quite understand why, but something in her gut told her not to ask. Kadence gave a hesitant smile.

After they switched seats, the light in Kadence's eyes returned. Though Kadence didn't say another word about it, her green eyes twinkled with gratitude. The two held one another's gaze, as though they were speaking in silence. Avery tried to calm her heart. This platonic thing was starting to be much harder than she thought.

"You can leave once we get to the studio. I'll hitch a ride with someone else. You've already done enough, Avery."

Avery frowned, gaze falling to the floor.

Kadence placed her hand on Avery's forearm. "I didn't mean it in that way. I appreciate everything you've done for me today. I just can't ask you to do even more for me. Mel will be off work soon, I can—"

"But I want to." Her amber eyes rose from the

ground.

Kadence studied her. "Okay."

They progressed down the road for a distance.

"So, how's the painting going?"

"It's good. You can stop by to see it if you want."

"I might do that."

"It's a good present. You should give Em some pointers. She needs ideas. A registry would help."

"I'll get on it." A frustrated sigh escaped Kadence's lips.

"Hey," Avery eased out. "Are you okay? Like, are you taking care of yourself? A wedding is a lot to plan for, especially with such short notice."

They stopped for a red light. With the car still, Kadence turned to Avery. "I appreciate you looking out for me."

Avery broke into a shy grin. "Anytime."

***

Avery sat at the back of the classroom with a drawing pad Kadence had insisted she bring along to occupy her time. She tried to concentrate on the figures she was drawing, but she was drawn more to Kadence's voice, breathy and light as she commanded the class with grace. It was hypnotizing. That and the fact Kadence had stripped down to leggings and a sports bra, leading the class into a sinful back arch. It was like sitting through sixty excruciatingly unholy minutes of torture.

"Expand your chest, inhale deep and slow."

Avery's thighs clenched at the emphasized words. *Bennett, you're a fucking perv. Keep it in your pants.* She swallowed hard, regretting not grabbing a water bottle on the way.

An hour later, Avery was tense as a bow, her pencil clenched in a white-knuckle grip. Her throat was parched and pupils dilated. She was so lost in her corrupted thoughts she didn't even notice Kadence settling on the floor. Class had dismissed and the room was now empty.

"What did you draw?" Kadence cocked her head to the side, legs crossed at her ankle. She leaned forward to glance at the tablet in Avery's lap.

"Oh, uhh…" Avery rotated the sketchbook so that Kadence could get a better glimpse at the rough outlines. Human figures, ambiguous in their features, decorated the page. They illustrated the yoga poses that had occurred during the class period. Spheres and lines created the illusion of faces while soft, delicate curves formed the bends and arches of backs, legs, and chests. Sharper angles laid out the elbows and knees of the various positions.

"These are fantastic! May I?"

Avery nodded, cheeks rosy as a result of Kadence's compliment. Kadence flipped through the pages Avery had filled, the lines growing a little bolder and darker as the poses became more intricate and subsequently, a little more sexual in appearance.

She felt her cheeks burn when Kadence scanned a page with dark impression lines and a figure with its legs spread wide into a split. Her amber eyes rested on Kadence's face, trying to discern her opinion.

"You make yoga look so beautiful." Kadence's fingertips traced the shading of the collarbones branching into outstretched arms and open palms.

You are. "It is," Avery agreed with a terse nod, voice thick and heavy. The room fell silent as the two locked eyes, a feeling of push and pull hovering.

Kadence tore her gaze away. "Care to give it another chance?" Kadence inquired, closing the sketchbook with finality, passing it to Avery.

"What do you mean?" Avery's stomach flipped when their fingers touched.

"Yoga. You seem tense."

No shit. "I'm not really built for that kind of movement," Avery said, rapidly sketching a clumsy-looking stick figure with a snapback falling into a contrived position. She then drew a second figure that appeared to have face-planted before drawing a cartoonish frown. "Me."

"Nonsense." Kadence chuckled, finger tapping the figure doing the splits. "You can be beautiful, too. There's a special yoga that I think you're going to like."

Before Avery could object, Kadence's bare feet padded to the storage closet, appearing after a few moments with two long strands of silk ribbon around her neck and a small step ladder in hand. Her eyes shone with excitement as she gave Avery a wink. A wink that absolutely did not set her cheeks ablaze. No, sir. Not at all.

Kadence proceeded to unfold the ladder, hooking the fabric onto the rungs anchored to the ceiling. "Ever hear of aerial yoga?"

Amber eyes trailed up the fabric with hesitance. "No?"

"You're going to love this. It's just like a swing set." She guided Avery to the hanging fabric, positioning it at waist level, pressing it to Avery's pelvis.

Avery choked down a cough.

"Just making sure it's the right height," Kadence said before letting go, allowing the silk to flow back. She repeated the process again as she prepared a station for herself.

"All right. The first step is easy. Bunch it up like this." Kadence demonstrated by gathering a fistful of the fabric into each hand. She stood on her tiptoes, shifting her hips so she could bring the bunched material under her waist.

"Now sit, then pull forward. You're basically making a seat for yourself." She traced the curve of the fabric, hands coming to the round of her butt. "See?"

Fuck. Yes, Avery definitely sees. Avery did as instructed, though she wasn't even half as graceful.

"Fun, right?"

Avery wobbled in the swing, hands clenching the fabric in her hands. "Not sure if falling on my ass constitutes as fun."

Kadence chuckled, shaking her head. "You're not going to fall."

Really not sure about that. Avery flailed, trying to regain her balance as her weight shifted around.

"Let's do a simple stretch," Kadence said, ignoring Avery's dramatization. "Here, take the fabric from under your knees and pull it forward to make a hammock." She pulled the silk from where it had been resting under her knees, leaning to bring it toward her ankles so her body was resting at a ninety-degree angle.

"No way," Avery gasped. "I'm going to rip my pants if I try that."

Kadence's rich, airy laughter filled the room and all of Avery's resolve cracked at the sound. "You won't."

Avery wiggled, attempting to follow Kadence's lead. To her surprise, the movement created a more stable surface for her sit in, the tension in her back slowly releasing. It felt *amazing.*

Kadence seemed to detect her relief. "Want to keep going?"

No.

Kadence shot her a smile.

"Okay." *Whipped.* Avery watched Kadence with attentive eyes.

"Let's slip out of this and into something more comfortable."

Did she just...? Avery's pulse spiked as Kadence poked her tongue between her teeth. Avery swallowed, eyes betraying her as they scanned Kadence's figure.

"That's better."

Avery couldn't tell if she meant the new position or the fact Kadence had gotten her flustered like she used to.

"Want to try an inversion?"

"I don't know what that means."

"I know." Kadence nodded.

"Am I gonna regret this?"

"I'll guide you." She approached Avery from behind as her fingers steered Avery's hips, positioning her in the silk cloth. Her palms found purchase on her sensitive sides. Avery tensed.

"Breathe," Kadence whispered in her ears.

Oh, no. Not again. "I...I'm trying," Avery whimpered, posture still stiff as a board.

"Relax."

Goosebumps shot down her arms as Kadence ran her hand up and down her spine before kneading the curve of her shoulders.

Fuck. Me. Game. Over. Press X to exit.

Kadence dipped lower, knuckles grazing to the small of her back. "I'm going to pull the fabric out." Kadence's warm breath puffed against Avery's ear.

"Lean back. The fabric will catch you."

Avery obeyed the command.

"Cross your arms and grab the edges right here."

Avery felt Kadence giving the cloth by her ears a gentle tug. Her fingers found the edge, but not before accidentally skimming Kadence's fingers.

Kadence cleared her throat. "Now, bring your knees into your chest and fall back as far as you can."

"What?"

"It's called a flip out. Your feet will find the floor, I promise."

"Kadence..." Avery tried to object, eyes widened in horror.

"You don't have to be scared." Kadence kept her voice level.

"I never said I was."

"Your eyes have been saying otherwise all day."

The tension of the room was suffocating. They were no longer referring to yoga anymore.

"I'm sorry."

Kadence just clicked her tongue, shaking her head. "Come on. Let's get past it." She pressed her hands between Avery's shoulder blades. She gave a gentle push and the momentum was enough for Avery to toss her feet above her head and land squarely on the foam mat below her.

Kadence seemed pleased. "See, I told you it was fun."

Avery managed to nod, legs somewhat shaky. Her skin sizzled everywhere Kadence had roamed. Their eyes locked and Avery saw Kadence searching for something, but she couldn't place her finger on what. Still, she was unable to break away.

"Umm, I think that's enough with the tricks for

today." Kadence's voice was tight. "Let's wrap up."

She placed Avery into a final position, a resting position that allowed her a moment of silence. Avery wasn't sure how long she was left alone to let her mind wander, but the next time she opened her eyes, her spirit felt renewed.

"Are we feeling a little more at peace now?"

Avery nodded. "I think so."

Kadence smiled back. "I think so, too."

Jessica Yeh

Chapter Sixteen

KADENCE'S HEAD THUMPED AGAINST the wall. She had just gotten off the phone with the repair shop. Her car was going to take three weeks to fix. She would have to resort to public transportation for the time being.

Normally she wouldn't have a problem with taking public transportation. After the accident, there was a period of time when she would only take public transport, too afraid to even set foot in a car, let alone drive it. But not having a vehicle while trying to complete maid of honor errands was terribly inconvenient.

Avery had called earlier that day to invite her to check out the painting's progress. During their conversation, she accidentally revealed that she was going to be car-less and had errands to run that afternoon. Avery didn't even let her finish her sentence before allowing her to borrow hers. The chivalrous heroine even offered to pick her up. Kadence didn't want to continue to burden her, so they agreed to meet in two hours, at Avery's place.

When she arrived at the third floor of the apartment building, she was surprised to find Emma, rather than Avery, at the door. "Hey, Emma! Is Avery here?"

Emma's smile fell from her face. "What did she do now? I swear, Avery is a good person, she just—"

Kadence placed a hand on her forearm to stop her from storming out the door. "Avery didn't do anything. We were supposed to meet up but I'm early. Is she here right now?"

The roommate shook her head. "I saw her leave the studio about half an hour ago. Said she needed a break. She hasn't come back yet."

"Do you know where she went?"

Emma shrugged. "Probably the park. But I'm sure she'll be back soon though. You're welcome to hang out here until she gets back if you want." She gestured in the direction of the couch and television.

"That's all right. I think I might go find her."

***

Kadence walked through the gated area toward the brambles and brush when she heard a husky laugh from across the basketball court. She stopped in her tracks, turning toward the sound that made her stomach bubble. *That's unexpected.*

What she saw was even more unexpected. Avery was running from a crowd of boys, laughing and squealing as they shouted after her. A ball bounced between her hand and the pavement before hitting the backboard, swishing into the basket in a near-perfect arc. The sun danced around honeysuckle curls as they sprung in time with Avery's steps. For someone who didn't like exercising, Avery was certainly putting in quite a bit of energy, eyes shining as the boys tackled her to the ground. They proceeded to pile on top of her and for a moment Kadence wondered if she should break them up and rescue her. But then a long arm broke through the mass of children, waving frantically.

The boys pulled themselves off her, a red-headed boy holding out a hand. Avery emerged ruffling his hair before addressing the group. Soon, all but one dispersed.

The red head retrieved the winning basketball, returning to Avery with an eager gleam in his eyes. Avery took the ball from his grip, placing it under her arm before holding up a finger. Kadence was too far away to hear what she was saying. With the ball nestled under her wing, Avery pointed to the tip of her finger. The child nodded ardently, eyes wide and eager.

What happened next had Kadence thoroughly impressed. Avery gave the ball a light toss, catching it on her left pointer finger. She whipped her right hand around its surface, spinning the sphere before allowing it to lose momentum. The boy jumped in the air, clapping enthusiastically. It elicited a boisterous laugh from Avery and Kadence found herself smiling at the sound of it.

Avery passed him the ball, gesturing for him to copy her trick. It fell out of balance, his expression dropping along with it. The youngster passed it back to Avery with his head hanging low. Avery placed a hand on his shoulder before repeating the motion. On his next attempt, the boy managed to catch the ball on his finger, but it wobbled before tumbling toward the pavement.

Avery recaptured the basketball before it hit the concrete. She spoke to the boy again, making a sharp swiping motion. The student mimicked her action, receiving a nod of approval. This time, he sent the ball spiraling on his finger. His face lit like fireworks and Avery placed her snapback on his head. She lifted him in the air with a hoot, his gangly limbs flailing as she did.

Laughter erupted from the pair. Kadence's grin widened.

When his feet contacted the ground, his eyes caught sight of Kadence and he pointed toward the intruder. Avery grabbed the boy, positioning him behind her. When she registered it was Kadence watching, her gaze softened. Kadence gave a shy wave in their direction.

Avery's shoulders slackened and she returned the gesture. Kneeling to place a hand on the boy's shoulders, she spoke to him before holding a hand in the air. He completed the high five, removing the snapback and returning it to Avery. Avery gave him a nod before he scampered toward the gate.

"Ryan!"

The boy pivoted.

"Forgetting something?" Avery held up the basketball with a laugh.

Ryan bolted to Avery, wrapping his arms around her waist. Kadence saw Avery's eyes shimmering before he detached himself, bidding her farewell. She grabbed a drawstring bag that had been resting against the bench before breaking into a brisk jog.

"Hey, Kae. What are you doing here?"

Now that she was closer, Kadence could smell the mixture of sunlight and fresh grass emanating from Avery's skin. A sheen of sweat coated her heaving chest. Kadence had never seen Avery exert herself this willingly, and for a bunch of kids. It was endearing, if not incredibly sweet.

"I came to find you."

"Shit. Am I late?" Avery started to rifle through her bag. "I didn't have my phone on me. Did Em not let you in? I'm sorry if..."

It took Kadence a moment to register what Avery had asked, her rambling words blurring together in the rush. She shook her head, gathering her bearings.

"You're fine," Kadence assured with a chuckle. "Don't apologize. I was early. Emma said you were at the park, so I decided to come find you."

"Sorry."

"Stop apologizing," Kadence rebuked. "Especially for just being yourself."

Avery flushed. "Sor...Okay. I didn't mean to get caught up with them."

"Are they your...friends?" They were a bit young, but Avery *did* have a youthful spirit about her.

Avery's fingers toyed with the straps of the bag on her shoulders. "I uhh...Logan used to coach them. We used to play with them when we were still together."

"That must be..." Kadence paused in search of the right word. "Conflicting."

"Yeah." Avery's smile deflated. "But I don't want to let them down, especially Ryan."

"The one who stayed behind?"

Avery nodded, a gentle fondness in her eyes at the mention of the boy. "He's wanted to learn that trick for a while. I promised I'd teach him."

"That's sweet of you to keep your promise."

"He's the sweet one."

Something about the way she said it with so much pride sent a jolt through Kadence's chest. But Kadence wasn't sure she was ready. There was still a lot of trust that need to be regained. Luckily, Avery was too caught up with singing Ryan's praises to pick up on Kadence's conflicting emotions. "Kid's an absolute angel. Really smart, too."

"You're very taken with him. And he's taken with you, too."

"He's a good one."

"And I can tell you are, too." Kadence hadn't realized she said it out loud. Both women tensed before shyly drawing apart. Kadence cleared her throat. "Does he know?"

"Know what?"

"You put the hat on him." Kadence eyed the accessory. "Your father's hat. It obviously means a lot to you. Did you tell him?"

"I...it... yeah, it does. It makes me feel closer to him. Ryan doesn't know that though. I don't want him to be sad."

Then it hit Kadence, the sheer significance of her father's hat. Avery had been genuine all along. Even though she had masked it with flirting, cocky comments, and pick up lines, she wouldn't have let Kadence keep her father's hat for so long if her feelings weren't genuine. It meant something to her. That fact shattered Kadence's resolve. She took Avery's hand.

"Avery?"

"Yeah?"

"He wouldn't want you to be sad either." It came out more breathless than expected. She willed herself to tear her gaze away from their hands, looking up to discover a pair of watery eyes. She gave Avery's hand a squeeze, hoping to convey who she was referring to by *he*. Her eyes searching amber eyes as they shared the quiet moment.

The sound of Avery's cell phone caused them to jump apart. Kadence brushed invisible lint from her shirt while Avery fumbled with her bag, pink tongue between her teeth as she silenced the deafening alarm.

"We should get going," Avery noted, eyes no longer bearing the same sadness they had carried a moment ago. "That was my cue to go and shower before you got here. Or if you want, I can give you my keys and you can go without me. I'll drive you home when you're done—"

"No." Kadence shook her head. "You and I made a deal. If I drove, you would be with me." She bit the inside of her cheek, realizing what implication her words might have. "In the passenger seat. It's your car, after all." *There we go. Just respecting her property. Nothing deeper.*

"I trust you with it."

Kadence tensed. She still felt the urge to be guarded against Avery. *How could Avery feel so opposite? Surely it wasn't that easy to just forget.*

"You coming?"

Her gaze flitted to the back of the Avery's figure and the sway of her hips. Kadence shook the image from her head and let her gaze fall to the sidewalk.

"Right behind you." Her voice cracked as her haywire heartbeat thrummed after Avery.

***

They arrived at the custom print shop to pick up the wedding order. Kadence combed through the list while Avery assisted with verifying each quantity— invitations, thank you cards, personalized envelopes, and gift bags with *Jordan and Melody* scripted on the handles. Once everything was accounted for, they made their way back to Kadence's apartment.

Unfortunately, the return paled in comparison to the journey there, literally. On the way to dropping

Kadence off at her place, they hit traffic. Within minutes, the blaring of sirens emerged. White knuckles gripped, no clung, to the steering wheel. Kadence's pupils darkened and eyes glazed over as she tried to ground herself.

"Kadence?"

Kadence's jaw locked, biting back tears of hysteria. It wasn't until she felt a warm pressure around her wrist that the sound of Iris' scream stopped echoing in her head. She startled to find Avery rubbing the stiffened joint, speaking in hushed tones. Slowly, the muffled words became clear enough for her to comprehend.

"Kadence, I'm here. You're here. We're present. We are present." As Avery repeated the soothing mantra, she never ceased to let go of Kadence's wrist. "Can you count with me? One...two...three..."

On four Kadence's trembling voice joined in.

"Five...six...seven...eight...nine...ten." They counted together. After a few moments of repetition and coaxing, the swelling in Kadence's throat relaxed. But her embarrassment escalated as the seconds ticked on. A tear fell down her cheek, plopping into her lap.

"Hey, Kae." The way Avery spoke her name felt like a pair of warm arms and Kadence wanted nothing more than to fall apart in them. "Do you know where you are?"

Kadence blinked and swallowed. Avery allowed her a moment to breathe before answering. "W...we're in DC. Off I-95, heading to my apartment."

Avery nodded. "Good. That's right. Do you want to pull over? I could drive if you'd like to take a break."

After a shaky exhale, Kadence shook her head. She needed to pull herself together. What would

Melody think if she knew she'd had another panic attack? "I think I'm okay now. Thank you, though." She turned to face the road. Neither brought it up, sitting in silence until the traffic sped to a crawl.

Kadence couldn't spare a glance at the wreckage as they moved beyond the scene of the accident.

"Looks like everybody's okay," Avery announced. "The cars took the brunt of the damage."

"That's good. They're lucky." Her voice cracked. She cleared her throat, masking it with an exaggerated cough.

"Kadence?"

Here it comes.

"Yeah?" She summoned all of her energy into speaking the single word.

"Can you please pull off at the next exit? I forgot that I need to grab something from the craft store."

With a wooden nod, Kadence flicked the turn signal. Avery directed them to the parking lot of a small shopping complex and Kadence killed the engine. Kadence unbuckled her seatbelt, but Avery stayed put, shaking her head. Kadence cocked her brow.

"Let's just sit here and breathe for a second," Avery said. "Like yoga."

Kadence hesitated. "Seriously?"

"Seriously." Avery released her seatbelt, making herself at home. She cracked the windows and leaned back in the seat. Eventually, Kadence's eyes closed as she inhaled. Her jerky breathing gradually leveled into a steady pattern. Feeling secure, Kadence chanced a glance at Avery, indulging herself in studying her mysterious savior.

She observed the slope of her nose and the bottom where it upturned the slightest bit. She tried to count each of her dark full lashes and the shadows they cast against her cheeks. Avery breathed with her lips parted just enough for Kadence to make out a tiny bit of ivory. When a pair of amber eyes ignited in the afternoon sun, Kadence felt her own breath falter, quickly recovering.

Avery offered her a smile. "Better?"

"Yes. Thank you." Her voice sounded worn and exhausted, but calmer now. *How did Avery know?*

"You can ask me anything, Kae." Avery's genuine gaze melted Kadence's pensive stare. Her heart began an erratic banging.

"How did you know?"

"My mom pulled me out of a few breakdowns." Avery dug her nails into her palms. "After my dad died, I used to call her on the phone. Especially when I had nightmares, I'd just call. I couldn't even say anything. It felt like knives in my chest."

"I...I didn't know." Kadence felt a matching ache in her heart.

"I've learned to live with it for the most part, though some days are easier than others."

Kadence nodded in agreement, allowing herself a second before speaking. "We never talk about stuff like this. Is this okay?"

"Is it okay with you?"

Kadence nodded again as they fell into a silent contemplation. "Hey, Avery?"

"Hmm?"

"How did you know about my wrist?"

"Your wrist?"

"How did you know rubbing it would calm me down?"

Avery blinked. "I...I don't know? Maybe I just had

a feeling?"

It was baffling. How could someone like Avery understand her so well after such a short amount of time? She wasn't one to believe in soulmates, but since meeting Avery, Kadence felt like she had awakened into a new life.

"Is there something I should know about it?" Avery tilted her head.

Kadence stifled the panic in her chest. "No, not yet."

Chapter Seventeen

AFTER THE INCIDENT, SOMETHING shifted between them. Every time she found herself looking at Avery, the woman was already looking back. She wasn't sure what it meant. It was genuine though, that much she knew. Because she could feel it in the way her amber eyes filled with pain matched with understanding. Avery would press her lips together, the smallest stitch weaving between her eyebrows. When that happened, Kadence would give her an uptick of a smile. With just one expression, Avery would relax, and Kadence would feel the weight lifting from her own shoulders.

Avery continued to lend her the car, despite Melody offering the same. "You don't want to owe her anything," her sister had cautioned, but Kadence reckoned maybe she already did. Instead, she insisted Melody keep the SUV to run wedding errands. After all, having two vehicles would allow them to cover twice as much ground.

The first week, Avery would come to Kadence's apartment, switching positions to allow her into the driver's side. But after a few inefficient days of Avery picking her up, accompanying her to every meeting, and dropping her off at her apartment, Kadence decided they needed a new plan.

Every morning thereafter, Kadence gathered her clothes into a duffle, packed two sets of lunches, and slung her bag on her shoulder before hopping the subway to Avery's apartment under the guise of convenience.

"You don't need to bring me fancy food," Avery joked. "I'm one hundred percent okay with canned spaghetti."

"That stuff is awful for you."

"The only awful is it is awfully delicious!"

Kadence had smiled then. She had a feeling there was an underlying meaning behind Avery's fixation with the canned food. If it even qualified as that. That was something she started to pick up on as she chipped away at Avery's exterior. There was always something deeper, and Kadence was growing increasingly more invested in discovering what those things were.

In actuality, she found herself spending more time with Avery in general, not even taking wedding preparations into account. It just seemed easier to spend her days at Avery's apartment. After all, the artist's studio was quite comfortable. It, like its owner, had its own messy charm that with time, Kadence grew rather fond of.

**

On Friday morning, the second since their new driving arrangement, Kadence had a yoga class to teach. She had just finished showering to find she had one missed call. The voicemail crackled before the sound of Avery's voice resounded off the bathroom tiles.

"Hey, Kadence..." Avery's voice was rough and scratchy. Kadence paused, hairbrush frozen in place above her part.

"Look, I know I promised to ride along with you

but I'm not feeling well." A lull followed by a fit of distant coughing tore through her lungs.

"Sorry, that was so gross." Her apology was followed by a congested sniff. "I don't wanna throw off your schedule, but you should probably take the car without me. I'll leave the door unlocked. The keys are on the counter as usual. I'm sorry." There was another strangled sound, then a fit of harsh, miserable coughs before Avery groaned and the message ended. Kadence frowned before scrolling through her contacts.

***

Kadence arrived at Avery's apartment and slipped off her shoes. Her ears detected the soft buzz of voices coming from Avery's room. She padded to the bedroom with a bottle of water and her bag, knocking on the doorframe.

"Avery?"

"Kadence?" Avery sat up. "Shit. Did I forget to put the keys out?"

Kadence chuckled, shaking her head. "They're there."

Avery eyed her bag. "Is everything okay?"

"Shouldn't I be asking *you* that?"

"I'm fine." Avery's reply would have been more believable if she didn't fall into a coughing fit as she said it. Kadence hustled to her, rubbing her hand against Avery's back. "Really. I'm fine. It's just a cold."

"Mmhmm." Kadence raised a brow in challenge before nodding to the bed. "May I?"

Avery shook her head. "I don't want to get you sick. I'm germy."

"Hey, Germy, I'm Kadence." Kadence suppressed

a smile as Avery scowled at her comeback. At least she wasn't too ill to lose her sass.

"You worry about your body, I'll worry about mine." Kadence gave a playful nudge. She could feel Avery's eyes focus on her figure at the mention of her body. She resisted the urge to snort.

"You're not dressed for class."

"No, I'm not. Thank you for noticing." Kadence rummaged through her bag, withdrawing a bottle of water, cough syrup, and variety of over-the-counter medication, lining them up on the nightstand.

"Geez, Kae. Did you bring the whole pharmacy with you?"

Kadence ignored her. "What have you taken today?"

Avery looked overwhelmed at the vast collection of medication. "Umm, nothing. I was gonna ride it out."

Kadence clicked her tongue, finding the jut of Avery's pink lips rather kissable. *Wait...Kissable?* She shook away the thought, focusing on pouring thick liquid into the small service cup. "Here." She held the cough syrup out to Avery.

Avery had scrunched her nose as the liquid gooped into the container. Kadence would have found the stubbornness sort of adorable, had Avery's health not taken precedence.

"Open."

"No! That stuff tastes horrible."

Kadence rolled her eyes. "You're on the brink of a fever, Avery. You have to."

Avery flat out *whined*. It was nothing like the cocky, confident woman when they first met. That woman was easy to get to bend to her will. The memory sparked an idea. Cocking her hip and lowering her gaze,

Kadence leaned down, lips hovering at the shell of Avery's ear.

"*Please*, Avery. For me?"

Avery gasped and Kadence slipped the contents of the cup between her parted lips.

Avery's eyes widened as she choked the liquid down, flailing dramatically. "I'm dying. Actually dying. Holy shit." She knocked the rest of the table's contents onto the floor as she pretended, she had chugged half the bottle.

Kadence resisted the urge to laugh at Avery's performance as she replaced the items. "You're so extreme. You're not dying. You shouldn't joke about that." She placed a hand on Avery's shoulder.

Avery leaned in, the warm press of heat tingling against her skin before she pulled away. Kadence cleared her throat, eyeing the time on her phone. "I'm going to make us something to eat. You haven't eaten breakfast...or lunch, have you?"

Avery's guilty pink cheeks gave away her answer.

"I want the rest of those meds taken by the time I get back."

***

Kadence busied herself in the kitchen. It startled her just how natural it felt walking in and finding her way around. She returned to the bedroom to find Avery's enraptured, droopy eyes glued to the television screen. A blonde girl with an ornate headpiece was running through an animated city.

"Hey."

"Shh," Avery hushed her, a dopey grin plastered on her face as she placed a finger on her lip, askew.

"Cartoonsareon."

From her slurring, Kadence realized Avery had mixed the daytime and nighttime pills that had spilled onto the floor. She pried the remote from Avery's hands with ease, pausing the program.

"Food first. Then you can go back to watching."

Avery frowned at the tray of food in front of her; a sandwich, soup, and more water.

Kadence held up a hand and withdrew an aluminum can from behind her back.

"For me?" Avery asked with a smile wide enough to split her face in half. Kadence giggled at the childlike expression. Drug befuddled Avery was elated.

"Yes, Avery. For you."

She placed the spoon inside the bowl before nudging Avery's knee. Avery wiggled, sliding so Kadence could join her, backs against the headboard. They resumed watching the anime reruns while Avery ate. She made it through half of the bowl of chicken noodle soup before her head started to bob, leaning into Kadence's side. Kadence welcomed the weight.

"How about you take a nap?"

"I don't need a babysitter." Despite her stubbornness, Avery yawned.

"You do." Kadence shifted off the bed, no longer supporting Avery's body. She fell to her side and into the pillows with a whimper.

"Come back." Avery kicked out her legs with a huff.

"Baby," Kadence teased, giving Avery a push under the covers. "Take a nap. I'll come back after I wash these dishes, okay?"

Avery sighed, eyes drooping as she faced Kadence.

"What?"

"I like when you call me that," Avery said with a lazy smile. "Baby."

Kadence's heart stumbled. She tamped it down, gathering the tray of dishes and making her way to the doorway. "Go to sleep, Avery."

"Hey, Cooper?"

"Yeah, Bennett?"

"Will you come back?"

"Sure. Anything you want." Kadence chuckled, hand hovering at the door handle. "Whatever will get you to sleep."

"I don't want anything," Avery mumbled through her exhaustion. "Just you."

Kadence's stomach whirled.

Her fingers coiled around the doorknob as she calmed herself. When she looked back, Avery's eyes had closed and her chest rose and fell with congested breaths. Probably better that way.

***

Kadence wasn't sure how she had fallen asleep, but she woke to the sound of the front door closing. She blinked at the light, sight coming into focus. At the door, a giddy Emma was pinned to the wall with Danny tethered to her lips. Kadence cleared her throat to make herself known. The lovebirds flew to opposite sides of the room.

"Uhh, hey, Kadence." Emma's cheeks were brighter than her hair as she waved. "I thought you and Avery were going to be out."

Danny ducked his head, bolting into the kitchen to avoid the awkward situation.

"Avery wasn't feeling well, so I canceled yoga."

"Oh, no." Before she could speak further, Emma hustled down the hall. Kadence followed in pursuit.

"Kadence?" Avery rasped as Emma propped open the door. Avery reached into the empty distance between the bed and doorway. That little tug returned to Kadence's chest.

"No, it's Em. But Kae's right behind me."

Not wanting to let her heart get out of hand, Kadence busied herself with preparing another dosage of medicine.

"What happened, Avery?" Emma cooed, placing the palm of her hand against Avery's forehead. "You were fine when I left this morning."

Avery turned to her side, clutching her stomach and burying an incoherent mumble into the pillow.

"Sorry, what was that?"

Avery's lips rose a millimeter above the fabric. "SmellslikeKadence." Her eyes pinched shut before her head flopped back into the sheets. "My head hurts. Where's Kadence?"

Emma turned to Kadence and tilted her head toward the sickly blonde. "Maybe you should take it from here."

Kadence tried not to flush at the wink Emma shot her before exiting the room.

"Hey, Avery," Kadence whispered, settling to her side. "I'm right here."

"Fix me," Avery whined.

Kadence combed away the baby hairs clinging to Avery's sweaty forehead. "I'm trying, Avery. I'm trying."

Avery released a heavy breath, relaxing under Kadence's gentle touch. When she finally fell back asleep, Kadence exited to find Danny sitting in the kitchen alone.

"Where's Emma?"

"Ran out to buy food," Danny said. "Apparently Avery was supposed to get groceries this afternoon but that obviously fell through."

"Oh." Kadence frowned. "You didn't go with her?"

"No." From the way he smiled, Kadence knew she was in for an earful. "I wanted to talk to you. Since when do you cancel yoga to take care of Avery?"

Kadence bit her lip.

"What's going on between you two?"

Kadence hesitated to reply.

"Calm down." He chuckled. "I won't tell Melody, don't worry. I know how she gets. She is my best friend, after all. Or Emma."

Kadence found it weird how interlaced the people in her life seemed to become. Her sister's best friend just so happened to be dating one of her students. And that student's roommate just happened to be...*What was Avery?*

A few weeks ago, or even a month ago, she would have said Avery was nothing more than a friend. But she was a friend that made her laugh, tried almost too hard to make her blush, caused her to roll her eyes, and feel so many emotions she forgot even existed, forgot she was capable of feeling.

On top of that, they had shared a kiss, one Kadence ran from after witnessing Avery's blinding rage. Yet, she grew to understand that heartbroken pain after Avery offered herself so selflessly to get back into her good graces.

"Kadence?"

Kadence shook the thought away. "Sorry, what?"

Danny grinned. "You like her."

Maybe, but admitting it this early is too risky. "I'm not sure how I feel about her. It's complicated."

Danny nodded, holding up his hands. "Emma mentioned you getting into a fight. It's not my business. I don't like getting involved."

"Thanks—"

"But if I *were* to get involved..."

Spoke too soon. "Danny—"

"Hold on!" He laughed. "Don't get defensive just yet. I'm just saying, everybody deserves a shot at happiness."

She was quiet so he continued.

"Remember Jeanne?"

She resisted the urge to cringe.

"Yeah, I know," Danny scoffed. "I was so hurt by her, but if I didn't let another person in, I wouldn't have found Emma. I'm not saying that you're in love with Avery, but you could give her another chance. Things have obviously changed between you two. And this could be really good, if you let it."

Kadence swallowed the bubbling in her chest. "Thanks, Danny."

"But, if anybody asks, we never had this conversation." He gave her a wink before ruffling her hair. "Especially Melody."

His impression of her sister's scowl only made Kadence laugh harder.

"She scares you, doesn't she?"

"She scares everybody, doesn't she?"

***

Kadence Cooper: *How are you feeling today?*

Avery Bennett: A lot better. Seriously, thank you. The canned spaghetti was the best part. It was like my dad was taking care of me again.

Kadence paused at the mention of John. She had no idea Avery's fixation, or rather attachment, to the food had been a result of her father. Again, she realized how much more there was to the artist. And to her surprise, how much she wanted to learn about her. A throat clearing caused her to jump. Melody leaned against the doorframe of her apartment with her arms crossed, keys dangling from her pinky finger.

Kadence Cooper: Melody's here. We're going to do wedding errands. Talk to you later!
Avery Bennett: Have fun!
Kadence Cooper: Thanks. Get some rest. Feel better!

She clicked off her phone. "Hey, Mel." She greeted her with a smile before taking in her older sibling's expression. "What?"

"You've been smiling at your phone for the past ten minutes."

Kadence's ears burned. "You've been here the whole time?"

Melody snorted. "Who were you texting?"

"Uhh…" She chewed her lip. "Avery."

"Avery." Kadence studied Melody's unreadable expression before jumping to Avery's defense. "She's not as bad as you think. She has been very helpful, especially with my car situation."

"Kae—"

"And did you know she plays basketball? I mean, I

knew she probably did, considering how many pairs of basketball shorts she has. But she's also kinda clumsy. So, I didn't know if she'd be good. But she is."

"Kae—"

"She plays in the park sometimes with the neighborhood boys." She recalled the way Avery's eyes had shone when the kids concluded the game by tackling her into a hug. "They all look up to her. It's sweet."

"Kadence," Melody shouted, startling Kadence out of her monologue.

"What?"

"I literally just said her name. Geez! You just went off with the rest."

Kadence ducked to hide the pink of her cheeks. "Yeah. I'm just grateful, that's all."

"Mmhmm. Whatever you say."

***

"It's nice to see you ladies again." April greeted them as the siblings approached the planner's doorstep. "How is everything going, Melody?"

"It's going." Melody drew her lips into a flat line, plopping into the chair across from the desk. An unruffled April chuckled, elbows resting on the table as she laid her chin atop laced fingers. "Well, I hope that everything I've arranged has been more than satisfactory."

"It has," Kadence jumped in with a nod. "Thank you."

"Now, we still have a few more odds and ends to wrap up. For example, the venue, seating arrangements, DJ, and songs. There's also...um, traditionally, there's a father daughter dance."

Kadence swallowed thickly as she felt Melody tense by her side.

"We're skipping it," Melody snapped, clenching her jaw.

The room remained in silence.

"Very well." April cleared her throat. "Do you have a playlist you want to use for the evening? Your couple's first dance?"

Kadence zoned out after that. The weight of their parents' headstones fell across her. The planning process only served to remind her of all the things she was gaining, but even more so, everything that she and her sister had lost. Soon they moved onto seating arrangements. She was still lost in her thoughts when Melody requested to add an extra seat for Kadence's plus one. She almost missed it. She probably would have, had April not looked at her with confusion.

Who was Melody referring to? Did she mean Avery? Why would I bring Avery? Well, why wouldn't you?

When the meeting concluded, Kadence lingered behind, turning to whisper quickly in April's ear.

"You're sure?" April asked warily, pen hovering at the notebook paper.

"Positive."

***

"So where to now?" Melody asked, hands resting on the steering wheel.

Kadence shrugged. "I was hoping to swing by Emma's."

"Isn't she with Danny at his place? They spend

Saturdays together."

"Oh." Kadence paused, hoping to remain impassive. "I guess I'll just…"

"You want to go to see Avery?"

Kadence shrunk in her seat, wishing to disappear from under her sister's searching gaze. She braced herself for another blow involving her distaste for Avery.

"Make her drive you home."

It was closest to her admitting that Avery wasn't all that bad. Maybe it would be the closest thing to Melody admitting she was slowly coming around to tolerating Avery's friendship with her baby sister. That wasn't to say she wouldn't still be ridiculously protective of Kadence, but it *was* progress. And progress, Kadence had recently learned, could be a good thing.

Chapter Eighteen

AVERY MUNCHED ON A bland piece of toast, a bowl of soup resting on the coffee table. She was still recovering from being sick.

"So, your dad is the one who got you into canned spaghetti?" Kadence asked, nestled on the couch across from Avery.

Avery nodded, pushing the bread aside and moving to the soup. "Whenever he was too busy, it was faster to eat that than make something from scratch. On most days, he didn't have enough time to eat lunch at work or couldn't step away from monitoring the chemicals in the lab, so he would just eat it cold. I picked up on it when I was younger."

Kadence laughed. "You are so unbelievably sentimental."

Avery set her spoon in the bowl to shoot Kadence the most serious expression she could muster. She tilted her chin in defiance, but quickly broke into a pearly white grin when Kadence copied her gesture.

"Don't tell anyone! I have a badass image to uphold."

Kadence snorted, rolling her eyes. "Sure."

"I do." Avery's pout made Kadence laugh again. Avery really liked the sound of her laugh.

"I don't see it."

Avery gasped in fake offense before glaring with furrowed brow. "You know some things you see with your eyes, others you see with your heart."

Kadence tilted her head in confusion. "Is that a quote?"

"Maybe…"

"What's it from?"

Avery rubbed at the back of her neck, scrunching up her face. "*The Land Before Time*."

"You mean like the children's movie?"

Avery's cheeks grew warmer.

"Oh, my god." Kadence burst out laughing. "I can't believe I ever thought you were cool."

"Hey, don't judge. Those movies were a pivotal part of my childhood, thank you very much."

"I watched them, too." Kadence held her hands up in surrender. "They were my favorite."

"You did?" Avery couldn't help how much her voice betrayed her bafflement.

Kadence paused to study her. Avery felt her cheeks brighten under Kadence's emerald gaze.

"God, no," Kadence deadpanned, the straight face only lasting milliseconds before she broke into a breathtaking smile that had Avery melting. She was a complete puddle once Kadence started giggling.

"That was cruel, Cooper." Avery tossed a pillow in Kadence's direction, though she was unable to harbor any sort of resentment. Nimble fingers caught the object with ease, propping it behind her back. Kadence's shift caused their feet to touch but neither of them made any attempt to draw away.

"What are you gonna do about it?" Kadence challenged, leaning even farther into Avery's space.

"Wouldn't you like to know?" Avery managed to think on her feet fast enough to retort, though she didn't have anything up her sleeve at the moment. Kadence was close enough now for Avery to get a whiff of her perfume and suddenly, everything was much more dizzying.

"I would. That's why I asked." Kadence's lips tilted dangerously to the side, morphing into a smirk. "Clearly."

"Okay. Just for the sass. I'm not gonna tell you." Avery attempted to shuffle back, but her spine was pressed against the arm of the couch. Her sudden movement made her foot brush against Kadence's.

"You're all talk," Kadence acknowledged, nudging back with her own foot. She sat up, slowing moving until her knees were pressed to Avery's shins. "Don't act so high and mighty."

Shit. Are we really doing this? "You have no proof," Avery shot back, swallowing the nerves bubbling in her stomach, acutely aware of just how close they had been.

"Don't need to. Your eyes give everything away."

"What? No, they don't." Avery flushed red as a tomato.

"They do." Kadence wedged her lower lip between her teeth. "They always have, it's endearing though."

"I...what? No. I'm not endearing. Take it back." Avery was beyond flustered.

"Make me," Kadence said, leaning just a little closer.

Fuck. She smells good.

They were pushing the boundaries of their friendship. Though the banter had always come easily for them, this was far beyond platonic. Amber eyes darted to Kadence's lips just as the front door opened and Emma strolled in. The pair flung apart, guiltily trying to calm the rapid fluttering in their chests.

Emma raised a brow, eyeing them with a suspicion. "Am I interrupting something?"

"N...no." Avery's reply was unsteady. "I was about to show Kadence something in the studio."

"You were?"

Avery shot to her feet. "Yup. You ready?"

Kadence nodded, sharing a confused look with Emma before chasing the speeder down the hall. She took her newly accustomed seat in the beanbag chair in the studio corner next to John's painting.

"You know, we never talk about your parents," Avery said.

Kadence's face fell.

"Sorry. Forget I—"

Kadence held up her hand, shaking her head. She inhaled slowly.

Avery braced herself.

"My parents passed away when Melody and I were just kids."

"Shit. You must think I'm such a brat. I sound so selfish for—"

"You're not selfish." Kadence shook her head with a sad smile. "You had someone that meant the world to you taken away from you, too." Kadence's finger trailed along the edge of the canvas. "Unfairly and unexpectedly."

Behind her sultry facade, Kadence would occasionally let the sadness of her past seep through the cracks. And as Avery chiseled away at her exterior, it made her heart ache for Kadence. She knew how irritating it was when people offered sympathy when her father passed. So many 'sorry for your loss' and 'he was a good man' comments always seemed contrived. Instead, she collected Kadence's wrist in her hand, smoothing patterns on the bone.

"Avery?" Kadence's voice wavered. "What are you doing?"

"I'm proud of you for being so strong. That's all."

"I..." Kadence seemed at a loss for words, but Avery just widened her smile.

"Will you paint for me?" Kadence requested after a moment.

"Of course."

The first time she had worked on the portrait of Melody with Kadence present, she was a bundle of nerves, but slowly, that vulnerability evolved into a certain level of trust and she allowed Kadence to sit and watch her work. And Avery wished that maybe, someday, Kadence would feel the same way.

***

A few days later, Avery's wish was granted. But not in the way she had hoped. She had just gotten in the shower after an exhausting day of sculpting a series of busts for a new project. Her body was sore and ached from bending at the worktable. Her neck was stiff, and her hands were cramped. Both arms were caked in dried clay and plaster, and her hair clumped into unflattering strands.

After drenching herself in the scorching spray, Avery climbed out of the shower, fingers wrinkled and pruned. She was about to climb into bed to binge-watch a season of mind-numbing television when she caught a glimpse of her phone. She had one missed call and a voicemail. She pressed play, taken aback by the lazy drawl in Kadence's voice as she spoke into the receiver.

"Hey! Come here. I have wine and no one's

here," Kadence singsonged before hanging up abruptly.

It was vague and somewhat out of character, but who was Avery Bennett to object to spending more time with Kadence Cooper?

Avery Bennett: *Sorry. Was in the shower. Do you still want me to come?*

Her phone buzzed almost immediately with a single word—*hurry*.

It wasn't until she arrived at Kadence's door, finding it already unlocked, when the possibility that this was a booty call crossed her mind. Should she have changed into something more appealing than just her skinny jeans and V-neck? Before she could second guess it, she heard a crash from the kitchen and immediately followed the source of the sound.

The sight was one she'd never forget and hoped to never see again. Kadence lay with her head in her hands, blearily eyed as she grasped for the wine bottle, red liquid and shards sloshed at her feet. Avery rushed to Kadence's side, coaxing her uncoordinated body away from the broken glass.

Kadence whimpered. "They're all gone."

Avery's heart broke when fresh tears tracked down Kadence's face.

"Gone. Gone. Gone." Kadence slurred, shaking a second, empty wine bottle clutched in her hands.

"Hey, Kadence," Avery urged, pulling the swaying girl. "I think maybe you've had enough." Avery took the bottle away before Kadence could cause herself any more harm and led her to the kitchen table, pulling out a chair. She gently pushed Kadence back until her knees hit the edge.

"Stay here, Kadence. Can you do that for me? Stay here?"

Kadence sniffed, nodding as she wiped her tears with the back of her hand. Avery searched for a mop and broom but came up empty handed.

"Kae, do you have an old towel or a T-shirt that I can use to wrap this stuff in before I throw it out?"

Kadence simply blinked before lifting the hem of her shirt.

"Whoa!" Avery rushed to her, quickly pulling it down, hands accidentally brushing against Kadence's abs. The drunk woman let out a small moan, causing Avery's eyes to widen. *Fuck. Don't do that.* She ground her teeth. Maybe it would be best to relocate Kadence to the couch. Once there, she switched on the television and placed the remote control in Kadence's lap. "Here, Kae. I'm going back to the kitchen."

"No," Kadence cried, green eyes wide with confusion and panic. She reached for Avery's hand with a rough tug. Avery came crashing down on top of her with a grunt. *The lord is testing me.* Avery scrambled to her feet, distancing herself.

"Please, Avery. Please stay. Everyone always leaves me!"

Avery frowned at Kadence's sobs. What was it like for Kadence to always be so alone? No family to speak of? An ex-girlfriend who (stupidly) left her? And a sister who was about to move to another country?

Kadence shook her head, whimpering becoming her only way of communicating.

"I'm here. I'm not leaving you," Avery promised the devasted woman, taking a seat on the couch. Kadence climbed into her lap, resting her head against Avery's shoulder, small puffs of hot breath hitting her neck as she cried softly.

Avery hesitated before wrapping her arms tightly around her. "Kadence, why are you crying? What's wrong?"

"Everything. I shouldn't." Kadence hiccupped her thoughts incoherently. "I can't. I'm *scared*."

Scared? "Of what?" Avery pressed her palm against the small of Kadence's back.

"If I love someone they leave. I can't love any more people." Kadence's bottom lip trembled.

"Hey, you don't have to love any more people," Avery assured, hoping to prevent another round of tears from falling from those brilliant emerald eyes. "No one is making you do that."

Kadence elevated her head, grasping Avery's face with both hands, eyes unfocused before she whispered softly. "But I want to."

Avery was at a loss for a reply. Luckily, Kadence let her head fall back onto Avery's shoulder, hand bunching up the fabric at the bottom of Avery's shirt, grounding her to Avery. They didn't speak. Soon, Kadence's eyelids grew heavy before finally falling closed.

Avery sighed, as she rubbed at Kadence's back, trapped underneath her weight. She was just about to fall asleep herself when the door opened and Melody strode in.

"Hey Kae, I stopped by to get some..." she called out, arms full of bags blocking her view of the pair. It was only after she situated them on the counter that she noticed. "What are you doing here?"

"Honestly, I'm not sure I know."

Melody placed her hands on her hips, surveying the kitchen floor. "What happened? Is she okay?"

"She called me earlier and asked me to come, so I did. When I got here, she was drunk and crying."

"What did you do?"

"Nothing." Avery held her hands up in defense. "Honest."

Kadence whined at the loss of body contact, which caused Avery to blush in embarrassment. "Ok. I mean. Not nothing. I've just been holding her. She was upset. But I didn't do anything like that. I would never. I was going to wait for her to fall asleep then clean up the mess."

Melody stared at her, and Avery wasn't sure if she was about to get murdered or not.

"Or, uhh, I can leave if you —" she tried to say, about to lift Kadence off her lap.

Melody jerked her head. "No. You stay. I'll go. She called you for a reason."

"What do you mean?"

"Did she tell you what day it is?"

Avery shook her head.

"Interesting." Melody hummed cryptically. "Give me your phone."

Avery scrambled to retrieve the device from her back pocket, handing it to her. At the shift in movement, Kadence clung on tighter, burying her face into Avery's hair.

"She trusts you," Melody noted, keeping an eye on her sister as she typed something into Avery's phone.

"Me?"

A faint buzz echoed from Melody's purse before she handed the phone to Avery.

"In case she asks for me." Melody's eyes softened at the sight of her sister, before locking with Avery's.

"But something tells me I won't be hearing from you." She stalked to the kitchen to retrieve one of the bags. "These are some of her favorite foods."

Melody brushed a lock of Kadence's hair behind her ear. Kadence drunkenly batted at her sister's hand. The strand fell a moment later and she sighed.

"Kae, stop. Melody's just trying to help," Avery said to the sleeping brunette, attempting to tuck the strand back in place. This time, Kadence let her do it, sighing in her sleep.

Melody half-smiled. "I'm clearly not needed any more."

"Melody, I wasn't—"

"Don't fuck it up this time," Melody said, the faintest hint of a smile on her lips as she approached the door. "We've only ever had one another. We take care of one another. Now I have Jordan, too. But Kadence, well..." Melody paused, chewing the inside of her cheek for a long time.

Avery was almost certain she was going to end the conversation there, but the words finally spilled from the tight line of her pressed lips.

"Maybe she could have you." Melody's hand hovered at the handle before she turned, offering a final word of advice. "She likes when you play with her hair."

The older Cooper slipped across the threshold. Avery stared at the now closed door, trying to process what had just happened. What did Melody mean by what day it was? What happened today and why did it make Kadence so upset? She had so many questions, but judging by Kadence's intoxicated state, they would have to wait.

"Kadence?" Avery whispered, combing her

fingers through Kadence's waves. "Kadence, let's eat something, okay?" Avery shifted her off her lap to gather the bag off the coffee table. She needed to find something to soak up the alcohol in Kadence's system.

"Nooo," Kadence whined incredulously.

Avery barely managed to get her to eat a sandwich and down a bottle of Gatorade. By the time the floor had been cleaned, Kadence was in a more sober state.

"Come on," Avery urged, pulling Kadence to her feet. "Let's get you to bed."

"No. No." Kadence stumbled after Avery, grasping the bathroom door, almost causing the two to fall. "We need to take our pills and count." She pointed at the medicine cabinet.

Pills?

"Ok. Hold on. Let me go see." Avery ushered Kadence down the hall, opening the cabinet to find a small prescription bottle. *To be taken for anxiety and minor depression.* Her eyes widened as she realized Kadence was not the person she thought she was. She was just lonely. Avery had always been self-focused, but for the first time, she wanted to focus on someone else. She wanted happiness for Kadence and even more importantly, she wanted to be the source of that happiness. The thought caught her by surprise. *Now is not the time, Bennett. Sort it out later.*

Kadence waited, palm outstretched, but Avery knew mixing medication with alcohol was not a good idea. Forcing a smile, she shook her head.

"No pills tonight, Kae. I'll be your happy place."

Kadence frowned. "I don't deserve to be happy."

"Of course, you do." Avery met Kadence's gaze in the mirror. She placed her hand on Kadence's wrist.

Kadence stared down at their hands for a long time, thoughts whirling in her head. Avery waited for her to speak again. And when she did, it was meek and dejected.

"I'm alive. It's not fair."

"What do you mean?"

Green eyes stared back at her, hooded and turbulent. The sight left Avery hypnotized, yet terrified.

"Iris deserved better." Kadence sobbed, body shaking with physical evidence of her emotional pain.

"What?" *Iris? Didn't she dump her? She'd have to have been a real moron to leave someone like Kadence. Kadence is the type of girlfriend you would die for.* Avery's stomach dropped.

Now it all made sense. Kadence's insistence on the seat belt, her anxiety when it came to driving, the strange moments when she would freeze up from something Avery hadn't even realized was a trigger. She had always thought Kadence and Iris just had a messy breakup that left Kadence scarred after she left. It hadn't crossed her mind that Iris had *died*. A car accident must have brought their relationship to an untimely end.

Her heart plummeted at the thought of Kadence having to go through something so traumatic. Kadence was so strong and put together all the time. But was it a result of numbness or caution? Probably both. Suddenly, Melody's words carried that much more weight. *Maybe she could have you.*

Avery circled Kadence in her arms, determined to take away her pain as Kadence fell into her for comfort, clinging to her shirt while Avery led her to the bedroom.

"I survived." Kadence whimpered as Avery sat her on the sheets.

Certain she could remain upright, Avery dug through the dresser drawers.

"But I'm just getting by…" Kadence trailed off.

"We deserve better than just trying to get by, Kae," Avery said over her shoulder, hoping to maintain conversation to prevent Kadence from falling asleep before she had changed. "'Don't you think?"

Before she could process what happened, Kadence was launching herself at Avery, clawing at Avery's clothing.

"Hey," Avery gasped, tugging her shirt down, leaning away from Kadence who was trying to kiss her neck. "Whoa. Stop!" She never thought she'd be turning down a hook up from Kadence Cooper, but she couldn't. Not like this. "No, wait." She caught Kadence's wrists in her hands, ducking to meet her eyes.

"You said it." Kadence's eyes were wild. "You said it just like Iris."

"I'm sorry." Avery apologized, unsure of what else to do. Kadence freed herself from Avery's grasp.

"You're not Iris." She blinked as if this revelation were new to her.

"No." Avery frowned, finally locating a pair of shorts and a T-shirt. "I'm not Iris." She held out the clothing for Kadence. She took them, studying the folded articles with fascination.

"But, you're Avery," Kadence deduced, managing to put on the T-shirt without much struggle. It was the shorts that caused her the most trouble and she eventually gave up, tossing them onto the floor.

Keep it PG, Bennett. "I am Avery, yes," Avery confirmed, tearing her gaze from exposed legs. "Can you get under the sheets for me?"

"Okay."

It took a moment for Kadence to get situated in her impaired state.

"You're not Iris...but...Avery is good, too," Kadence murmured, snuggling her cheek into the pillow.

Avery fought to ignore the way the words sent a glimmer of hope to her heart. "Go to sleep, Kae. We can talk about this in the morning."

"Sleep here," Kadence insisted, holding the comforter in the air.

"I don't know if—"

"But you promised you would stay." Kadence jutted out her lower lip.

"Okay."

Thankfully, any further protest seemed to leave her mind for the rest of the night. Kadence resituated under the sheets without a fuss. Avery moved a trashcan to the bedside, before finally allowing sleep to take her for a few brief hours.

Chapter Nineteen

KADENCE WOKE HALFWAY THROUGH the night with a throbbing headache, and a hand moving through her hair. A warm body pressed against her aching frame, secure and comforting. Avery's eyes were closed as she ran her fingers through Kadence's locks. Kadence knew she should separate herself, but her bones had turned to lead, and her nerves were unable to register anything. Soon, her eyes fluttered shut as she succumbed to the feeling of Avery's touch.

The next time she opened her eyes, it was morning, bright and blinding morning. Spotty memories of the previous day flashed to the front of her mind. The day had snuck up on her. It wasn't until she was signing the studio's monthly utility bill that she realized the date matched the password on her phone. Her stomach churned and she spent several minutes hovering above the sink before finding the strength to stand on her own two feet again. She immediately fell into a somber mood, which spiraled into loneliness. No family. No lover. Melody was getting married. Everyone was *leaving.* As much as she wanted her sister's happiness, she couldn't help but wonder if happiness was ever in the cards for herself.

Kadence clenched her fist to ward away the negative emotions, only to find it pressed flush against something soft. Clenching it again, she heard a groan, or rather, a moan. Her eyes burst open, burning her retinas in the light. When her pupils adjusted to the searing sun, she found Avery staring back at her, mouth agape with anxious, amber eyes. Kadence looked at her hand, specifically the one she had clenched. She had been *groping* Avery in her sleep.

"Oh, my god!" She pulled her hand away, cheeks aflame. "I am so sorry. I didn't mean to." She ricocheted from the bed. Her hands grasped at her skull in a futile attempt to keep the room from spinning. *Where are my pants?*

"Easy there." Avery inched toward her, placing her hand on Kadence's forearm. "You had a lot to drink last night."

Kadence nodded, trying to collect her bearings and last shred of dignity.

Avery seemed to read her mind. "We didn't do anything. I just held you and played with your hair a little. Your pants are there." She gestured to the floor. "You didn't want to put anything else on. And I didn't want to force you while you were drunk."

Kadence sighed, head still in a daze as Avery nudged a trashcan by her feet.

"Thanks," Kadence managed to mutter.

They sat in silence, and *not* the comfortable kind. She could feel Avery's eyes pinned to her, bottom lip pulled between her teeth. Kadence knew she owed her an explanation, regardless of how embarrassed she felt.

"I'll be back." Avery swung her feet across the bed, breaking the silence. She was still dressed in her typical day clothes. That meant she had no intention to stay.

Stay. Hazy memories flashed behind her eyes. Avery holding her, rocking her, humming to her. She thought she had heard Melody's voice last night as well but couldn't recall seeing her. Surely, if Melody had come, her sister would have stayed, right? But Melody was nowhere in sight. It was just she and Avery in the apartment.

The wooden floorboard released a small squeak. Avery stood in the doorway, hair disheveled from sleep and one sock slipping off her foot. She carried a glass of water in one hand and a bottle of pain killers in the other. A hurricane swirled in Kadence's stomach. And not from the alcohol.

"I hope you don't mind, I went looking through your cabinets." Avery handed her the remedy. Kadence downed the pills, gulping every last drop of water. Avery extended her palm. For a moment Kadence almost laced her fingers between Avery's before realizing she was offering to take the empty glass. She cleared her throat, hoping the blush on her face would go unnoticed as she surrendered the cup.

"I'm sorry for my behavior last night..." She bit her lip, voice weary. "I'm sorry you had to see that."

Avery placed a hand on her knee. "Hey, I'm here for you."

Her skin scorched under Avery's palm. Maybe she was still a little drunk. Confused by her body's reaction, she shifted away, but not before catching the way Avery's expression fell, though she feigned a quick smile.

"Last night, you asked me to come here. Do you remember why?"

Kadence paused for a moment. She recalled wanting to be with someone, yearning to be able to love again. She remembered the hunger in her chest to just be close to somebody. To *Avery*.

Kadence nodded, feeling ashamed. "I shouldn't have put you in that position. It was—"

Avery shook her head, fingers slipping around her wrist. "I'm glad you did."

Kadence flexed her jaw. "I'm usually not like that. It's just..." She could feel Avery's eyes on her as she choked on the words. The warm glow of her stare made it that much harder to continue.

"I'm not going to make you talk about anything you don't want to. I just wanted to say *thank you*."

"What? Why? Shouldn't I be—"

"Because you let me in." Avery's smile was enough to send Kadence's heart twirling. "I don't know all the details and you don't have to tell me them if you don't want to. If you're not comfortable enough around me. Or if you don't trust me..." Avery averted her gaze as she trailed off.

Kadence hated the way the words made her own heart constrict.

"Anyway." Avery sighed. "If you *do* though, I'd be honored to listen to anything you want to share."

Overwhelmed by her sincerity, Kadence threw her arms around Avery's neck. Her response was rigid at first, but soon dissolved as she wrapped her arms around her waist. Kadence nestled her face into her hair, whispering an honest thank you. Their embrace lingered until a warmth crept into Kadence's cheeks and a rosy flush coated Avery's skin.

"I was just—"

"Sorry, I—"

They both said at the same time, blushing even harder.

"Sorry, you—"

"No, you go—"

The two spoke over one another a second time, bashful of their clumsy conversation. Avery placed her left hand on her own mouth, waving her right in a circular motion for Kadence to go ahead. The sight made Kadence feel young again, giggling at Avery's theatrical behavior.

"Yesterday was Iris' birthday." The words were thick on her tongue as the name of her former lover weighed on her heart. "She would have been twenty-seven."

Avery nodded, allowing Kadence a moment to collect herself.

"We met when we were still in college. She was two years older than me. Iris was the epitome of the girl next door."

Avery offered her a sad smile as she reminisced. Kadence found her attention drawn to the downward curl of her lips and wondered how she could possibly fathom thinking about someone else while speaking about Iris. She blinked away the distraction, trying to properly pay tribute to the girl who once was her world.

"She was so pure and kind." Kadence let out a single puff of air through her nose, a laugh, but a sad one, full of yearning and loss. "I'll be turning twenty-five this year...older than she ever made it to."

She saw Avery calculating in her head, the side of her hand grazing against Kadence's clammy one.

"Two, almost three years. I know, I should be starting to move on."

Avery shook her head, placing a hand on Kadence's shoulder. "It doesn't matter how long it's been. It will *always* hurt. My dad died years ago, but I still miss him, some days more than others. But I still miss him. *Every. Single. Day*. And sometimes, it's nice. In a sick kinda way, I guess. Because it keeps his memory alive."

Kadence could relate all too well. "It's haunting." She subdued the lump in her throat.

"It doesn't have to be a memory that burdens you."

Kadence disagreed. "Love is just a burden. You're just asking to get hurt."

Avery paused, as a challenging tension fell on them. She sought out Kadence's eyes, searching with tenderness. "Do you believe that?"

All the bubbling in her stomach and pounding in her chest surged toward the surface, rendering her speechless. Kadence knew she could no longer stave off the way she was gravitating toward Avery. Their eyes connected. The amber twinkle sent an urge to her lips as she felt Avery leaning. Kadence fought to retract herself.

"Do you wanna get breakfast?" Kadence stood abruptly.

Avery blinked. "Uhh, sure."

"Let me treat you. As a thank you for yesterday before I have to get ready for yoga."

It was a lie. She didn't teach on Tuesdays. And Avery knew it, too. She'd been taking Kadence to and from classes long enough to know her schedule by now. Avery didn't call her out on her fabricated excuse. Though she felt guilty, Kadence needed time to think. The two eventually parted ways with a strained, yet comforting hug. Kadence hated the way she chased after the heat of Avery's arms.

***

Kadence needed familiarity, and she knew exactly the person to help ground her. She made her way downtown. She knocked twice, fiddling with her hands as she waited for the door to swing open.

"Hey." She could sense Melody observing her with something on the tip of her tongue. But her sister refused to say it out loud. "I've been thinking about you."

"Really? Why?"

Instead of answering her questions, her sister responded with a set of her own. "What are you doing here? Why aren't you at Avery's? Or at least with her?" Melody tugged her inside, making them both a cup of tea.

Kadence settled at the island, observing the open-concept apartment. A pile of cardboard boxes had accumulated in the corner of the living area. A few were already sealed with tape—boxed up memories, good and bad, ready to find a new home. What used to make her stomach twist in knots now filled her with jittery anticipation.

"How's that coming along? Need some help?"

Melody followed her line of sight, taking one last sip of her drink. The clink of her mug against the granite was the only sound. "I know you're not here to help me pack, Kae. What's up?" Melody's fingertips drummed against the side of her mug, hand hooked under the handle.

"I can't spend some time with my beautiful big sister? My favorite blonde in the whole wide world?"

Melody rolled her eyes. "Sarcasm is not appreciated. Besides, I'm not your favorite blonde."

Kadence knew what her sister was insinuating. Kadence quickly dropped her gaze to her cup. She swirled the steaming liquid, watching it funnel into a spiral before evening out again.

Melody's eyes were still on her. She could feel them. "Avery's your new favorite blonde." The statement was accompanied by an expression Melody had never worn before, something caught between a scowl, a smirk, and a glimmering endearment.

It made Kadence's cheeks flush red. "We're uhh...just friends." Hiding her blush behind her cup, she took another long drink.

Melody snorted. "That's why you called her last night instead of me."

That caught her attention. "So, you were there?" Her theory had been correct. But then, that meant Melody willingly left her with Avery.

Her sister observed her with an amused look. "Wow, forgetting me already? I haven't moved yet, you little shit."

"I—"

Melody held a hand up, cracking the slightest tilt of smile on her pressed lips. "You even shooed me away."

She then proceeded to mimic what Kadence assumed were her hand gestures from the previous night, swatting at the air with a chuckle. Except, it wasn't *just* a chuckle. It was a laugh. A genuine, *real* laugh. Kadence was speechless. It was as though Melody had transported three years earlier, before the entire ordeal. And they were just sitting in the kitchen making breakfast after a long night out, laughing about their night of wild antics.

"I'm going to be straight with you for a second. And yes, I'm aware that you are gay."

Kadence glared, poking her tongue out.

"I'm not your first choice anymore, Kae," Melody said with a pause, brown eyes probing for something Kadence couldn't identify.

Suddenly, Kadence felt a blend of guilt and self-consciousness. She forced her body to sit taller, despite worrying a lip. Her sister offered her a gently outstretched hand, linking their fingers across the countertop.

"I'm not your number one," Melody repeated, softer this time. "And I haven't been for a while."

Kadence itched to say something to console her sister, but Melody just smiled, running her thumb across Kadence's knuckles.

"I'm not saying it in a bad way, believe it or not. You know I didn't like her at first, and I'm still not a hundred percent about her, to be honest. But I trust you." Patient eyes bore into Kadence's. "And you trust her. So...it's okay if you're depending on her more—"

"I just didn't want to burden you."

Her sister glared at her choice of words. "You're not a burden."

Kadence gave her hand a squeeze. Melody didn't miss a beat and reciprocated the gesture. A part of her wanted to prove to her sister that she was still her go-to person, her number one. But another part of her, the distressed and conflicted part of her, yearned to be comforted by warm arms covered in acrylic paint. Things were changing all around her, and the place she found her stability was now becoming a beanbag in the corner of an art studio, surrounded by canvas lined walls. She shook the thoughts from her head, refocusing her attention to the conversation at hand.

"I want you to be able to focus on your future." Kadence lied to her inner self. "You're moving with

Jordan and I have to be independent."

"And *your* future?" From Melody's narrowed stare, Kadence knew she didn't believe her either.

"I'm okay. I don't mind being alone." The words left an unpleasant taste in her mouth.

Again, her sister saw right through her walls. The same walls Kadence was trying so desperately to resurrect. Although deep down, she knew they had already been lowered. All thanks to a certain pair of amber eyes.

"But you don't have to be." Melody raised an eyebrow. "You don't want to be. I know you don't."

"What do you mean?" Kadence made a half-hearted effort to play dumb and avoid the subject but couldn't suppress the heat in her cheeks. As much as she tried to run from her feelings, Kadence knew that in this race of the heart, it was becoming evidently clear that Avery Bennett was going to come in first.

"You know."

Kadence swallowed.

"Shall I spell it out for you? There's another blonde in your life, the one you spend every day with."

Kadence picked at her nail.

"You have feelings for her. You have feelings for Avery Bennett."

Kadence's breath hitched. She was positive Melody could hear her heart pounding in response to the words.

"You're..." Chestnut eyes scanned hers. "Scared. Not of getting hurt, but because you're afraid that what happened to Iris might happen to Avery," Melody declared with deadly accuracy.

Kadence didn't know how to object. She couldn't.

"Look, Kae, you need to stop saying things you

think I want to hear. You're trying too hard to make everyone else happy and get their approval. But honestly, I *am* happy." Melody's thumb fiddled to twist her engagement ring around her finger.

"I just want you to be happy. With whoever brings you that happiness." She ducked her head to meet Kadence's with sincerity. "I know Avery makes you happy, as weird and stupid as she may be." Melody released an eyerolling chuckle. "But, Kae, you're being stupid, too. You're running away and hiding because you don't want to take a chance. Or you're afraid to offend me. Or hurt someone's feelings."

She couldn't find it in her heart to defend herself because as always, her big sister knew her much too well.

"And it's just going to result in you hurting yourself in the end. And I don't want to see you do that. I'm not saying she's perfect, because trust me, I can find about a billion things I'd like to change about her."

Kadence frowned.

"Okay, maybe just a dozen things." Melody flashed a devious smile before shifting to a staid expression. "But you obviously see something in her. And she sees something in you. Don't complicate it more than it needs to be. Our lives are already complicated enough." She nodded toward the stack of boxes in the corner.

The two shared a bittersweet smile. Melody was right. It was time to move on.

Chapter Twenty

AVERY RETURNED TO HER apartment, exhausted and confused. Emma had taken one look at her appearance and immediately ushered her to the couch, placing a steaming mug of coffee in her hand. Avery curled onto the cushion, ankles crossed. Her forearms rested on the plush surface, the warmth of the cup pressing against her palms as she explained the events of the night before, sans the pills in Kadence's medicine cabinet.

"I just don't get why she would lie about it. I've taken her to yoga for two weeks, and we see one another practically every day."

"You do see one another every day." Emma took in her roommate's dejected expression. "Right. Sorry. Not helping. Continue."

"It just doesn't make sense." Avery gnawed her lip. "I know she doesn't have to teach today."

"Maybe she was embarrassed."

"Well, I know she was. But I thought we were getting past that. Even Melody said she trusted me. And that's huge. I mean, come on. It's Melody."

"That is a pretty big deal."

"Do you think I did something wrong? Am I being too pushy?"

"I wouldn't say that. You comforted her when she asked. Knowing she was too drunk, making sure she was safe was the right thing to do."

"Then why doesn't this feel right?" Avery gestured to an imaginary space in the middle of herself, practically spilling the coffee on her lap.

Emma reached out just in time to steady the mug, taking it from her grasp. "Maybe…" Emma shook her head, placing the mug on the coffee table. "You're not going to like what I'm about to say."

"Say it anyway."

It came out like a whisper. "Maybe she doesn't want you to save her."

The words hit Avery straight through the heart. But instead of causing the usual pain, it brought about a new flood of emotions, a driving, burn set aflame in her chest.

Kadence didn't need to be saved. She needed, well, something sweeter. Something to make her laugh on the days when she felt lonely. Something to keep her warm and safe when her panic attacks arose. A reason to wake up in the morning and smile. A someone.

"I'm not trying to save her, Em! I'm trying to love her."

Both roommates' eyes widened at the revelation.

"Holy shit, did you just…?"

"I didn't mean to!" *But you did, Bennett. And you know it.*

"Okay. I see the problem now."

An uneasy feeling tumbled to the base of Avery's stomach. She had seriously fallen for Kadence Cooper. She wanted her, and not in a sexual way. In a deeper, altruistic way and Kadence had run away. Her shoulders slumped in defeat.

"It's okay." Emma wrapped an arm around her. "We'll figure this out."

Avery nodded with a sigh, taking a sip of her

coffee. Even with the sugar added, it still tasted bitter.

***

She hadn't heard from Kadence in almost two days. It didn't seem like a lot, but it was when every little thing reminded her of Kadence. Avery's fingers itched to dial Kadence's number. They had gone from seeing one another daily, texting dozens of messages per day, to complete silence. It was driving her mad. But Avery had taken Emma's advice, urging her to give Kadence space. As difficult as it may have been.

Imagine Avery's surprise when she found Kadence standing in her doorway, enchanting as ever. Her raven hair was pulled into a loose fishtail braid, with small baby hairs coming undone near the crown of her head. Her winged eyeliner drew direct attention to her emerald eyes. Avery was entranced.

"Uhh, to what do I owe this pleasure?" *Really, Bennett? To what do I owe this pleasure? Can you learn to talk like a normal person in front of your crush for once? What are you, twelve?* She shook her head. "What's up? Wanna come in."

Kadence fidgeted in the doorway. Green eyes trailed her figure, taking in Avery's paint-stained limbs.

With red-hot cheeks, Avery crossed her arms, flashing a cheeky grin as she attempted to cover her messy state. She scratched the flakes of dried acrylic caked above her chest. When she looked up from removing the residue, Kadence's gaze darted away. She rocked back on her heels.

"Uhh, I was wondering if you're free right now."

"Now? I'm kinda covered in paint."

"You look fine, Avery. Great, actually." A blush

crept across Kadence's face. "I mean...I like it. It's very...you."

"It's very...me?"

"Yes." Kadence bit her lip.

Was Kadence Cooper nervous? "Okay. Let me just grab my shoes and we can go." Avery managed to find a pair of sneakers, slipping them on without having to unlace them. "All right. I'm ready if you are."

"Wait." Kadence held out a hand, maneuvering toward Avery's room. Avery caught a whiff of her perfume as she passed and her knees went weak. Before Avery had time to even collect herself, let alone question Kadence's actions, Kadence returned with John's hat in her hands. Nimble fingers placed it atop Avery's wavy blonde curls.

"There. Perfect."

Avery did her best to calm the accelerating pace of her heartbeat.

***

Kadence threw the car into reverse, backing out of the apartment complex lot. "I have a few wedding arrangements I want to get done before the bachelorettes come for the fitting next week."

Avery blinked. Time had been flying by.

"That fast, huh?"

"You know, that's life." Kadence paused, bottom lip tucked between her teeth. "Sometimes things just happen that quickly." Kadence's gaze darted to hers before tearing away. "Overwhelmingly and terrifyingly quick."

Avery's heart skipped. She forced herself to look out the window, afraid her expression would give away the confession she'd made to Emma a few days ago. *Settle down, thirsty. She's talking about the wedding.*

Kadence drummed the steering wheel with her thumbs. Music filled the space between them until the pair arrived at a small flower boutique.

"Centerpieces?" Avery guessed before noticing how Kadence's steps hesitated as they crossed the lot. The closer they approached, the slower she seemed to move.

Avery wrapped a careful hand around Kadence's hand. "Are you okay?"

Kadence nodded, frozen in place.

Avery shuffled forward. "Kae, please talk to me."

Instead of vocalizing her needs, Kadence cast her gaze downward. Avery seemed to understand her request, lacing their fingers together. She hoped her palms weren't sweaty. Kadence didn't seem to mind as she tightened her grip.

The shop door opened with a ring. She could feel Kadence tensing at the sound. Though Avery wasn't sure of why this place seemed to be triggering to Kadence, she was honored Kadence trusted her enough to bring her along.

Ramona, according to the nametag on the flower shop owner's apron, smiled at Kadence as though seeing an old friend. Her gentle gray eyes studied the pair as she greeted them. Under the woman's gaze, Avery wondered if she should drop her hand, but Kadence simply held on tighter.

"Oh, Kadence! It's been so long!" Ramona's eyes shone with a bursting excitement tainted by sorrow. She tucked her shearing scissors into her apron before rounding the counter, arms outstretched. The elderly woman's feeble fingertips trembled as the pair embraced. Avery wondered just how long it'd been.

"I'm sorry it took so long to come back."

"When someone goes from purchasing weekly roses to just a single lily, I've learned to expect that they won't be coming back." Ramona's wise eyes were tinged with sadness.

Avery decided that maybe the conversation wasn't meant for her to hear and moseyed out of earshot. While she allowed the two a private moment, Avery lost herself in the blending of the pastel petals. A unique, but subtle form of art went into flower arranging that she had never taken the time to consider. A hand on her bicep caused her to jump with a yelp and a stifled giggle sounded from behind her.

Kadence smiled. "Sorry, Avery. I just realized I never introduced you. Avery, this is Ramona. She's going to be Melody's florist."

The woman's hands were aged and calloused, but despite her frail appearance, her grip was steady and welcoming. "Nice to meet you, Avery. You weren't the blonde I expected to walk in with Kadence, though you're just as beautiful."

Avery's complexion could rival a fire engine.

"I told Melody to focus on packing. I can handle this." Kadence's voice wavered. Ramona didn't seem to notice, but Avery did. She skimmed her fingertips along Kadence's forearm in silent reassurance. Kadence's lips quirked upward.

"I thought Avery could help. She has a better eye for these kinds of things. She's an artist."

"An amateur at best."

"That's not true."

Ramona smiled between the two of them, a twinkle in her eye. "You two are just lovely. Avery, dear, do you think you'll be able to help me pick something out?"

Before she could answer, Kadence jumped in to respond. "Avery's great at picking up minor details. Shapes, colors, patterns, you name it. She can do it."

Avery's stomach bubbled at the compliment. "You want me to pick something for Melody's wedding?"

"No pressure, Avery." The way she said her name was softer, different than in the past. "I'd just like to get your suggestions. Mel will be the one to make the final decision, but I'd love to know what your thoughts are."

Avery felt herself glowing. She recalled the details from their previous errands as her mind spun with ideas. "How about a white flower with gold glitter sprinkled on the petals. It could be classy. Or maybe something with black tulle ribbon. You could paint the outside tips of the petals gold. It might be tedious, but I think that could be classy, too. Or maybe dip-dying? Braiding gold or black ribbon around the stems?"

"Well, Avery, it sounds like you might have this all taken care of," Ramona chortled with a wave of her hand. "You might even put me out of my job. Should I be worried?"

A strand of blonde dislodged from where it had been tucked into her hat as Avery shook her head. "No! I can assure you that my true love is with 2D mediums. No offense. I mean...but florals are nice."

Ramona chuckled and turned to Kadence with a smile. "She's sweet," she whispered, though it was still loud enough for Avery to hear.

Kadence leaned in, whispering just as loudly in reply. "I know."

Avery wasn't sure what inside joke the two seem

to be acknowledging, but the compliment caused her to redden.

"So, Avery, do you want to help me with some sample mock-ups?" The woman redirected her attention to focus on the cherry-faced artist. Avery nodded, following the two women into the dedicated work area.

After a half hour of collaboration between the creatives, accompanied by intermittent compliments from Kadence, the trio conjured up their top three options. Kadence snapped a few photos, texting them to her sister.

"Google the meaning behind them." Ramona smiled with a wink, sending the pair off with two white gardenias. "Take care."

"We will."

"Of one another," the woman tacked on.

Kadence's steps slowed at that. Her eyes met Avery's. Avery noticed the way Kadence's jaw pivoted, lips parted. A moment passed, far too long to be consider a coincidence, before Kadence looked over her shoulder.

"We will." Kadence looked back at Avery, her eyes warm, and the two made their way to the car. They didn't talk about the moment they shared, but neither woman could deny that it was definitely not platonic.

"So, what does it mean?" Kadence asked.

You tell me. "What does what mean?"

"The flowers. What do the gardenias symbolize?" Kadence inquired, not taking her eyes off the road.

"Oh, right." Avery dug her phone out of her pocket. "It says that gardenias are given to convey you're lovely. It is a flower that can be gifted to lovers, friends, and family. Other common associations include trust, hope, renewal, and alignment."

Kadence smiled from the driver seat, but otherwise said nothing else. They fell into a comfortable silence as they made their return to the artist's apartment.

***

Avery entered her apartment in a complete daze, still buzzing from the feeling of Kadence's lips against the apple of her cheekbone. She hadn't expected the goodbye gesture. But she wasn't complaining. A vibrating from her back pocket drew her from her euphoria. It was Adam, the gallery owner.

"Hello?" she answered, feeling a strange texture against her face. She pulled the device from where she had smashed it against her cheek and a flower fell at her feet. *Kadence.*

She hadn't even noticed Kadence slip the gardenia behind her ear. She was too caught up with petal-soft lips upon her skin. Kadence was so smooth without even trying. It made Avery's belly fill with butterflies.

She bent to pick up the flower, shaking it off. A few of the petals had creased, but nothing a little love and care couldn't fix. It wasn't broken by any means, just a little damaged. Something about its appearance paralleled her own life at its current state.

"Avery?" She heard her name in her ear.

"Sorry, sir. Could you repeat that?"

Adam chuckled. "I hope that silence is a result of your excitement. I asked if you'd like to be featured as one of our most promising artists."

Avery's jaw dropped. "You want me to be an MPA?"

Only the most prestigious exhibitors were asked to display their works at the follow up. It was an elite showing where the highest-paying, VIP patrons were invited to bid.

"Your last series was incredibly well-received, and you were given very high compliments amongst my colleagues."

"I..." It took a moment for her to find any other word besides *hell fucking yes.* "I... I would be so honored. Thank you."

"Then it's settled. I'll reserve your spot in the gallery. We can check the details of how much area you'll need to display your works closer to the date of the exhibition."

"That sounds perfect. Thank you so much."

The second the line beeped in conclusion, Avery pumped her fist in the air, arms flailing and legs shooting out in every direction. She bopped her way down the hall, pouncing on her unsuspecting roommate as she unlocked the apartment door.

Emma yelped, the contents of the popcorn bowl in her lap flying everywhere. "Umm, hi?"

"Hi!" Avery grinned, shining her pearly whites.

"You're in a good mood." Emma flexed her thigh muscles. Avery shuffled on her hands and knees before settling across from her, beaming as she watched her roommate pluck popcorn out of her hair.

"I am." Avery stole a piece of the salty snack and placed it in her mouth.

Emma rolled her eyes at her primal behavior. "Out with Kadence?"

"I was, but that's not why I'm happy."

Emma raised a brow.

"Okay, fine. She's part of the reason why I'm happy." Avery dipped her fingertip into the center of the flower, tracing the softness of the petals. "But there are other things, too." She waited for a beat. Then another.

Emma slapped Avery's arm. "Spit it out, woman."

Avery made a show of pretending to be injured, cradling her forearm. "Careful! I'm going to need that if I'm going to be making stuff for the MPAs this year."

"You're such a baby." Emma shrugged, reaching to salvage whatever popcorn was left in the bowl. Her hand froze. "Oh, my god! Did you just say the MPAs?"

"Maybe…"

The bowl was hurled into the air, as Emma squealed in excitement. Popcorn rained around them, scattering on the living room floor. They were a mess, but she couldn't care less in that moment.

"I'm so happy for you." Emma bounced against the cushions. "Congratulations!"

"Thanks, Em. It's humbling."

"Good." Emma gave her a nudge. "Sometimes your ego needs deflating."

Avery blew a raspberry.

"Really mature." Emma laughed, hands held up in defense. "I'm just saying. The Avery I've seen the last few weeks has been great. I definitely approve."

Avery softened her gaze. "Me, too."

"So?" Emma glanced at the popcorn kernels wedged between the couch cushions and scattered across the floor. "We need to celebrate. I'm gonna have Danny stop by the liquor store on his way. Party time?" Emma accompanied her proposition with an obnoxious wiggle of a brow, prompting Avery to burst into laughter.

"It's so last minute. Who would even come?"

Emma shot her a devious grin. "Oh, I can think of a few."

"Am I going to regret this?"

Emma shrugged. "Maybe. Maybe not."

"All right then. Let's do it."

Chapter Twenty-one

KADENCE SAT AT THE table with her cell phone on speaker.

"Are these for the wedding?" Melody asked.

"Yes."

"And is that…" Kadence could only picture Melody squinting at the phone before pinching two fingers outwards. "Did you go to Ramona's?"

"Yes."

"And…" There was hesitancy in her voice. "Are you okay?"

"Yes."

"Are you capable of more than one-word answers?"

"Yes," Kadence responded, muffling a giggle. She heard an audible huff on the other end of the line. "So, do you like any of them?".

"I do. But go back. You went to Ramona's?"

She could tell her sister wanted details. "I asked Avery come with me, but yes. I finally went to Ramona's."

"Wow." She could hear the amazement in Melody's voice, even through the phone. "You know you didn't have to do that. I was going to go next week."

"Anyway, the arrangements?" Kadence didn't want to argue. She was happy she went, proud even.

"The first one looks nice."

"I like that one," Kadence agreed.

"And the second isn't bad either."

"No, it's not. I like that one, too."

"And the third's pretty."

"It is."

Melody snorted.

"What are you laughing at?"

"You."

"Me?"

"Avery arranged all of those, didn't she?" A hint of amusement lingered in her tone.

Kadence was grateful Melody couldn't see her blush through the phone. "No?"

"Oh, Kae." She could practically hear Melody shaking her head. "You're an idiot sometimes, but I love you."

But Kadence couldn't bring herself to feel any sort of irritation, her entire chest consumed by the fluttering in the pit of her stomach.

***

"Back so soon?" Ramona asked, dusting the potting soil off her hands.

Kadence blushed with a nod. "Things are going well. I need something for our date tonight."

Ramona chuckled. "She must be quite special for you to come here every week."

It was Iris's idea. Date night every Friday. It made things simple.

"She is."

She had been coming for three months straight. Things with Iris had always gone smoothly. She was soft and gentle, tender and slow. Sweet.

"How's she doing?"

"She's good. Really good! I have a picture to show you." Kadence retrieved her phone. She scrolled to a picture of Iris with her arms out, gesturing around her. In the photo, she was surrounded by flowers of all sorts, some gifted by Kadence, some gifted to Kadence. They both went to Ramona's, sometimes on the same night, to pick out bouquets for the other. It was a bit excessive, but they had fallen into the routine. And it was comforting, aside from the apartment turning into a jungle.

"You could open up your own flower shop if you wanted."

"I would never."

"I know." Ramona studied the picture before whispering. "She's very pretty."

"I know," Kadence whispered in return, admiring her girlfriend's bright eyes.

"I hope you have a beautiful time tonight." Ramona handed her the wrapped bouquet. "One day, I expect you to invite me to the wedding."

Kadence flushed crimson. "It's only been a few months. It's a little early don't you think?"

"Love does not have a timeline, darling. Either I'm a guest, or I'm the florist. Take your pick." Ramona's words were demanding but accompanied by a warm chuckle.

"Of course, Ramona." Kadence laughed along with her. "Of course."

Chapter Twenty-two

TWO HOURS LATER, DANNY arrived with several bottles of soda as well as various bottles of rum, vodka, and whiskey. The apartment was flooded with an impressive number of guests, especially for a Tuesday night. Emma and her magical ways even managed to put together an elaborate sound system.

"Jesus, Em," Avery shouted above the music. "How many people did you invite?"

"Just a few dozen of our nearest and dearest friends."

"I'm impressed, if not a little overwhelmed."

"Ehh, just enjoy the party. By the way, turn around." Emma nudged Avery in the side, hitting her most ticklish spot and she jumped with a yelp.

Avery attempted to glare at her roommate but found herself unable to even remember what she was upset about. In that very moment, the apartment door opened, and Avery caught sight of gorgeous charcoal waves, sinfully tight skinny jeans, and a light tank top with sequin neckline draped on a goddess-like frame. Avery's knees went weak. All she could focus on was Kadence. All she wanted to focus on was Kadence. *You are royally fucked, Bennett. And you love it.*

Their eyes met from across the room and Avery gave a cheeky wave. Kadence offered her a quick wink in return before turning to the woman at her side. She leaned in, whispering something into Melody's ear before giving her sister's elbow a squeeze.

"Hey stranger. Long time no see. It's been what? Six hours?" Kadence gave a one-hundred-watt smile.

"Thanks for coming. Good to know you're not too tired of me yet."

"Nah, but I'm getting there." Kadence laughed, while Avery pretended to pout. The betrayed hostess stuck her tongue out, scrunching up her nose.

Kadence crossed her arms, waiting for Avery to finish her theatrics. "You done yet?"

Avery shook her head, blowing a raspberry in Kadence's direction. "Okay, now I am."

Kadence rolled her eyes good-naturedly before muttering a sarcastic, "Cute."

"I thought so." Avery grinned. The two chorused into giggles.

"So, I hear Adam picked you to be one of his most promising artists. That's a pretty big honor, right?"

"I guess." Avery dug the toe of her shoe into the carpet. "I'm one of three that the VIP patrons will be able to purchase works from. The pieces I submit will be displayed at the showcase and then auctioned off. Last year the highest bid went to a painting that sold for fifteen thousand dollars."

Kadence whistled. "Maybe I should get an autograph before you get too famous."

Avery shook her head. "I don't think I could be in that sort of spotlight. Despite what you may think about my asshole ego."

"Stop doing that."

"What?"

"Putting yourself down like that. Your ego is fine. There's nothing wrong with being confident in who you are. Give yourself more credit." Kadence's tone was insistent, a flare of passion burning in her eyes with each word.

Avery's chest tightened. "Yeah. I guess it's just humbling. I was worried a party would seem like I'm trying to brag about it. I know we haven't hosted a party in a while, but the congratulations part wasn't necessary. We could have come up with another excuse to have a party." She stopped herself from rambling any further by taking a gulp of her drink. *Slow down, Bennett.*

"You may not be in the spotlight, but you still shine in your own way."

Was it the alcohol or was Kadence leaning closer?

"For the record, *I'm* impressed. No one deserves it more than you. I've been lucky enough to see your work and watch you work. And I think you're pretty special."

Is this really happening?

"I mean..." Kadence bit her lip. "Uhh, your art is special. I wasn't trying to—"

Avery cut her off, fingers ghosting across Kadence's arm. "Thank you."

Green eyes fell to where Avery's skin seared against Kadence's. Their eyes connected before breaking away, the two flushing a matching shade of crimson.

"Umm." Kadence glanced around the apartment, focus wandering to someone in the distance. "I can't wait for her to see it."

Avery followed her line of sight to Melody and Danny mingling in the kitchen. "Oh! I forgot to tell you earlier, but I finished it. Do you..."

Before she could invite Kadence to see her latest

completed piece, Melody seemed to sense being watched, cocking a brow at the two. Her pseudo-nemesis beckoned with a finger.

"Is she talking to me?"

"I think so."

"Should I be worried?"

"I'm not sure."

"Shit." Avery downed the rest of drink before scurrying to the older Cooper sibling.

"Uhh, hey, Melody!" Avery rubbed the back of her neck. "What's up?"

"Why aren't you offering my sister a drink?"

Avery felt like a deer in headlights. She glanced to Danny for assistance, but the broad-shouldered bartender remained silent. *Thanks for nothing, dude.*

Melody furrowed her brow.

"Umm. Was I supposed to?" Avery fidgeted with her empty cup. "I didn't know if...well, with what happened the other night and all, I wasn't sure if it would be a good idea to—"

Melody barely reacted to her bumbling, only narrowing her gaze.

Oh, my god. She's going to kill me.

After a prolonged pause, Melody's lips gave way to a lopsided smile. It was more cunning than Kadence's smirk, but without a doubt, a trademark expression of the Cooper family.

"Good answer." Melody held out a hand, wiggling her fingers at Danny. He placed a cup of something that looked like a makeshift cocktail into her hand. "Here." She thrust the cup forward. "Give her this."

"Oh." Avery blinked. "Thanks. I will."

They remained standing there, and again, Avery grew antsy under the older woman's inquiring eyes.

Luckily, Danny came to her rescue, nudging his best friend, who scowled in response.

Danny, unfazed by Melody's abrasive behavior, continued to prompt her. "Mel, didn't you want to ask Avery something?"

"I can do it myself." Melody rolled her eyes, hip checking him in the process.

Danny laughed, shaking his head in amusement before directing his attention to mixing drinks.

Melody turned, almost threateningly, toward Avery. "Don't book anything for the first weekend in August."

Avery's brows knit together. "Why?"

Melody just shrugged, grabbing a cup from Danny's grasp before walking away.

Avery turned to Danny in confusion. "What just happened?"

The man grinned. "That's Melody for you. She means well, but she's pretty horrible at expressing it."

"The first week of August? Is that what I think it is?"

Danny chuckled at her expression of disbelief. "Depends, do you think it's the date of her wedding?"

Her jaw dropped. "Holy shit."

Danny looked on, entertained.

"She just...I was just...I did...I...I just..."

Emma bounded to them in the middle of her ineloquent speech, wrapping her arms around Danny's waist. "What's wrong with Avery?" She raised a brow as Avery continued to mentally flop like a landed fish.

"I can't...I, wow..."

"Who broke her?" Emma asked her boyfriend.

Danny leaned down to place a tender kiss on her forehead before laughing. "Melody, actually. She just invited Avery to the wedding."

"Wow. So, you're going as Kadence's date then?"

Before she could respond, a fourth partygoer emerged from around the corner, causing the group's conversation to end abruptly.

"Oh, hey, Kae!" Emma nudged Avery in the side and, as per usual, the ticklish victim let out a squeak in reflex before her friends made themselves scarce.

"What were you guys talking about?"

"Oh, nothing."

Kadence shrugged. "If you say so. So, what did you want to tell me earlier?"

Avery tried to recall their previous conversation, still in shock about the spontaneous wedding invite. "Oh, right. I forgot to tell you. I finished Melody's portrait before you came. I was just caught off guard when you showed up and forgot to tell you."

"Sorry," Kadence apologized. "It was inconsiderate of me to just drop by."

"No." Avery's reply was so forceful, it startled Kadence. Avery cleared her throat. "I like spending time with you."

Kadence's lip slanted to the side, blushing at her own admission. "Likewise."

Avery tilted her head in the direction of the studio. "Want to see it?"

The two trailed into the darkness of the hallway. The knuckles of their hands skimmed against one another as they walked. Avery offered a bashful smile and Kadence brushed their shoulders together.

"Tada!" she gestured, arms outstretched as they entered the studio. Kadence stood at her side, taking it in.

"Amazing," Kadence said breathlessly, fingers

tracing the texture of dried oil against the canvas.

You really are.

From far away, on the surface, everything seemed beautiful, fine, composed, and perfect. But that beauty could only be created from the indentations and crevices formed from each layer of paint, every color, and every painstaking stroke.

"I'm at a loss for words. You always seem to do that." Kadence paused, glaring at the cup in her hand, before shaking her head. "Your art, I mean. Your art always seems to do that."

"Thank you." Avery hid her bashfulness behind a large swig of alcohol from her own cup. But to her dismay, Kadence's awestruck features soon changed, taking on a somber expression.

"Hey." Avery took a step closer, the index finger of her free hand drawing light circles around Kadence's healed wrist. "You all right?"

"Yeah." Kadence chuckled to herself. "As my sister would put it, I'm just being an idiot."

Avery furled her brow. "Penny for your thoughts?"

Kadence glanced at the piece in front of them. "Now that you've finished your masterpiece, I have no excuse to come see you." Kadence's cheeky attempt to sound light-hearted fell short as Avery detected the real sense of disappointment in her eyes.

"You're *always* welcome to come hang out." Avery rotated her hand until her palm pressed against Kadence's limp fingers, hand hanging at her side. Gentle digits entwined with hers.

"You know, it's not fair. You should be there when she gets it. Or at least be able to see her reaction somehow. You put in so much effort."

"I might be."

Emerald eyes brightened. "Really?"

Avery nodded. "Melody sort of invited me."

Kadence grinned. "When did she do that?"

"Just now." Avery attempted to sound unfazed, but the astonishment was still there. "Informally, of course. I didn't get an invite or anything. I don't know." She paused, wheels turning in her head. "Do you think she was trying to prank me?"

Kadence hummed. "No. I don't. Melody doesn't do pranks. She teases, but she doesn't prank."

"Okay."

That didn't stop Avery from feeling nervous regarding the entire situation, Emma's implications of it being a date, and more specifically, *Kadence's* date, hovering in the back of her mind.

Kadence was quick to pick up on her hesitancy. "Do you think you'll come?" Kadence's lips tugged up in the smallest smile.

Avery knew she was just trying to relieve her hesitation with coy banter. She gratefully played along. "I don't know. Do you want me to come?" The light tone veiled her seriousness.

The alcohol in their systems must have increased her confidence, because Kadence stepped closer until their chests were pressed together. "What do *you* want?"

Avery swallowed, eyes darting to the plump curve of Kadence's bottom lip. Her stomach tumbled and her heart hammered in her ears.

A bang on the door caused the two to jump apart, Avery with a small yelp, and Kadence to scramble back with darkened pupils. There was a faint scuffling on the other side. Avery glanced back at Kadence, sending a wide, toothy smile. The two women broke into laughter.

"We should probably get back out there."

"Agreed."

***

Somehow, between dancing and the congratulations, Avery ended up with another drink in her hand. And another. And another. And another.

"All right, guys," Kadence declared as Avery choked on the next cup offered that night. Calming fingertips ran up and down her spine. "I think Avery's had enough."

"Ugh. Thank you," Avery sputtered, tossing her empty cup in defeat onto the coffee table.

"Stay here." She patted Avery's knee before standing. She returned a moment later, handing Avery a red plastic cup. Avery eyed it with disdain.

"It's just water." Kadence tilted the container so Avery could see the clear liquid inside. "And it might be a good idea to tap out for the night and find you some food."

"Yes!" Avery groaned. "Please."

They spent the rest of the night in the kitchen. Avery occupied her slurring tongue with canned spaghetti while Kadence pandered to her drunken ramblings.

"Did you know," Avery singsonged with drooping eyelids. "There's this dude, a prisoner in the nineties, who asked specifically for *canned* spaghetti as his last meal?"

Kadence quirked a brow, amused. "Is that so?"

"They gave him *regular* pasta instead." Avery

threw her hands into the air. "What a horrible way to go."

"Horrible."

Avery, in her drunken state, didn't pick up on Kadence's sarcasm and continued with her tirade. She pointed her spoon at Kadence. "It is. Consider yourself educated."

Kadence shook her head with quiet laughter, refilling Avery's cup with water. "And you can consider yourself wasted."

Avery sighed, downing the glass before mother nature sent her rushing off to the bathroom for the third time in an hour. She relieved herself before returning to the kitchen to find Kadence and Melody sitting on the barstools.

"Hey." Kadence seemed to sense her arrival. "Still doing okay?"

Avery nodded.

"All right, well, Mel was just telling me she's ready to head out." Kadence toyed with the keys in her hand. "Do you think you'll be okay on your own?"

"My own?" Avery looked around in confusion. She had been too frantic in her quest to get to the bathroom she hadn't noticed the entire apartment was empty, save for the two Cooper siblings.

"Emma went home with Danny," Melody said.

"You're kidding," Avery exclaimed. "Abandoning me at my own party."

Melody snorted. "You're at your own apartment. You're fine."

"I can stay with you if you want." Kadence offered, biting at her bottom lip.

Avery blushed. "I, uhh, you don't have to..."

"It's okay. I want to."

"Are you positive?"

"If you still need me…"

Avery fought back a smile. "I'd love that. But are you sure?"

"Oh, my God." Melody let out a frustrated groan. "Kadence. You're staying. I've decided for both of you dumbasses. Okay? Bye." She rushed out without another word while the duo stared with slack jaws at the apartment door closing.

"Uhh, shall we?" Avery asked, now suddenly a lot more sober. She didn't think Kadence would take her suggestion seriously. And now, well, now she was incredibly nervous.

When they made it to her bedroom, she found Kadence's focus transfixed on the flower that had now found a home in a vase on her bedside table.

"Kadence?"

Kadence broke her trance, eyes full of affection. "You kept it."

"I did."

"You're cute."

Avery couldn't help but blush. Tension crept into the atmosphere around them.

Green eyes drifted to the bed. "I didn't think this through."

Avery swallowed. "I can take the couch. You can have the bed. I appreciate you offering to stay but I'm okay. I was just being a brat. I'm not that drunk. And now you're stranded here."

Kadence shook her head. "I can't make you do that."

"Well, do you wanna take my car keys?" She tried another solution, though not ideal. "Are you sober enough to drive home?"

"No." Kadence shook her head again. "It's not that. I just..." Her eyes darted to the mattress, blankets untucked.

"We've slept together before." Avery tried to reason before realizing the insinuations she made. "I mean, in the same bed before. It uhh...wow. I am so sorry. I didn't..."

Kadence broke into a fit of giggles. "Why is this so hard for us?"

Avery was relieved that Kadence found the situation more humorous than awkward. "Do you think we can we just...cuddle?"

Avery melted at the adorable way Kadence flushed at her own proposal. "Of course! But be warned, I'm gonna cuddle the shit out of you. Get ready for the best cuddle of your life."

"That's perfectly acceptable." Kadence's shoulders relaxed.

After changing into T-shirts and shorts, they settled under the sheets. Neither of them touched, yet somehow it was the most intimate they'd ever been.

"How are you feeling?" Kadence asked.

"Good."

"Drunk good or...?"

"Not drunk good." Avery shook her head. "Just...good."

Kadence wrapped her arm around Avery's waist.

Avery gave an involuntary yelp.

Kadence relinquished her hold in alarm. "Did I hurt you?"

"No." Avery shook her head. "It's just...I'm just, umm, really ticklish."

"Oh." Kadence backed a few inches away.

No. Come back! "Here." Avery gestured for

Kadence to rotate onto her side. She switched their positions, so Kadence was the little spoon instead. "Comfy?"

Kadence nodded and Avery leaned forward just enough to get a whiff of her perfume.

Kadence let out a contented sigh. The room fell silent, and for a moment Avery was almost certain Kadence had fallen asleep. But then she shifted.

"Thomas Grasso," Kadence whispered into the darkness.

"Sorry?"

"The guy who didn't get his canned spaghetti. His name was Thomas Grasso." Kadence yawned.

"You knew?"

Kadence turned to face Avery with a sleepy nod. "I may have looked up random canned spaghetti facts one day."

Though the room was dark, Avery could still distinguish the smile on her lips. "Seriously?"

Kadence hummed. "With the amount of that stuff that you ingest, I needed to make sure I didn't have to worry about the you getting cancer or something."

"Oh, my god. I might be in love with you." Avery laughed until she realized what she had just said.

Kadence didn't seem bothered by the words. Her eyes didn't even open. But she *did* slide closer.

"Kae?"

"You asked for cuddling, so come and get your cuddle on."

Avery pressed forward, holding Kadence in her arms as the sleepy woman burrowed into her chest. It was the best sleep either had gotten in a long time.

Chapter Twenty-three

THE PAIR WOKE IN a tangled mess of limbs and warm skin. Sometime during the night, they had managed to wrap themselves further into one another's arms. Avery's arm was cradled on Kadence's hip, palm pressed flat against the small of her back, while Kadence's face was tucked into Avery's chest, nose buried into her neck as she inhaled the smell of acrylic that permanently emanated from Avery's skin. It should be unappealing, or at the least, somewhat dizzying. In a way, Kadence guessed, it was dizzying, but in the most thrilling way possible.

Kadence lay in the sheltering embrace, her heart being catered to by protective arms. She reveled in it until she felt a pressure in her lower stomach, reluctantly extracting herself from the sheets. Avery shuffled, blinking awake. The sight of amber eyes reflecting in the morning light caused Kadence's breath to catch.

"Everything okay?" Avery's husky voice croaked.

Kadence added it to the growing list of things she was starting to adore about Avery Bennett. "Just need to go to the bathroom. I'll be back."

"M'kay." Avery nuzzled her nose into the pillow where Kadence's hair had been splayed. The sight made Kadence's chest swell.

After a quick trip to the bathroom, she settled

back under the sheets, bed dipping under her weight. Avery's front pushed against her back in an instant and the pair released dual sighs of content. Kadence boldly pulled Avery's arm to snuggly encircle her waist, linking their hands as she clasped their fingers. Kadence knew something had shifted between them. She could feel it. She felt *closer*. Being with Avery physically, without being physical, felt nice. *Really nice.*

By the way Avery was holding her, it was obvious she felt it, too. But neither of them made the first move to discuss it. She started to drift off again, lulled to sleep by the rise and fall of Avery's breathing.

The next time she woke was to Avery running her fingers though her hair, carefully unknotting the tangles in her bedhead curls.

"That feels nice," Kadence purred, enjoying the feeling of being pampered, a satisfied mewl escaping her lips.

"Really? I couldn't tell." She could hear the smirk in Avery's words. She gave a playful shove backward, feeling the puff of breath from Avery's soft laughter on her neck.

"Hey, Kadence." Avery's words vibrated off Kadence's skin. "Thank you for spending the night. You didn't have to."

"It was my pleasure." Kadence smiled, tightening her grip on their entwined fingers. "I wanted to."

"Well, let me repay you. Can I make you breakfast? Do you like pancakes or waffles?"

"You don't have to do that."

"It's my pleasure," Avery copied. "I want to."

Kadence snorted. "You're cheeky in the morning. I guess pancakes wouldn't hurt."

"Good! Don't leave." As Avery unraveled from

their tangled position, Kadence did her best not to chase the warmth.

"As long as you promise not to." Kadence rolled to face the retreating blonde.

"Well, it *is* my apartment." It was a joke, but the sincerity in Avery's eyes told her that she understood what Kadence meant to say. "I'm not going anywhere."

After borrowing some clothes and taking a quick shower, Kadence returned to the kitchen to find Avery dancing to an old-school ninety's playlist, hips swaying to the beat. A current of affection coursed through her veins.

"Nice moves." Kadence appeared at the unsuspecting chef's side, causing her to jump. Her spatula flew from her hand. Kadence shot forward just in time to catch it and save it from landing on the ground. Despite her quick reflexes, she still collided with Avery's body, pressing her against the counter.

"I take that back. *Very* nice moves," Kadence repeated with an amused upturn of her lips. She handed Avery the spatula as she chuckled.

"Like you could do better."

Kadence smiled. "I can." She spun before Avery could even register the movement and ground her body against the dumbstruck woman.

"Oh, fuck me," Avery choked.

With that, Kadence dipped once, throwing a wink over her shoulder before sauntering to the stove. She pried the spatula from Avery's grip in one smooth motion and resumed attending to the pancakes. "You wish." She shot the most devious look to the baffled blonde.

"Oh? She has jokes now."

Kadence shrugged. "Guess your cheekiness is

rubbing off on me."

"Maybe it's my clothes."

"Maybe. I certainly smell like you."

"Oh, yeah? And how exactly do I smell?"

She scrunched up her nose in feigned disgust. "Like burritos and paint thinner."

"Wow." Avery gasped. "Cheeky and rude."

Kadence threw her head back, laughing freely. It echoed through the entire apartment as a feeling of ease seeped into her chest.

"No, you smell clean. Like something new and fresh." She gave a little tug at the fabric hanging from her frame. "And..." Kadence sniffed her hair, dampened by the shower. "Sort of like gummy bears."

"Gummy bears?" Avery raised a brow. "No way."

"Smell." She gestured for Avery to lean in.

Just as Avery was about to inhale, the apartment door opened with a smash. The spatula clattered to the floor as the two shot to opposite sides of the room.

"Umm? Are we interrupting something?" Emma glanced between the pair, eyes scanning Kadence's attire before cocking a brow at Avery.

"We're just making breakfast." Kadence scrambled for the fallen cooking utensil.

"Pancakes. Want some?" Avery asked the newcomer.

"Uhh, duh!"

***

After breakfast, Avery slipped into the shower as Kadence bustled about the kitchen with Emma, cleaning the plates of the savory syrup and fluffy pancakes.

"Looks like Avery's becoming a part of you,"

Emma noted as she took in her attire.

She really has. "She let me borrow some clothes." Kadence hoped her voice sounded steady, though she was not oblivious to the way her heart leapt into her throat at the mention of Avery.

"Are you two dating or something?"

"What?" Her eyes widened. "No!"

"Oh." The peppy redhead seemed to deflate. "But she asked you to stay the night?"

"It...it's not what you think." Kadence held up her hands in defense.

"No. I know it's not. It's just..." Emma seemed to debate whether or not to reveal her next set of words. "Well, Avery never asks people to stay. It's a rule about commitment or something that she has. Well, had, I think is a little more appropriate."

Kadence's stomach lurched, unsure of how to compute the new bit of information.

Emma shrugged. "It's not my place to be talking about this. Just know Avery really cares about you."

Kadence couldn't fight the rosy tint of her cheeks. "I care about her, too."

Emma reciprocated her grin before stacking the last dish into the cupboard and heading out the door. Kadence sat in the silent apartment until Avery returned, a towel wrapped around her hair and a fresh shirt on her shoulders.

"After a wild morning like that, it's quiet now, don't you think?" Kadence surveyed the apartment.

"Wow. Am I not good enough?" Avery jested.

Kadence caught her wrist, speaking softly. "You are more than enough."

Avery flushed scarlet. "Do you wanna hang out today?" She sounded rather nervous, though they had been doing this for weeks. To be fair, Kadence felt it, too. The air buzzed with tension.

"We can still hang out even if the painting is done. Nothing's changed."

"Right." Kadence bit her lip, fighting the shared smile the two hardly succeeding at hiding. "Of course not."

They both knew it had.

***

Hanging out consisted of cleaning. Simple, uncomplicated cleaning. They made it a game, chasing one another around the apartment while competing to see who could fill her trash bag quickest. One point for each proper item of garbage, while two points were deducted if a bottle or can was not recycled. Loser had to sort through it all at the end.

Their harmless competition was accompanied by bubbling laughter and girlish squealing as they tried to sabotage one another, bumping the other out of the way, or in Kadence's case, tickling Avery. The giddy feeling from hearing Avery's laugh was just a bonus.

It had been a rather uneventful, lazy day. And yet, Kadence was positive it was her favorite day they had spent together by far.

***

The next few days were not. Most definitely not. That was, in part, due to the fact Kadence didn't see Avery after Talia and Claire's arrival for the bridesmaids fitting. Melody had arrived with her fiancé's sisters bright and early to get breakfast before making it to their appointment.

Jordan's sisters weren't particularly rude people, but they were intense and unfiltered. At times, their bluntness could be mistaken as offensive. They got on great with Melody for that same reason, but sometimes their behavior overwhelmed Kadence. Now was one of those times.

They had already been to two other boutiques but hit a roadblock each time. Melody was growing frustrated, Claire was hungry, and Talia's indifference was making it more difficult to decide, rather than easier. As such, it brought them to their current situation where Kadence sat in the waiting area with Claire while Talia and Melody worked with the sales associate to pull dress options to try on. The soles of her feet thanked her for finally getting a rest.

Her phone vibrated in her purse. Despite the discouraging morning, she couldn't help the smile when she saw the sender's name.

Avery Bennett: How's dress shopping going?
Kadence Cooper: Not too well.
Avery Bennett: How come?
Kadence Cooper: Melody is angry.
Avery Bennett: So basically, like any other day then? :P

Kadence sniggered, smiling at the message.

Kadence Cooper: Careful. I might show her your text.
Avery Bennett: No! I want to live!
Avery Bennett: I take it back!
Avery Bennett: I'm sorry!

Avery Bennett*: How can I make it up to you?*

Kadence giggled behind her hand as Melody and Talia returned with a plethora of gowns laid across their outstretched arms.

"Who are you texting?" Claire, Jordan's youngest sister inquired.

Kadence locked her phone. "Umm, no one."

It vibrated again.

"Doesn't seem like no one." Claire craned her neck, trying to peek at Kadence's screen.

Avery Bennett*: Kaaaaeeeee!!! Please!*

"Just a friend." Kadence hoped the vague response would be enough to satiate the young teen's curiosity so she'd drop the subject. Claire rolled her eyes with a shrug.

Luckily, the saleswoman finished hanging up their options, mumbling something about chiffon and satin being more ideal materials than silk or some other fabric Kadence didn't quite catch the name of, still distracted by the buzzing in her lap.

Melody directed Claire into a dressing room, pointing to the arrangement of dresses on the hook.

"Claire, you're up."

Avery Bennett*: Your silence means I'm about to die, aren't I? Melody wants to kill me.*

Melody caught Kadence's grin.

"Are you texting Avery?"

Claire peeked her head from behind the curtain. "Ooo! Who's Avery?" "Oomph!" She gasped suddenly.

"Talia! Not so tight!"

Talia's grumbling voice could be heard from behind the squirming eavesdropper. "Stop moving then."

"Like I said, she's just a friend."

Talia pulled Claire back into the room, adjusting the dress with hushed whispers and the shuffling of fabric. Kadence chanced a glance at her phone.

> **Avery Bennett**: *Should I start writing my will? I want to leave all of my art possessions to Adam, my guitar and books go to Emma and Jayce Walsh, and my father's hat to Kadence Cooper. #RIPMe*

Kadence chuckled at the melodramatic reaction, remembering a time not too long ago when jokes about dying would make her cringe. But now, Avery made her smile. She found herself able to bask in the humor of the statement, rather than sulk at the solemn exaggeration of it. She equated it to Avery and her silliness, which normally Kadence would find immature. But Avery, with her childish, happy-go-lucky personality, coupled with her deep concern and genuine heart, was nothing but endearing.

> **Kadence Bennett**: *You're so dramatic.*

Claire exited with Talia trailing behind her. She twirled, holding out her hands for Melody to take it in. It was definitely gold and matched the color scheme for the wedding, but also looked extremely frilly. By the scrunch of Melody's nose, Kadence already knew what the answer was going to be

"No." Melody shook her head with a flick of her

wrist. She gave a nod toward the next dress in line.

This time Talia emerged in a golden gown with a taupe princess cut at the chest.

Melody narrowed her gaze, turning to her younger sister for a second opinion.

"The cut is nice, but the colors clash. The gold is just a little too far on the color wheel from the taupe and it looks like the designer was colorblind, rather than making the choice intentionally."

Claire, having changed out of the first dress, nodded, impressed. "Wow! Kadence, I didn't know you knew that much about color theory."

Melody snorted. "She doesn't. Avery does."

Kadence's ears burned.

Claire nodded as Talia returned to the changing room. "So, are you seeing anyone after Iris?"

"Oh, my god!" Talia marched out with her dress half unzipped, holding it up by the fabric near her breasts. Her free hand quickly shot to her younger sister, bopping her upside the head.

"Oww!" Claire hissed with a glare. "What the fuck?"

"Go change!" Talia demanded, pointing to the next dress in the lineup.

Kadence looked at Melody, overwhelmed by the sisters' method of argument. Talia was even more intense than Melody.

"You'll have to excuse Claire," Talia apologized, turning to Kadence. "My sister is dumb and," she raised her voice loud enough for Claire to hear, "doesn't know when to shut up. It's like she has zero filter, one hundred percent of the time."

"It's okay. No, Claire," Kadence called out. "I'm not."

Claire pulled back the curtain to send her sister a deadly stare before Talia flipped her off, returning to her own dressing room. Kadence slumped in her chair, releasing an exhausted sigh.

Melody flopped down in the seat next to her. "So, what's the problem?"

"Well, I think since Claire is shorter, most of the dresses don't fit her the same way they do on Talia and me. And the different shades of gold are..."

Melody shook her head. "I don't wanna talk about that."

"Mel." Kadence placed a reassuring hand on her sister's knee. "I know this is stressful, but we're here to help you. It's your big day. Don't overthink it. We just want you to pick something that you like. We'll wear anything."

Melody scoffed. "That's because you look good in everything. And I don't overthink. That's your job. I wasn't even talking about this." She waved her hand nonchalantly to the remaining few dresses. "I meant, what's the problem with you and Avery."

Kadence blinked. A problem with her and Avery? She wasn't aware that there was one. Everything felt pretty right to her.

"I don't overthink. And there is no problem. We're good friends."

"Mmhmm. Sure." Melody rolled her eyes so hard Kadence worried they'd get stuck. "If that's the case, here." Melody reached into her purse, withdrawing a stiff piece of cardstock with metallic gold trim.

"Why are you giving me this?" Kadence asked, befuddled by the invitation in her hand.

"I thought you said you weren't going to overthink it."

255

"But I know when the wedding is."

"It's not for you." Melody flicked her, channeling the Talia of just a moment ago.

"Oww!"

"Invite Avery to be your date."

"What?" Kadence gasped. "I can't...we are..."

Melody gave a pointed look just as Talia and Claire reappeared in their street clothing.

"So, what's next?"

"Yeah, Kadence, what's next?" Melody said subtly.

Kadence bit her tongue, grabbing the next gown and retreating into the dressing room. From inside, she could still hear Melody cackling. Changing swiftly, she returned to the trio and displayed the shining gold dress with a black lace neckline.

"Oh, come on!" Melody threw her hands up in the air. "You would look this good."

Kadence blushed.

"Take it off before I feel inadequate about myself in my wedding dress."

Kadence laughed. "You're not going to look inadequate."

"Says you, Talia. Claire, you two try it on." They ended up reserving three of them and getting alteration measurements taken. Kadence let out a sigh of relief. On to the next task.

Chapter Twenty-four

AVERY TAPPED HER FOOT against the wall as she laid on the hardwood floor in her bedroom. Her cellphone was grasped in her hands, hovering at the tip of her nose. She had spent the majority of the afternoon in that position, doing nothing in particular while engrossed in sending texts back and forth with Kadence.

Kadence Cooper: Melody is about two seconds from canceling the wedding and eloping to Vegas.
Kadence Cooper: You think I'm joking. But she's dead serious right now.
Avery Bennett: That bad, huh? So, no dress then?
Kadence Cooper: I already got my dress.
Avery Bennett: Really? No alterations?
Kadence Cooper: Nope. Just got the one off the mannequin modeling it and it fit like a glove.
Avery Bennett: That's because your body is perfect.

She froze, smacking herself in the forehead for being so forward.

Avery Bennett: Sorry. Ignore that.
Kadence Cooper: Thank you. You're sweet.

Her cheeks grew warm.

"Tell Kadence I said 'hi.'" Emma appeared in the doorway.

The phone collided with Avery's nose.

"Damnit! Stop eavesdropping." Avery rubbed at her injury.

Emma laughed. "That isn't a verbal conversation." She rolled her eyes, tilting her head toward the device. "You can't eavesdrop."

"Then how did you know I was talking to Kadence?"

"Because you're always talking to Kadence. Simple deductive reasoning." Emma shrugged. "If you're not together in person, you're still texting or on the phone."

"Are not!" Avery flushed at Emma's all-too-accurate observation.

"Whatever you say. I just wanted to let you know, Danny and I are planning on going on a camping trip next week with Jayce and Lola. You should invite Kadence to come. Maybe Melody could take Jordan, too, if he isn't traveling for work again."

Avery knew for a fact he wasn't, Kadence had told her as much. The future in-laws were planning to pick up wedding favors and get suit measurements with the groomsmen later that week.

"I don't know, Em. You're all couples. Kadence and I are just friends."

Emma's brows reached her hairline. Avery almost laughed at how comical it was to see her roommate so serious.

"Puh-lease. You've already shared a bed. You can share a tent. It's not a big deal. The worst thing she could say is 'no,' but I doubt she will."

"All right." Avery couldn't argue with that logic.

"I'll give her a call later."

"Yay!" Emma clapped, launching herself at Avery and pulling her into a tight hug. "I'm glad you're so whipped for this girl. I could never get you to go camping otherwise."

"Hey!" *Damn, Bennett. She sniped you.*

Emma gave a smug grin, puffing her chest. Avery thrust a pillow at her, but her heart still skipped at the idea of a potential getaway with Kadence.

***

"I'd love to," Kadence chirped into the phone. "Just let me check with Melody. She's pretty overwhelmed with everything, but you're right. We could definitely use a break."

"And you're okay with the tent situation?" Avery picked at her cuticle.

"Maybe," Kadence purred into the phone. "It depends."

Is she flirting? "On what?"

"Are we cuddling?"

She is definitely flirting. Avery grinned. "Definitely."

"Good." Avery could hear the smirk in her reply.

"Good," Avery parroted back.

"Okay."

"Okay." At the giggle in her ear, Avery increased the volume on her phone.

"Kadence is the best."

Avery didn't miss a beat. "Kadence is the best."

Kadence laughed. "Okay, enough of that. I have an invitation for you, as well."

"Oh?" Avery quirked her brow, interest piqued.

"And what's that?"

"Are you home right now?"

"I am."

A knock on the apartment door interrupted their conversation. Avery groaned. "Hey, Kae. Hold on a sec. Someone's at the door." She placed her phone on the kitchen counter, skidding to a halt in front of the apartment entrance. Rising to her tiptoes, she peered through the peep hole.

"Kae?" She unlatched the door. "What are you doing here?"

Kadence's lips quirked to the side. "Inviting you, of course."

"To?"

"Melody's wedding." Kadence held out an envelope.

Avery's head tilted in confusion at the cardstock wedding invitation. "But I was already invited."

"You were invited as a guest. I..." Kadence ducked her head. She inhaled before straightening to meet Avery's gaze directly. "Avery, I want to invite you as my date."

"Oh." Avery's skin grew hot. "Okay." A grin spread across her face.

"Okay?" Kadence said with twinkling eyes, her own features following suit with a grin.

"Okay."

Kadence laughed. "Are we really doing this again?"

"Yes. But it'll be better this time. I promise I won't be a complete dick like I was back then."

"Not a complete dick." Kadence smiled in understanding. "You were good for the majority of the evening. It was just toward the end when things got a bit, umm, messy."

"You can say that again."

"You were hurt." Kadence reached out to grasp Avery's hand, giving it a squeeze. "But I know you now. We're okay."

Avery gnawed the inside of her lip.

"You do believe me, right? You trust me like I trust you?"

Avery gave a bashful nod.

"Good," Kadence whispered, hovering closer.

"Good," Avery replied just as gently. Her gaze fell to soft lips and for a moment, Kadence's did, too. Emerald eyes twinkled. Waiting. *Just go for it, Bennett. You're gonna miss your chance if you...*

"Umm." Kadence shivered. "I should probably get going."

What did I tell you?

"Claire and Talia are still at Melody's and I'm not being a very good maid of honor by ditching them."

"Oh, of course." Avery nodded. "I mean, not of course to you being a good maid of honor. I mean, a bad maid of honor. I meant that you're a good maid of honor. You're a good everything...wait. I just mean that..."

Her idiotic rambling was rewarded by Kadence stepping forward and placing a soft kiss to her lips, cutting her off. Stunned, Avery barely managed to reciprocate before Kadence pulled away. Everything tingled.

"I...I..."

Kadence giggled again, pecking her cheek. "You're cute."

"You..." was all Avery managed to sputter in her awestruck wonder.

Green eyes sparkled as Kadence tucked a stray hair behind Avery's ear. "Goodnight, Avery." Kadence bid her a gentle farewell.

The softness of her tone wrapped itself around Avery, filling her with warmth. She was unable to get her jelly legs to move until Kadence descended the staircase and vanished out of sight. She spent the rest of the night tracing the outline of her lips, remembering the press of soft, warm skin against them.

***

They didn't talk about the kiss. In fact, they barely talked at all with Kadence being so busy hosting her two future sisters-in-law. Avery knew she shouldn't fret. But she wanted to discuss it—*them*. And the press of petal soft lips, coconut scented perfume, and the subtle caress of fingertips across her cheek as they tucked hair behind her ear. The unusual lack of communication caused her to worry that Kadence thought the entire thing was a mistake.

Avery needed to ensure that Kadence had no doubts about her intentions. That her feelings were genuine and that she was ready to make the effort. To make the first move, even. As long as her stupid, thirsty brain didn't turn into mush around the green-eyed goddess.

A week went by before their next reunion. It was humid outside when the three vehicles finally made it to the campground. Avery was thankful her unruly hair was secured under the snapback on her head as she climbed out of the backseat. Like magnets, her eyes sought out Kadence standing by the familiar red SUV. She was in the middle of braiding her hair into a long, single French braid that rested on her shoulder.

The simple beauty of the woman made Avery's breath hitch, cheeks tinting a hue bright enough to rival the vehicle Kadence stood next to. As if Kadence detected her catch of breath, she turned to meet her gaze. Avery offered a shy wave. Kadence, hands occupied with her hair, responded back with a full-blown smile and a wink that made Avery's heart rate run amok.

The band of friends sought out a level area to start assembling their tents and unloading their bags of gear. They then broke into task forces to finish setting up their weekend home.

"Hey." Avery greeted Kadence after she and Emma finished building the fire. The Cooper siblings were sorting through their meals, having been placed in charge of food. This, admittedly, had been due to the fact that Avery couldn't be trusted around snacks and Lola had an irrational fear of fire.

Kadence turned at the sound of her voice and the movement swayed her braid perfectly across her shoulder in the process. Avery swallowed thickly. They had been in the same position a few months ago, but Avery had been too shallow, her one-track mind too distracted by a toned body and long legs.

You're still distracted by those things, dumbass. Shut up! But now, things were different. Now, she was invested. And though there was no denying Kadence's figure was definitely captivating, there was also an incredibly beautiful part of her that Avery had fallen even deeper in love with.

"Hello, Avery." Kadence blushed as she hunched over one of their supply bags, zipper peeling apart where it was held between her index finger and thumb.

"Wanna help me start cooking lunch? You can be sous-chef?" She bit her lip to hide her smile, both of them knowing Avery was the more talented cook of the two.

"Absolutely." Avery grinned, crouching down to sort through their various options.

"There are beef patties in the cooler."

Avery retrieved them. "Are these as good as Five Guys?" she asked, watching the memory flash in Kadence's green eyes.

Kadence smiled. "Hopefully better this time."

"Better," Avery repeated, the two sharing a moment as they sifted through their stash of food. When they reached the bottom, Avery caught sight of a familiar red and white label, fighting back a smile as she turned the can in her hand.

"Shh." Kadence placed a finger on her mouth with a mischievous grin. "There's only a few of them for you. We'll hide them in our tent later."

Avery felt the inside of her chest expand. "Secret's safe with me." Avery nudged her playfully but the touch between them felt electric, both cheeks matching with the same rosy hue.

"What's taking you two so long?" Emma called from the fire pit.

"We should probably…"

"Yeah I…"

They both said at the same time, as they inched their way to the waiting roommate perched on a stump near the crackling flames.

***

They stirred up a few veggies while Avery flipped the burgers, the smell wafting into the warm summer breeze, making her stomach rumble. Rounding up the gang, the group circled the fire with their canteens and granola bars.

"So, we're thinking of going out for a hike after lunch, now that the tents are set up," Jayce said, taking a bite of the jerky that Lola split with him. He gave a grateful thank you, smiling like a lovesick fool. Avery immediately found herself looking at Kadence the same way.

"I would be down for that," Emma piped in, turning to Avery. "Avery, you in?"

Avery blinked, having only partially paid attention to the conversation, mouth preoccupied with stuffing the cheesy burger into her mouth while her eyes were glued to the delicate way Kadence held her burger between her fingers.

"Yo, Bennett!" Melody kicked some dirt in her direction, a few chunks getting stuck in her laces. "Pay attention." The instigator scoffed as Avery cowered back.

"Mel, stop it." Kadence rolled her eyes. "She likes you," Kadence said, leaning to reassure Avery with a soft whisper. "She just doesn't like that she likes you."

Avery muttered a quick negation before shaking her head. "I think I'll pass on the hike. I've only got so much energy stored up for this weekend. I've got to spend it wisely." She patted her stomach.

Kadence giggled at her side while Emma shrugged, leaning into her boyfriend. Avery surveyed their circle of friends, resisting the urge to groan in jealousy as all of the couples expressed their affection for one another. She felt, more than saw, Kadence tense as well, clearly noticing the same.

"Me, too, actually," Kadence added a second

later, a sort of stiffness to her voice.

"Kadence, really? You never turn down hiking," Danny gasped. "Avery, what have you done to my friend?" He looked between the two before securing his arm around Emma's shoulders.

Kadence let loose an airy giggle. "I promise I'll go on the next hike. But I have my own reason, not equated to laziness." Kadence grinned as Avery's jaw dropped. Her green eyes twinkled as she gave Avery a gentle nudge to assure her it was all in jest.

"I wanted to go find the lake and sit by the water for a bit. Maybe meditate, do some yoga, go for a swim..." She trailed off as she listed the possibilities.

"Yeah, that one definitely won't be joining you for that, then." Emma pointed a finger at Avery.

"Hey," Avery exclaimed indignantly. "I resent that. I may not be able to swim, but I'm becoming quite the yoga guru. Tell em, Kadence."

"Of course, Avery. Whatever helps you sleep at night." Kadence grinned with a wink as the entire circle broke into chuckles.

Avery didn't mind the teasing though, because after they settled and the laughter died down, Kadence's hand found a place on Avery's knee.

***

After lunch, Kadence found a secluded area by the lake and perched on one of the large rocks that had been smoothed by the lap of water. Avery had intended to draw a little and hopefully speak privately with Kadence. But as she approached, realizing how peaceful Kadence looked in the serene landscape, she felt as though she was intruding. She pivoted to return back to the tent, only to stumble on a fallen branch, the wood breaking apart with an ear-splitting crack.

"So, you decided to join me, after all," Kadence said without opening her eyes.

"How'd you know it was me?" Avery asked astonished, if not incredibly impressed.

"I didn't." Kadence inhaled for a beat, holding it as Avery counted out three seconds in her head, before exhaling. "Just hoped." Her eyes fluttered open.

Avery blushed, watching the corner of Kadence's mouth quirk upward. "Oh. I, umm, I was going to sketch the scenery. Is it cool if I join you?"

"Of course. Please do." Kadence gestured to the space beside her.

Avery situated her supplies, flipping her sketch pad to a clean sheet of paper. Her wrist flicked as she made long, quick strokes on the page, outlining the clusters of trees and their reflections dispersed across the lake's clear surface. Her eyes darted back and forth between the landscape and the tablet in her lap. About a dozen exchanges later, she noticed Kadence peeking at her. She ceased the scratching against the page.

"Umm, is this bothering you?"

"No. I just like watching you work."

"Okay. As long as it's not distracting."

"Oh, it is." Kadence smiled. "But it's a welcome distraction."

Avery nearly dropped her sketch pad in her flustered state. "Look, Kae, about the kiss. I—"

Her words were cut off by rustling from behind them. Both women straightened. "Uhh, Kadence?" Avery hissed, eyes trained on the bush as she shifted closer to Kadence. "What are the possibilities of that being a snake?"

Kadence crouched up. "Snakes aren't that loud." She inched toward the source of the sound as though she were being tossed into a horror movie and their demise was descending upon them. Why was Kadence walking toward the potential source of danger?

"Kae, come back. It could be a bear."

"Bears don't live at this altitude," Kadence reasoned, taking another step closer. "Besides, it's a commercial campground. There's no way the park rangers would allow people to stay here if there were bears."

"Kadence," Avery yelped as a fuzzy creature darted from the shrubbery, rushing between Avery's legs. The telltale pattern of gray and black fur grazed against her shin. Avery rushed to Kadence, grasping her arm as the critter ascended up a tree. The reaction rendered a laugh from the all-too-calm woman at her side.

"Aww," Kadence cooed. "Not a fan of baby raccoons?" She nudged Avery's side and she flinched in response to the ticklish sensation in her ribs.

"Stahhpp!" She groaned in embarrassment, burying her face in her hands. "I wasn't scared. I was just taken off guard."

"Mmhmm." Kadence scoffed. "Just like the snakeskin."

"No. Not like the snakeskin."

"There, there. I'll protect you, little one." Kadence readjusted Avery's hat with a pat to her head. Delicate fingers wrapped around her hands, tugging them away from shielding her reddened cheeks. "I know what will make it better." She smiled, pulling Avery back toward the lake. She retrieved Avery's sketchpad from where it had been left on the bank, placing it on the rock she had been sitting on. She then proceeded to strip.

Fuck. What is this? Shit. Look away, Bennett! Look away! She ripped her gaze away with such monumental effort, she deserved an award for it.

"Avery?"

Avery chanced a glance at the gorgeous figure in just a black sports bra and matching black underwear.

"You coming?" She waded into the water, nodding at Avery's still dressed form.

Yes. So hard. "Um, Kadence, what are you doing?" Avery squeaked, lungs fighting for even the slightest bit of oxygen.

"You want to prove that you're brave, right?" Kadence mused. "Come on then, I'm going to teach you how to swim."

Avery's eyes widened, hands hovering at the hem of her own T-shirt.

"Let's go, Ms. I've-Never-Skinny-Dipped-Before." Kadence dipped into the water until only the skin above her collarbone was exposed.

Avery's eyes immediately betrayed her, following the sight.

"I'm already cutting you a break since we're in public." Kadence cocked a brow, challengingly. "Otherwise, we'd be naked."

Fuuuuuccckkk! Mustering up every bit of strength, she relented, shedding her clothes and slinking toward the shore. The soft pull of the waves lapped at her toes.

"A little farther," Kadence encouraged, swimming back toward her, holding out a hand. Droplets of water tracked down her abs. If Avery's grip was a bit too tense, Kadence didn't say anything. Instead, she pulled her deeper into the lake until her chest met the crest of the water.

"There you go." She beamed. "Now lift your feet off the ground and start kicking them."

Avery did as she was told, treading for a few seconds before having to place her legs back onto the ground.

"Nice." Kadence nodded in approval. "Now, add your arms like this." She demonstrated the movements for Avery to mimic.

Avery tried to follow, but quickly found herself sinking. Kadence moved toward her, catching Avery before her mouth could fill with water, arms secured around her waist.

"Good effort."

"Yeah, right." Avery rolled her eyes. "I told you, I can't swim."

"You're not that bad," Kadence said, unfazed by her stubbornness. "Just need a little more practice." She gave Avery's hips a squeeze.

It was then that Avery realized their position. Her arms were wrapped around Kadence's neck as she held her afloat. And the amount of clothing between them or rather, lack thereof. *Come on, Bennett. Make a move!* "You're not bad yourself."

"Focus, Avery." Despite Kadence's scolding disapproval, there was still a rosy hue to her cheeks. She waded deeper into the water. "Let's see if you can do this again. Let yourself relax." Kadence relinquished her hold. Avery sputtered water into the air, splashing about. Slender arms swiftly returned to her sides while rich laughter rang across the surface of the lake.

"This is cruel and unusual punishment." Avery huffed at the grinning instructor. "I'm so glad you find my misery amusing."

"Just a little."

"Well," Avery said, frowning. "I can't help it if I like it better on the ground." She realized the unintentional innuendo when Kadence cocked a brow with a devious grin. "Okay, listen." Avery narrowed her gaze, though their position compromised her ability to truly remain serious. "I stick to the ground. I enjoy having my feet balanced on the ground. It's nature. I'm a grounder."

Kadence chuckled. "That is not a real term."

"It is in baseball."

"Yeah?" Kadence readjusted her arms to hold Avery tighter as she smirked. "And what base are you trying to get to, exactly?"

Avery wrapped her legs around Kadence's waist. "I think I'm pretty content with this one."

Smiling, Kadence carried her as they waded around the lake, water helping her remain buoyant. A comfortable silence fell between them. Avery pressed her forehead to Kadence's, content to just look into her eyes.

**

They remained in that position until all of their body heat was pulled away with the current and they shivered. The two returned to shore hand in hand.

"We should probably change into some warmer clothes."

Was that an invitation? Are we at that point yet? Avery swallowed. "You go ahead." She gestured to their shared tent, not wanting to pressure Kadence into changing at the same time.

"You sure?" Kadence asked, eyeing Avery's

goosebump-covered skin.

"Yeah." Avery nodded. "Go ahead."

"Okay. I'll be quick."

Kadence emerged minutes later in a large pullover, leggings, and slipped back into her sneakers.

"You're up." She climbed into the hammock while Avery took her turn. She returned to find Kadence with her eyes closed, face tilted up to the sun and hands propped behind her head. She looked so soft and beautiful, and most of all, cuddleable.

Avery cushioned her knee into the sway of the hammock, feeling the feminine curves next to her. Everything happened in a flash from there. The fabric swung sharply, causing her to tumble out, a body falling atop her in the process.

"Shit. Are you okay?" Avery immediately rolled off the previously dozing woman, now fully awake.

"Yeah." Kadence propped herself up on her elbows. "Umm, what was that about?"

"It seemed a lot cuter in the movies." Avery pouted, cheeks burning. "And a lot easier."

Instead of annoyance, Kadence beamed. "So, you wanted to cuddle?"

"Maybe?"

Their giggling subsided, and the space between them shifted. Before she knew what she was doing, Avery leaned forward and connected her lips with Kadence's. Kadence stiffened, and Avery immediately pulled away.

Had she misread? "I shouldn't have done that. I'm so sorry. We never talked about the last—"

Kadence didn't let her continue with her doubts, cupping Avery's face with both hands before kissing her again. Firmer, yet softer. Avery relaxed, the slightest smile on her lips as their lips moved in sync. The press was gentle and comforting, their touches growing surer as they progressed. Her heart started racing and butterflies erupted from deep in her stomach.

"Don't apologize," Kadence said, when they finally broke apart, eyes still closed. They fluttered open as she reached for Avery's hand, pressing the trembling palm to her chest. Brilliant green exploded from behind her eyelids, glowing in the sun. Avery's breath caught.

"Especially not for doing this to me." She pressed her hand on Avery's, allowing her to feel the rapid thrumming of her heart, leaning in for another mind-reeling kiss.

"So, this is okay?"

"Definitely." Kadence pecked her lips. "But I'd much rather we not do this on the ground."

"Aww. But I kinda like it on the ground." Avery wiggled her brow teasingly.

"Get off." Kadence laughed, pushing up to stand. They repositioned themselves in the fabric, enjoying the intimacy between them as they napped under the sun. They remained that way until a pressure in Kadence's bladder forced her to untangle from their warm press of skin.

"I'm going to the bathroom," she said, placing a quick kiss on Avery's forehead. "Holler if you need me." She barely made it ten yards away when Avery let out a piercing scream. Kadence started at the sound.

"Avery?" Kadence turned on her heel in a frenzy. "What? Is everything okay?" She rushed back, skidding to a halt, almost colliding into Avery in the process.

Avery wedged her lip between her teeth. "Yup. Just checking to see if you were being serious."

Green eyes rolled to the back of her head.

"You're such a dork." Kadence laughed before turning to go back down the trail.

"Kadence, wait." Avery tugged her wrist.

Kadence tilted her head in confusion, noticing the vulnerable expression on Avery's face, a complete contrast to the cocky jokester from before. Avery dropped her wrist, wringing her hands in her T-shirt.

"I...I really do need you."

Kadence softened as she a step forward, tilting Avery's chin up to meet her gaze. "You have me, Avery."

Chapter Twenty-five

A SHRILL CRY ALERTED them of approaching hikers. They had settled back into their cocoon, only awakening upon their friends return. Kadence sat up in an instant while Avery yawned lazily and stretched.

"How was the hike?" Kadence asked, before noticing Jayce carrying Lola on his back. "Is everything all right?"

Jayce nodded. "Lo's got a weak knee and it decided to give out so we figured it would be best to come back earlier."

"Here," Avery piped in from beside her. "Take the hammock."

Jayce assisted her into a lying position. He then climbed in, perching next to Lola's leg, massaging it lightly.

Kadence smiled in adoration at the couple, as Avery shuffled closer to her side. Their eyes met.

Emma placed her hands on her hips. "Okay. What's up with you two? Avery's been acting weird all week, and now you are, too. Are you two fighting again or something? Because I swear to God, I won't be able to—"

"Calm down, Em. It's okay," Avery jumped in. "We're not fighting. Far from it."

"Right. We're getting along quite nicely." Kadence flashed a smile in Avery's direction, the pair sharing a fond gaze.

"Okay." Emma eyed them skeptically. "I'm gonna

figure out whatever it is you're hiding eventually." She shrugged before heading off to find her boyfriend.

"That girl goes from zero to one hundred eighty in a second." Avery chuckled, shaking her head.

"And you don't?"

"I can." Avery spun around to give Kadence a view of her backside, attempting to twerk obnoxiously.

Kadence chortled, shaking her head. "Dork."

Avery stuck her tongue between her teeth, squinting her eyes before lifting her hat, taking a bow. She placed the hat on Kadence's head before wandering off to spend some time with the rest of the group.

***

"So, what did you two get up to while we were gone?" Melody nodded her head toward Avery, currently making some strange sort of gesture, hands flying wildly around her face as she spoke enthusiastically with Lola.

Kadence watched with endearment as the injured woman threw her head back, laughter escaping into the air. The pain etched into her features dissolved with the sound. Avery beamed and Jayce gave her a grateful smile in return for making his girlfriend feel better.

"Hello?" Melody waved her hand in Kadence's field of vision. "Earth to goo eyes." Her sister snapped her fingers, drawing Kadence out of her daze.

"Sorry." She cleared her throat. "I spent the afternoon doing some meditation then I tried teaching Avery to swim."

"Oh, yeah? And how did that go?" Melody gave Avery an incredulous glare.

"It went well." Kadence hoped Melody wouldn't

ask for any further details.

Instead, the older woman pressed her lips tight as she gave a disbelieving nod. "And can she swim now?"

"Umm." Kadence fiddled with her fingers. "No, not quite."

"Well, then, what kind of shit instructor are you?"

Kadence flushed as her sister sniggered in amusement.

"Oh, I know. You were just trying to get her wet."

Kadence's jaw plummeted to the ground. "Melody!"

Her sister cackled. Kadence burned brighter than a tomato, heat creeping up the back of her neck, all the way to the tip of her ears.

"Oh, my god! Your face right now," Melody gasped, tears forming in the corner of her eyes.

Kadence hadn't heard Melody laugh like this in so long. And if Avery, and by extension, herself, were to be the reason for it, then so be it. She brushed off her sister's lewd comment, diverting the subject to the afternoon's events. "Anyway. How was the hike?"

"It was good, the weather's nice and the trail wasn't too harsh. Probably going to try again tomorrow or something. Give Lola a night to recover and see how she feels."

"That's probably a good idea. They're going to the wedding together, right?" Kadence nodded toward the couple in the hammock.

Lola was poking Jayce in the side, her boyfriend entertaining her behavior for a few seconds before finally grasping her wrist, pulling her upright until they were face to face. Lola then proceeded to stick her tongue out, licking his nose as he pulled away with a groan. His features scrunched in disgust as he wiped off the offending spit with the back of his hand. Lola crowed with laughter and Jayce rewarded her with a kiss.

"Yeah." Melody snorted, having also observed the entire exchange. "I thought they were just friends with benefits but I guess some things change."

"They do." Kadence's gaze lingered toward Avery.

"Ya know, they're almost as nasty as you two."

"Hey!" Kadence frowned. "Avery and I are not nasty."

"No. Just gross."

Kadence gave sister a shove. "We aren't even dating."

Melody rolled her eyes. "You two skipped dating and went straight to domestic. You practically live at her place. And she's your date to the wedding. That is what people usually call dating."

Kadence couldn't deny her sister's claims. "Speaking of the wedding. It's in a month. Can you believe it?"

Melody groaned. "Don't remind me. I feel like there's still so much to do."

Kadence placed a reassuring hand on her sister's knee. "We've pretty much gotten everything taken care of. Dresses should be coming in within the next week. You and Jordan already took care of the caterer. I spoke with Ramona, everything's all set to be delivered and prepped the day before. And the venue deposit was already put down by Jordan and his mom weeks ago." She continued to check off the list mentally in her head. "Everything else, April's handling."

Melody nodded. "Jordan told me about the fitting for his tux and that you went along with him and the guys. You didn't have to."

Kadence smiled, brushing it off with a wave of her delicate hand. "It was fun! The gold vests are going to look so classy. Don't worry, everything for your big day is going to be just fine."

"Yeah..." Melody trailed off as her eyes found Jordan.

"Now look who's being gross." Kadence's teasing earned her a noogie and a head full of messy hair.

***

The group concluded the evening by stargazing into the night sky. Lola and Jayce huddled in the hammock, a blanket draped over their legs as they shared a canister of hot tea. Danny found a tree to sit against, Emma settled in front of him, between his legs as she leaned her back into his chest. Melody and Jordan were propped against a fallen log, the bride-to-be resting her head on her fiancé's shoulder. Kadence and Avery remained on their own blanket, lying side by side.

Kadence wanted to reach out and clasp their hands together, but they hadn't discussed where they stood in terms of public displays of affection. She opted for subtle, just barely extending her pinky to rub against Avery's wrist. Their eyes met as Avery turned her head. The stars seemed far duller in comparison to the brightness of Avery's smile, white teeth glowing in the moonlight.

"You tired?"

Avery shook her head, but a yawn escaped from her lips at the suggestion of sleep.

Kadence stifled a giggle behind her hand before pushing herself upright. "I think we're going to call it a night."

A chorus of goodnights rung out amongst the band of friends as they shook off their blanket. Avery grabbed one set of corners while Kadence grabbed the other, walking toward one another to meet in the middle.

"Hey."

"Hi."

Avery grinned. Kadence grinned. No one else noticed. She bit back a smile as they returned to their tent, and Avery kicked off her shoes. Kadence chuckled, straightening them next to her own while Avery zipped the tent flap. Avery flipped the switch on the small lantern in the corner of their tent before turning sheepishly to Kadence.

"Look." She revealed a large leaf that had been chewed up by the insects in the forest.

"Avery, why did you bring that in here?"

Avery quickly rearranged the light, holding the leaf just in front of the source, creating different sized specks that danced on the interior of the tent.

"Now we have our own stars."

Green eyes soaked in her makeshift skyline before locking with amber eyes.

"Beautiful." The single word escaped her lips with a catch of breath.

Avery's cheeks turned pink. "Cuddle?"

Kadence chuckled. "Of course."

They arrange themselves into a comfortable position. Avery's arm secured around Kadence's hip, both women snuggled under the blankets so far that only their noses poked out.

"Cold feet." Avery nudged Kadence.

"What?" Kadence hummed sleepily.

"You have cold feet," Avery whispered.

Kadence loved how easily their limbs had tangled together. She slid her hand across Avery's leg, fingers pressed to the warm skin. "Not about this. Not about you." With her eyes still closed, she pressed her feet against Avery's warm shin. Everything in her heart vibrated as Avery dropped a kiss onto Kadence's cheek.

"Goodnight, Kae."

"Goodnight, Avery."

***

A low grumble and the tossing and turning of Avery in her arms brought her out of her slumber. Kadence inhaled sharply before rubbing at her eyes. "I take it back, there are bears here," she muttered, rubbing her thumb on Avery's skin as she cuddled closer. "Quiet down, little bear."

"Sorry." Avery apologized into the darkness. "Go back to sleep. It'll pass."

When Avery's stomach growled, Kadence tied her hair into a messy bun as she retrieved her phone. She then proceeded to use the flashlight application to assist her as she squinted, eyes adjusting to the brightness as she shuffled through her belongings. Within seconds, she produced a can of spaghetti, tossing it in Avery's direction.

Avery popped open the top, eyes widening at the sight of processed tomato and sodium drenched noodles. Kadence sat beside her, leaning her body into Avery's as she handed her a spoon. Avery started munching away. Kadence switched off the light, resting her head on Avery's shoulder as she rested her eyes.

"Thank you."

Kadence nodded with a hum.

"Want some?"

"Bleh." Kadence squished her face in disgust.

"It's good."

Kadence let out a puff of air through her nose in disapproval.

"You sure you don't wanna try some?"

Kadence replied with a grunt.

A cold, sticky material slithered between her lips.

"Avery," Kadence sat up with a yelp, smacking her lips as Avery unsuccessfully suppressed her laughter.

"Sorry. I couldn't resist." Avery grinned, finishing off the spoonful of pasta that Kadence had batted away.

"Oh, that's it." Lithe fingers snatched the utensil from her hand. She scooped up her own spoonful, aiming for Avery's face.

"No," Avery squealed, tripping as she attempted to untuck her legs from the sleeping bag. Kadence followed quickly, chasing her around the tent. They looked absolutely mad, falling on one another and their belongings in the confined space. They were so distracted by their foolish antics that they failed to notice the tent flap opening until the beam of a flashlight scanned across them.

"What the?" Emma looked between them. A can of shaving cream was nestled in her hand.

"What are you doing?" Avery pointed to the aerosol.

"What are *you* doing?"

"We were having a spaghetti fight." Kadence grimaced at how ridiculous it sounded.

"Uhh, okay. Cause that's normal."

"You still haven't told us what you're doing up,"

Avery pointed out, ignoring the jab.

"Well, I was gonna prank you. I already got Jayce, and I wouldn't dare do Melody, so you were next on the list." She smiled evilly, holding up the spray can.

"Psh, you're gonna have to do better than that," Avery challenged lightly.

"Yeah." Emma snorted. "Not sure if I want to. I'd rather have caught you two making out. That would have been *way* less weird than whatever you're doing."

Kadence felt her face flush.

"Go away," Avery groaned, taking her spoon and holding it between her fingers, ready to fling the spaghetti at the intruder.

The tent flap closed a second later as Kadence let out a nervous chuckle.

"Well, that was..."

Avery rubbed the back of her neck. "Yeah. Do you think we should tell her?"

"Do you?"

Avery shrugged. "I guess she'll figure it out eventually."

"True." Kadence nodded. They re-zipped the tent door, attaching the interior lock this time.

Kadence let her finish up her meal before they settled back into their previous position. "You wouldn't have anyway."

"Wouldn't have what?"

"Wasted canned spaghetti by throwing it at Emma."

Avery's lips turned up at that. "You're right." She snuggled closer. "I only give it up to people I like."

Kadence chuckled. They laid silent. Along with the crickets, Kadence chirped the faintest "I like you, too."

***

They made it exactly eighteen hours before anyone suspected anything, or at least, that was what Kadence thought. She had kept enough distance from Avery during their hike, mainly because Avery had lagged in the back with Lola while she and Melody marched up front with Emma, Jordan, and Danny.

They were fine at breakfast. They shared the same log as they sat by the fire, but so did all of the other couples. It was the only logical option. Kadence believed everything had been discrete, even her stolen glances at Avery. But as the group started to say their goodbyes, Kadence leaned to place a kiss on Avery's cheek, as Avery turned and pressed forward. Their lips met just in time for the entire group to witness their unintentional display of affection, garnering a vast array of reactions.

"I fucking knew it." Emma pointed between them while Danny hushed her, adding he was happy for them both.

Jayce congratulated Avery with a muttered finally and a friendly thumbs up to Kadence while his girlfriend raised her brows.

Jordan smiled while Melody pretended to violently retch, shouting gross as she gagged.

But to be honest, the best reaction, was Avery's, who simply leaned forward, and kissed her square on the mouth again.

Chapter Twenty-six

THEY ALTERNATED BETWEEN ONE another's apartments. On the days when they were at Avery's place, they spent the majority of the time in the studio, Avery drafting ideas and Kadence working on paperwork or wedding tasks. At Kadence's, they would cook together, watch television, or just enjoy the other's company. Occasionally, Avery would dash to the kitchen to grab a napkin to doodle if she suddenly came up with an idea for her showcase, but all in all, things were easy.

"So, how's the speech writing going?" Avery asked as Kadence rounded the couch, handing her a plate. While Kadence settled into the corner of the couch, Avery took a bite of the meal Kadence had prepared. She pulled Kadence's legs into her lap. It was a recently developed habit of theirs that they sought comfort in, partially because Avery loved Kadence's legs, but also because she just liked having Kadence close. She set the plate with her lunch on the armrest, using her left to eat her sandwich while the right rested against Kadence's shins.

Kadence chewed and swallowed before answering. "It's okay." She shrugged, but Avery saw the turmoil behind her eyes. "I keep rewriting it. I just think I'm overthinking it. Every time I think it's good, I come up with something else, or remember that I forgot something and have to rewrite it."

Avery rubbed her knee. "It's a lot of pressure. I

can try to help, if you want. Though I'm not very good at expressing myself unless it's with a paintbrush."

Kadence gave an appreciative smile before her face lit up. "Actually, speaking of, I was thinking…" she trailed off with an impish smile that had Avery both nervous and excited.

"Uhh oh. Don't hurt yourself now," Avery jested lightheartedly.

Kadence balled up her napkin and threw it in Avery's face in retaliation, kicking her feet to nudge Avery in the side. Avery shrieked, squirming as her ribs tingled from her most ticklish area being stimulated.

"Okay! Uncle! I'm sorry, continue."

Kadence gave a satisfied grin as Avery retreated. "As I was saying before I was so rudely interrupted," Kadence rolled her eyes and a gave subtle smile. "I've dragged you to yoga willingly and unwillingly."

"Mostly unwillingly."

"Exactly. So, I was thinking that maybe we could do something more along your line, like…I don't know. I was hoping maybe we could paint together." Green eyes shone with sincerity. "I know it's your thing. And it's personal so I understand if—"

"Yes!"

Kadence's face brightened with eagerness. "Really?"

"Absolutely. Just let me know when and I'll—"

"Does now work?"

Before Avery could reply, Kadence was already swinging her legs off her lap, grabbing both of their plates before leading Avery to her bedroom.

"Wait, aren't we going to my—"

Kadence stood next to an arrangement of newly wrapped canvases, an assortment of paints, brushes, and pallet, all resting on top of a large tarp on the floor.

"Kadence," Avery said breathlessly, in awe from the sweet gesture.

"I know it's not your studio or anything professional, but I just thought you'd like to have some supplies here, too. You know, in case you get inspired. That way you don't have to keep drawing on napkins or searching for random pieces of paper I have lying around the apartment."

The way Kadence chewed her lip was so adorable. Avery's chest swelled. "I...I'm...I..." She fought the three words threatening to blurt from her mouth.

Kadence grinned. "Very articulate. You're right. Words are not your forte."

Avery opted to express her feelings in another way. She stepped toward Kadence, wrapping her in her arms before leaning to press her lips against Kadence's plump ones. The world stopped spinning and her heart pounded against her ribs.

Kadence, having finally recovered from the momentary surprise, moved in tandem, lacing her hands behind Avery's neck. Avery let her fingers trail to the small of Kadence's back, pressing her palms to bring them even closer. When Kadence broke again, she loosened her hold, only to find emerald eyes locked on her.

"Wow." Kadence breathed as the syllable left her tongue. Somehow it was both powerful and gentle at the same time, reverberating in her ear.

"I'm inspired." Avery ran her fingers up and down the ridges of Kadence's spine.

Kadence flushed so red Avery could feel the heat emanating from her cheeks as she pressed her lips to each of them, then her forehead, and finally against her nose. Kadence's arms dropped to encircle her waist.

"We should start while your inspiration is still fresh on your mind."

Avery smiled. *It'll take more than a few seconds for that feeling to disappear.* But she obliged. They changed into some old T-shirts and settled on the floor, legs crossed under them as they start to unwrap the new supplies.

"So, what are you thinking of painting?"

Kadence stared blankly at the vast amount of white space in front of her while Avery, in contrast, had already laid out the entire landscape of her painting.

"I don't know." Kadence tapped her brush against her knee. "You're right. Coming up with ideas is hard."

"Why don't we start with something simple like flowers or a bowl of fruit?"

"Flowers would work."

"Okay, do you have a specific kind in mind?" Avery asked, already pulling out her phone.

Kadence pondered for a moment. "Pink roses."

"All right." Avery searched for a reference photo. She sketched the general form of a rose on Kadence's canvas for her to use as her guide.

"There you go."

After a few minutes, Avery observed Kadence's posture and the frown on her face.

"You all right?"

"Yeah, I just don't think I'm doing this right." The green-eyed beauty shrugged. Avery found herself frowning.

"May I?" Avery tilted her chin at the painting.

"Please." Kadence handed her the brush. Avery shook her head, flipping it back into position and gently readjusting the tool where it rested in Kadence's grip.

She then placed her hand on Kadence's, guiding it to the canvas.

"Don't hold it so tightly. You should hold it kinda loose, but like a pencil. Keep your hand a little higher on the brush." Avery gave a few light strokes with a darker shade of pink. She used her free hand to uncap a bit of maroon and black. She swirled the color until it reached the right hue and consistency before returning their joined hands to the canvas. She used the deep tone to add depth and shadows to the piece.

"Oh, wow! It looks so much better already."

Avery blushed, turning her attention to her own painting, allowing Kadence to experiment with her brush strokes.

After another half hour, Kadence decided to take a break and observe Avery's progress. "I can't believe you did all that in less than an hour! Why doesn't mine look like that?"

"Just need a little more practice," Avery encouraged the sulking beginner.

"Or…" Kadence smirked. "Maybe I just have a crappy teacher who is hiding all her talent for herself."

Avery gasped. "Well, maybe you're just a shitty student."

"No, you are most definitely a shittier student." Kadence laughed, contorting into what was, admittedly, an accurate imitation of Avery attempting to do a basic yoga pose. Kadence wobbled, falling to the floor with a dramatic thud.

"I already told you, I like it on the ground," Avery threw back, pointing her brush at Kadence. Except Kadence moved at the same time to resituate herself, causing the brush to go straight to her face, streaking a deep green line across the rise of her cheekbone.

"Oh," Kadence grinned. "It's so on now."

"Kadence," Avery gasped as Kadence lunged for her. "It was an accident." Her cries went ignored as Kadence wrestled her to the ground. Avery's hat was knocked off as her back hit the floor. Admitting defeat, Avery relented to letting her smear a glob of pink across her forehead.

"There. Now we're even." Kadence grinned, quite pleased with herself.

Avery rolled her eyes before sitting up. Kadence refused to budge from her position, minimizing the distance between their faces, just centimeters apart. Amber eyes tracked between green crystals and inviting pink lips before deciding on the latter. She tucked a fallen strand behind Kadence's ear, cupping Kadence's cheek and bringing them together for a slow and tender kiss. Her thumb glided in the damp paint on her face, and she felt Kadence smile into her mouth.

When they broke apart, it took a moment for either of them to fully open their eyes, blinking slowly. Avery swallowed at the sight of Kadence's heavy lids, holding her gaze as they flickered with flaming adoration.

"You know, paint is a pretty good look on you."

Kadence didn't miss a beat, the corner of her lips tilting to the side. "Maybe, but it's perfect on you."

Avery's simple reply was to kiss until the paint evened out on both sides. Even with the clashing colors across her skin, Avery still found Kadence radiant. In fact, Kadence had never looked more striking than in this moment, truly taking Avery's breath away with her inner and outer beauty.

Chapter Twenty-seven

THE WEDDING VENUE WAS small, and the ceremony was short. A petite brunette walked in first, accompanied by a tall, muscular man. By Kadence's stories, she could only infer that the young girl was Claire, Jordan's baby sister. Next was Talia, based on the process of elimination, with another man, just as built as the first.

Were all of Jordan's friends so jacked? The thoughts evaporated when she saw Danny walking in with Kadence on his arm. Time stood still and her lungs constricted. She looked on in awe with her throat parched and her tongue feeling too loose in her mouth. An elbow to her side caused her to jolt.

"You're drooling," Emma said.

Avery straightened with a scowl, cheeks bright, but she couldn't help it. When Melody was escorted down the aisle by a man with a salt and pepper beard, Avery knew all eyes should be on the woman of the hour, but her eyes keep drifting to Kadence. She couldn't focus on anything else. They say the bride is supposed to be the most beautiful woman in the room, but oh, god. *Kadence.*

You need to keep it together, Bennett. Avery swallowed. As the officiant made his opening remarks, Avery used the time to drink in the maid of honor. The dress was a soft champagne color that hugged her curves in all the right places, a black lace neckline accentuated the gentle slope of her shoulders, and the strapless cut gave Avery a view of far too much skin for her brain to process. With the chandeliers overhead and the dancing crystal reflection in Kadence's eyes, Avery couldn't stop staring.

As the couple exchanged their vows, she found Kadence watching her, tilting her head as if to say 'pay attention.' Avery blushed, turning her focus to Melody, who was currently sniffling through her speech. It was the first time she had witnessed Melody like this. Something about it caused Avery to get teary eyed, as well. The second Melody's voice cracked in the middle of her vows, Avery was a goner, wiping cascading tears from her face. When she finally collected herself enough to look back up again, she found Kadence glancing at her with a tender smile.

When the final "you may now kiss the bride" was spoken, Avery felt the need to shield her eyes. Something about it felt invasive. She had never seen the pair this intimate before. Even when they were camping, it was only subtle touches and occasionally leaning on one another's shoulders. As different as this felt, she couldn't help but love the idea of it, wanting to be able to have something like this, as well.

"Today marks the beginning of a beautiful, young partnership," the officiant said. "In life, in love, and in family. May this ceremony entwine your connection and tie you in a knot that can never be severed. May your hearts be blessed with a love that will last for all of your days."

As the officiant made his closing remarks, amber eyes magnetically found green ones staring right back.

***

The guests transitioned to the reception area. Avery lingered behind with Emma while they waited for their dates to take photos. The shoot consisted of arranging and rearranging the wedding party into as many combinations as possible, adding in a few key family members here and there. Avery sipped a cocktail until the MC announced a five-minute warning for the reception to officially begin. The temporary models dispersed, and the two roommates navigated to their table.

"Hello, everybody. My name is Charlie and it is my honor to be the master of ceremonies for Mr. and Mrs. Hanson," a man with glasses and a pointed nose announced as his microphone echoed from the stage. "Thank you all for joining us on this magical evening when two lovers finally unite! Before we get to the main event, I'd like to introduce you to the people who helped make this possible. Ladies and gentlemen, if you would please turn your attention to the double doors in the back and help give a warm round of applause for the wedding party of Mr. and Mrs. Hanson."

The clapping commenced as he announced the trio of pairs.

"First, let's welcome Ms. Claire Hanson, sister to the groom. Claire is accompanied by Jordan's college roommate and close friend, Alex Oak."

The room applauded as the two entered and proceeded to the front of the room.

"Next up we have another beautiful sister, Talia Hanson, escorted by none other than Jordan's childhood best friend, Nicholas Carpenter."

"And finally, a big round of applause to this dedicated pair who helped put this entire ceremony together on such short notice. Please welcome sister of the bride and maid of honor, Ms. Kadence Cooper, accompanied by Mr. Danny Foster, Jordan's best man."

The room erupted into tumultuous applause and a few loud whistles. Emma, having a few too many drinks, placed two fingers in her mouth and released a whistle shrill enough for Danny to turn crimson. He shook his head with a chuckle. Avery decided to join in, cupping her hands around her mouth, shouting out a rowdy 'hot damn!'

Avery grinned sheepishly as Kadence flushed red.

"That's my date!" She puffed out her chest, pointing at Kadence. A few attendees laughed at her outburst before settling for the final announcement.

"And finally, I would like you to give me your loudest applause for this evening's newlyweds, Melody and Jordan Hanson!" The crowd burst into a chorus of clapping and congratulatory salutes.

"And now," He paused for effect before gesturing to the DJ, "Our couples' very first dance together as newlyweds."

A gentle acoustic guitar played, melodious and sweet as Avery watched Jordan pull Melody close. He placed both hands on her waist as she linked her arms around his neck, swaying to the gentle beat. Despite their rocky beginning, her heart warmed at the sight of Melody smiling as she looked into her husband's eyes. Avery glanced at Kadence to find her own glistening with pure elation as she fought back tears. She looked elated. Avery offered her a wink.

After the song faded, Melody and Jordan resumed their place up at the center of the table in front of their family and friends. As they delivered their welcome speeches and thanked those who had attended, Avery turned her attention to her date. As

Avery studied the glowing figure, Kadence looked up. Like a moth to a flame, Avery was hypnotized. Kadence's lips ticked up, brow raised. But instead of feeling the embarrassment of being caught, Avery copied her expression with a challenge in her eye, daring her to look away. It wasn't until she heard the applause around them, she finally broke contact, ending their little game.

A team of servers soon arrived with plates of food stacked high resting on their shoulders. The crowd began intermingling as the meal progressed. Avery barely got to speak to Kadence before she went to assist Melody with her dress as she and Jordan made their rounds in greeting the guests personally.

Dinner passed in a whirlwind. Before long, Charlie was standing by the DJ's booth again, motioning for Kadence. She took the cue as he passed her a microphone, raising her glass.

"Hello everybody! If I could have your attention." She took her knife, tapping it against the crystal. The room quieted.

"First of all, I want to say again, thank you all for joining us today. It means a lot to me and I know it means even more to Melody and Jordan. Their happiness means the world to me, so I'd like to take a moment to give a toast to my beautiful big sister, who has always been there to take care of me, and her husband, who I know will do the same for her. Melody, you will always be someone that I respect and look up to." She turned to face the couple, locking eyes with her sister.

"And Jordan, the moment I met you, I knew Melody had finally met her match, in more ways than one." She addressed her brother-in-law. "Though your relationship had a rocky, albeit, humorous start, you've come a long way. I remember when Melody first told me about you and your, I quote 'stupidly handsome face' and 'annoying smug grin.'"

The room erupted with laughter. Melody buried her face in her hands while Jordan pecked her cheek, placing an arm around her shoulder.

"I knew from the beginning, you would be the perfect pair of, pardon my French, sassholes. She told me all the stories about your fights and bickering, yet she just couldn't stop talking about you, no matter how much she tried to explain that it was just out of spite. But suddenly, with Jordan in her life, colors were brighter, she laughed a little louder, and smiled just a smidge wider. You have your differences, but in the end, it all works out and, as a result, you're both stronger as individuals, and as a team."

Kadence turned to face the audience. "It's funny, don't you think? It can't be a coincidence that everything we do, when it boils down to it, can be categorized into two things, what we do for love and what love does for us. And most of the time, we hope that those things fall into both buckets." She scanned the room.

"Loving someone is not just about finding them attractive. It's something so much bigger than that, something greater. It's about loving them for who they are. Seeing and appreciating the way that they exist in the world. It's about watching them interact in it, even if it's different from how you would. Because when you love someone, you're simply happy for them the way that they are. And you hope that you can be a part of that." Her eyes met Avery's.

"You'd do anything to see them smile, sacrifice

whatever you have for them. You're vulnerable because of them. *Not* because love leaves you exposed, but because you choose to be. You choose to surrender yourself and give them that piece of you. It's okay to be vulnerable when you find the right person. And it's okay to let someone in. It's your love for them and the trust you share that you hope makes them stronger. And their happiness, in return, makes you strong, too."

Avery was melting. Kadence sent her a smile before returning her attention to the couple.

"Love allows you to build one another up while simultaneously having the power to tear one another down. It's the most terrifying yet rewarding thing. And the payoff at the end is something I hope you two always find worth it. Jordan, Melody, I'm glad you two found one another. And I wish you a lifetime of building, growing, and existing together as Melody and Jordan but also as mister and missus."

As the attendees applauded, Melody, forgoing formalities, rose to her feet and wrapped her sister into a tight hug. Kadence rubbed her back, as the crowd aww-ed at the sibling's touching embrace.

"Come on, you can't smear your makeup." Kadence wiped gently at Melody's tears. "Ladies and gentlemen, I'd like to hand the mic to the best man, Danny. If you'll excuse me, I'm going to find some tissues."

She hopped off stage, handing him the microphone before dashing toward the door.

Danny's speech was the perfect mix of playful and sentimental. But it was the way he concluded it that stole the show. Or maybe that was just Kadence.

"Now, in a traditional wedding, we would normally start with a father daughter dance..."

Melody's eyes widened in apprehension. The room became suffocating.

"But unfortunately, Mr. Cooper couldn't make it." He said with a sad smile. "But though he is no longer with us, we were lucky enough to find a last-minute replacement who was willing enough to step into his shoes, or should I say, suit." He gestured to the back of the room. Kadence stepped out of the shadows and all heads turned in her direction.

The bride's jaw fell open as the room gasped. Melody stumbled to her feet as Kadence met her in the middle of the dance floor. Kadence withdrew a pocket square from a tailored blazer, making a show of straightening out her tie while Danny passed her the mic.

Kadence's heart was so big.

I am so lucky, Avery thought.

"K...Kae..." Melody was speechless.

Kadence responded a gentle smile. "Mel, just because you're a Hanson now doesn't mean we'll ever stop being a family. I know our parents couldn't be here physically, but I know they're here in spirit. And I'm here on their behalf to tell you one thing...that we will always love you, no matter how far apart we may be."

Their pseudo-father-daughter dance was an endearing mess of sobbing and giggling. And by the end of the song, there wasn't a dry eye in the room.

***

"Let me buy you a drink." Avery grinned, finally finding Kadence free of her maid of honor duties. She did her best to play it cool, leaning an elbow on the bar as she gawked at the beauty in front of her. It was the first time she had seen Kadence sitting.

Kadence had been running around doing typical maid of honor duties, refilling glasses, playing hostess, conversing with guests, fixing bobby pins, and readjusting loose strands of hair. It was a wonder Kadence hadn't gotten dizzy from all the circles she'd been running. Despite her eyes growing duller and more muted as the night wore on, Kadence still looked great. Exquisite, even.

"It's an open bar, Avery." Kadence ran her fingers through her hair with a sigh. They caught in a tangle.

"Shh." Avery quipped, pressing her finger to Kadence's lips before reaching out to free the fingers from the small knot. "Just let me have this."

"Okay. Thanks." Kadence's eyes fell to her lips. Avery wanted nothing more than to lean forward and kiss her. But she wasn't sure if she should do so in front of all of her friends and family. Instead, she elected to get Kadence a glass of champagne. They sat in comfortable silence, watching the crowd while Kadence rehydrated and rested her feet.

"So…" Avery bounced her knee, nerves getting the better of her. "Your toast…did you really mean all that or was that just nice wedding fluff?"

Kadence pivoted in her seat to face her, her knees brushing against the exposed skin. "You know I did."

Color rose to her cheeks. "Dance with me?"

They managed to get two songs together before Melody tugged Kadence away to the photo booth. To Avery's surprise, the bride grabbed her wrist as well, dragging them both along as she tore them away from the dance floor.

The first picture they took was relatively normal,

Jordan and Melody sandwiched between Avery and Kadence, flanking them on each side. The next, Kadence suggested should be a silly pose. Just as the camera started counting down, Avery dashed to the bride, smiling devilishly.

Melody read right into her intentions and glared. "Avery Bennett, don't you fucking dare."

Too late. With what little upper body strength Avery had, she attempted to lift the bride, bridal style, of course. Jordan and Kadence quickly caught on, assisting her as they hoisted her into the air. it was a chaotic, fantastic photo. The final picture was of Melody, arms crossed and scowl on her face as she glared daggers at her husband and his sidekicks. Avery paid her no mind, leaning to place a chaste kiss on her date's cheek just the flash went off.

Melody and Jordan placed their copy in the memory binder on the table while Avery and Kadence pocketed theirs. The bride then gave Avery a shove, grumbling at her for almost ruining the dress, but not before Avery caught a hint of a smile on her face. Melody stomped off with Kadence hot on her heels.

"You remind me of myself." Jordan chuckled, nursing his beer. "I used to be a little bit of an ass. You're not as bad though." He laughed. "I mean, I was a total tool. You are just ..."

"Immature." Avery supplied with a defiant grin. "Purposely irritating."

"Your words, not mine." Jordan shrugged, though she caught the slightest uptick of a smile on his face. "She's cool with you, you know?"

"I don't know...she's texted me otherwise."

Jordan lowered the bottle from his lips. "Wow."

"What?" She tilted her head in confusion at his

sudden amusement.

"She definitely likes you." He continued to laugh. "You've known her for how long? Melody wouldn't even give me her number until almost six months after we started talking. I had to email her using our school IDs. Do you know how embarrassing it is to ask a girl out using an email address that you know is going to be screened by every administrator?"

This time, Avery chuckled, clinking her beer with Jordan. "I've made a fool of myself plenty of times for a Cooper girl."

"They sure are something, aren't they?"

"They're pretty special,"

"Can't live with em, can't live without em," Just as the words left Jordan's mouth, Melody emerged from the crowd, overhearing him. She grasped him by the ear with a relaxed tug.

"You're literally moving to another country to live with me. You better be able to live with em," she scolded halfheartedly.

"Ow," Jordan yelped. "Yes, babe. I know. It was a joke."

"Not a funny one," Melody grumbled, giving him another tug.

At the suggestion of living together, Avery found herself imagining a living arrangement with Kadence and startled herself at how easily she could picture it. Kadence knew her way around the apartment. Avery cooked for her. Kadence cleaned. Their belongings were mixed. They shared clothes and stayed the night.

"Hello? Earth to Bennett." Melody waved a hand in front of her. "What are you thinking about?"

She blinked. "Sorry, what?"

Melody rolled her eyes and Jordan gave a

knowing smile.

Luckily, she was saved by her date wrapping her fingers on her bicep. "Sorry about that. After I left with Melody, Jordan's mom found me, and I got caught up in a conversation with her and Claire about some guy. Long story short, there's a big mess of approval and disproval that I don't..." Kadence cut herself off. "Sorry. You don't want to hear about that anyway."

"I like hearing whatever you have to say."

"Yeah, but I've been MIA all night. I'm being such a crappy date even though I'm the one who asked you to come."

As if on cue, Talia came striding toward them, summoning Kadence to the DJ booth.

"Be right there," Kadence assured her sister-in-law before turning her attention back to Avery with a sigh. "And now I have to go again. I'm sorry I've barely spent any time with you tonight."

Avery refused to accept her apology, offering her a warm smile. "Call me sappy, but—"

"Sappy butt," Kadence interjected with an airy giggle, still having enough energy left in her for one last joke.

"Okay. I'll let you have this just once because you're the maid of honor and I know you've been busy."

"Okay, go on. What were you gonna say?"

"That I think I have a pretty good date. And she's been wonderful so far, despite what she may think."

"Yeah? Well, mine is better." Kadence shot forward with a peck to her cheek before dashing off.

***

The reception concluded with cutting the cake,

which took a momentary turn, verging on the edge of a food fight when Melody slapped a sheet of fondant onto Jordan's cheek. The sticky substance got caught in his beard as she cackled madly. When he made to retaliate, Melody ducked, causing the handful of cake to go into his mother's face instead. It was ridiculous. And it was fantastic. All in all, it was a perfect evening and after the grand exit, Avery lingered behind to help with cleaning up and tearing down.

"Avery? What are you still doing here?"

"Emma waited for Danny." Avery shrugged.

"Oh, right. You carpooled." Kadence rubbed at the corner of her eye. "Sorry, I'm a little slow right now."

"Em's driving Danny home. I was hoping that—"

"Yeah. I can give you a ride."

"I wanted to ask if you'd let me drive you home." Avery chewed her lip nervously. "I'll take an Uber to my place afterwards."

Kadence blinked.

"I...umm, I know you've had a long day and you've been up since before dawn," Avery explained, her speech increasing in speed. "And I also know that you always want to drive, which I understand your reasons why, but I would just feel better if I knew that—"

"Okay." She took Avery's hands in her own. "Thank you."

Avery leaned in, brushing their noses together before connecting their lips. It had been hovering for the entire span of the wedding. She relaxed, easing into the kiss that both of them had spent the night craving.

"Stay tonight?"

"I'd love to."

Chapter Twenty-eight

THEY SLEPT SOUNDLY, AT least, until an irritating buzz drew her out of her peaceful slumber. Avery reluctantly withdrew from where her arms had been wrapped around the beautiful woman under the sheets. She propped herself up against the headboard, placing a kiss on Kadence's temple and a whispered apology before answering.

"Hello?" Her voice was still a bit groggy and Kadence moved beside her, reaching out to link their hands.

"You have twenty minutes to get here," Melody threatened on the other side of the line.

Avery rubbed her eyes. "What? Why?"

"Twenty minutes. Come alone." Melody disconnected the call abruptly.

She blinked dumbfounded at her phone.

"Who was that?" Kadence rested her head on Avery's thigh. Avery's fingers stroked through her hair.

"Your sister."

"What did she want?"

"My life, possibly." Avery was only half joking. "She told me to head to her place."

"Okay. When does she need you to come?"

"Well, now, actually." Avery rubbed at the back of her neck. "She said I had twenty minutes or else."

"Or else what?" Kadence snorted, unfazed by her

sister's threat.

"I don't know. The or else was implied."

Kadence chuckled. "You're both so dramatic," she teased, propping herself up onto her knees so she was at eye level with the upright blonde. Avery watched her with curiosity until Kadence leaned in, nose brushing against hers.

"Good morning, Avery," she whispered.

"Good morning, Kadence." Avery parroted before catching her lips. It was languid and lazy, and Avery didn't want the moment to end. But Kadence pushed against her shoulder with a light shove.

"You better get going."

Always the responsible one. "I might not make it back. When you see canned spaghetti, think of me." She threw an arm on her forehead with an exasperated gasp.

Green eyes rolled at her. "You better come back to me," Kadence said firmly before ushering her toward the bathroom with another peck to the cheek.

Avery readied within minutes, changed into a spare set of clothes she had kept at Kadence's place before borrowing Kadence's car to make it to the newly married woman's place.

***

Melody managed to open the door right as Avery lifted her fist to knock against the door, resulting in an incredibly awkward situation where her knuckles made contact with the older blonde's sternum instead. Her eyes widened in alarm.

"Fuck, Melody. I didn't mean to..." Avery flubbed with cherry red cheeks and burning ears.

"Get inside." The unaffected woman rolled her eyes, stepping aside for Avery to enter an apartment full of boxes and shipping supplies.

The second the door closed, she was pulled forward as a set of arms wrapped around her neck, squeezing tightly.

Her brain turned fuzzy. Melody Cooper, or rather Melody Hanson, was hugging her. *You must still be dreaming, Bennett.* She squeezed her eyes shut, but when they reopened, she was still staring at cardboard containers. *Definitely not dreaming.*

When Melody let go, her eyes returned to their dangerous, sharp form. "If you tell anyone what just happened, I will end you."

Avery saluted with a nod. "Fully noted."

"Good," the woman replied gruffly, stepping to place some distance between them again.

"Melody?"

"What?"

"Umm, what was that for?"

The woman gestured down the hall, at the unwrapped canvas leaning against the wall. Avery hadn't noticed it when she walked in.

"Oh."

"And for everything else," Melody added a moment later. "Kae's happier than I've seen her in years."

Avery blushed, comprehending the massive weight of the implication. It was a big deal. Not only for Melody to thank her personally, but for everything Kadence and Avery had become. The pink in her cheeks deepened to a scarlet flush.

"I was worried about Kae being the only Cooper left, but the reality of it doesn't feel as daunting anymore. I think she's ready for a new chapter in her life and you better make sure it's a damn good one to read." Melody tilted her chin to the couch.

Avery shuffled off her shoes, leaving them neatly by the door. She could imagine how Kadence would be laughing at her sudden change in character as she attempted to impress her sister.

"You know, there was a point in time when I hated you."

"Oh, trust me. I know." Avery frowned. "But now...?" She nudged Melody in the side.

"Don't push it."

Avery held up her hands in defense. "Okay, okay."

The slightest uptick of Melody's lips eased her doubts, though she may not have spoken it out loud.

"In all seriousness, I hated me, too, back then," Avery said levelly. "I was in a bad place and I know that's no excuse. But I'm glad Kadence gave me a second chance."

Melody nodded. "She's a good person. Sometimes too good of a person."

"I'd attest to that." Avery chuckled. "Like you said, she's too good for me." She recalled their first confrontation along the muddy hiking trail.

Melody's lips pressed into a thin, restrained smile, but it was genuine enough for Avery to consider it a win.

"Yeah," Melody agreed with a hum. She looked around the apartment in its scattered state, releasing a sigh. Avery saw the bittersweet feelings swirling in her eyes. She truly was Kadence's sister, both of them having incredibly expressive eyes that spoke the most telling thoughts when their voices failed to do so out loud.

"I promise." Avery held up a hand in pledge. "I promise to take care of her for you. I know I'm not perfect. But I do care about her. I lo—" she caught herself just as Melody's eyes darted up.

Avery swallowed. "I just mean I'll do my best not to mess up. I want to treat her right. Kadence deserves it."

Melody nodded in approval. "She does."

A pause fell between them, a lull in the conversation. In her eyes, Avery saw Melody turning the next words she wanted to say.

"You, too."

Avery found herself speechless as the two simple words tumbled from Melody's lips. Thankfully, Melody appeared unfazed by her having gone quiet and instead shrugged. "You should get back."

Avery tilted her head in confusion, still not fully recovered from the heartfelt words that Melody so sparingly used.

"You were at her place this morning, weren't you?"

Avery bit her lip, unable to deny the accusation.

"Get to cuddling with my sister," Melody said. "I have a hubby to attend to. It's honeymoon time."

That did not end as badly as Avery had thought.

***

When she returned to Kadence's apartment, she placed the keys on the counter, making sure to slip back into the bedroom as quietly as possible. She found Kadence, who had since fallen back asleep, with her face buried under the covers and just her nose and closed eyes peeking from the edge of the blanket.

Avery padded to the bed, wrapping herself around the human heater.

"Mmm, hi," Kadence mumbled with a lazy smile as she shuffled closer to press into Avery's chest. "That was fast."

Avery nodded. "You told me to come to you. And here I am."

Kadence giggled into her neck as they both settled into one another comfortably, releasing a contented sigh. For a moment, Avery felt her heart about to burst, loving the feeling of Kadence next to her. Loving Kadence next to her.

She reached out to trace her thumb along the bottom of Kadence's pouty bottom lip.

"What are you doing?" Kadence whispered, eyes still closed.

"Nothing." She trailed back the other direction, applying the slightest bit of weight from her hand, causing her lips to follow her movements. "Go to sleep."

Kadence parted her lips, catching Avery's thumb, nibbling it playfully before releasing it with a smile. Green eyes exploded in brilliant forest hues of magnificent trees and grassy meadows.

"Can I paint you?" Avery found herself blurting as she drowned in the ethereal woman by her side. Kadence grinned, rolling onto her side to prop herself on her elbow, lips hovering as she waited for Avery to close the distance.

After admittedly too much procrastinating (kissing) they finally set up a tarp and Avery helped Kadence position herself into a comfortable, yet artistic pose. Avery gazed at the woman, studying her form.

Everything from the joint of her wrist to the angle of her jawline all the way up to the sparkle in her emerald eyes. Everything about Kadence was perfect.

Chapter Twenty-nine

KADENCE LOVED WATCHING AVERY work, brows stitched as she concentrated, paint-stained T-shirt hanging from her shoulders, and pallet in hand. She was so enraptured in her element, that she didn't even notice her own stomach grumbling. But Kadence heard it loud and clear amongst their comfortable silence.

"Do you wanna take a break and eat something?"

No response. An absorbed Avery's tongue poked between her lips as she continued with broad brush strokes and a steady hand. Her amber eyes tracked the lines she was creating.

"Avery?" Kadence tried again, attempting to lure the concentrating blonde to the present so she could attend to her stomach's needs. "You want some lunch?"

Silence again. She chuckled. Maybe a pet name.

"Want me to make you canned spaghetti, babe?"

Still nothing. She shook her head, walking to Avery whose eyes were glued to the canvas. She placed a hand on Avery's shoulder and the artist jolted, pallet clattering onto the ground, skirting down her lap in the process. The brush went flying. Kadence fought off laughter as Avery flailed.

"Fuck!"

"Sorry." Kadence hid a giggle behind her hand, squatting to pick up the fallen brush and pallet, placing them on the table to Avery's side. "I was just trying to get your attention. You were in the zone."

"You scared the shit outta me."

"Oh, really?" Kadence leaned to gaze around at Avery's backside. "Let's see it then."

"What?" A wrinkle formed between Avery's brows.

"The shit I scared out of you." Kadence grinned.

Avery groaned. "You're disgusting, Cooper."

"Thank you." Kadence laughed, puffing out her chest with pride.

"I hate you."

"No, you don't."

"Fine, I don't. But you still made me look like an idiot." Avery crossed her arms, wiping at the acrylic residue.

"Yeah?" Kadence grabbed the tattered cloth to her side, assisting the artist in cleaning up the mess streaked across her legs. "Who do you have to impress?"

"Oh, you know…" Avery mused with a sly grin. "Just some girl that I'm friends with."

"Just friends, hmm?" Kadence took a step closer.

"Well, we do kiss sometimes." Avery leaned in.

"And how's that working for you?"

"Good." Avery's mouth was millimeters away. Kadence could feel the breath from her lips intermingling with her own.

"Just good?"

Avery pulled back. "What do you mean?"

Realizing the misconstrued implication, she clarified. "Why not make it more?" Emerald eyes dropped to rose petal lips.

"Kadence?"

"Don't you wanna be more than friends?"

Kadence couldn't believe she was doing this. Here. Now. So spontaneously and wildly. She never would have thought she would ever get to this point again. And definitely not without a plan or a grand gesture to accompany it. But this was Avery. And everything with Avery was wild, spontaneous, and full of color. *There's no turning back now.* "Girlfriends, Avery."

"Are you...?" A grin spread across Avery's features. It only served to make her even more endearing. "Kadence Cooper, are you asking me to be your girlfriend?" she inquired with a light-hearted arrogance.

"I might be." Kadence stole Avery's hat off her head and placed it on her own, snapback spun backwards.

Avery laughed, kissing her.

Finally. "So, is that a yes?" Kadence smiled when they broke apart. "Are you my girlfriend now?"

A playful glimmer flashed behind amber eyes before she responded with a mischievous grin. "I might be."

Kadence rolled her eyes before grabbing Avery's collar and pulling her to her lips, finding it too difficult to properly kiss her girlfriend because neither of them could stop smiling. If someone were to ask if she was in love with Avery Bennett, she would have one response. She might be.

***

Kadence left the yoga studio a few days later and was surprised to find a woman with damp golden curls waiting outside her apartment. "Avery?" She squinted into the pouring rain at her soggy girlfriend. "What are you doing outside? Are you trying to catch a cold?" She unlocked the door, ushering Avery inside.

"No. But I wouldn't mind catching something else." She snaked her hands around Kadence's waist, pulling her close.

It was a bit awkward with her bag slung on her shoulder, but being in Avery's hold felt safe, and Kadence was not about to deprive herself of that. Even if it meant that the water from Avery's soaked attire was seeping into her own.

"Oh, yeah?" Kadence bit her lip lustfully as she concentrated her attention on Avery's amber eyes, and not her transparent T-shirt. "So, then what are you trying to catch?"

"Your eye."

Kadence chuckled unexpected at the response, unraveling herself as she set her things down, motioning for Avery to follow. They moved down the hall where Kadence retrieved two towels from the closet, wrapping one around Avery's soaking shoulders before cloaking herself.

Avery toweled off her hair as Kadence gestured for her to remove her wet clothing and set them in the hamper. She did the same as well until they were standing in nothing but their undergarments. They crawled under the sheets to warm themselves, tangling their legs and hooking their ankles.

"Okay. You've got my eye," Kadence said, recalling their previous conversation. "What next?"

"Well." Avery paused. "I was thinking...maybe I could take you out on a real date?"

"We could make it official?" She scooted closer. "Kiss? We could go dancing? Or kiss? Or maybe if you want, we could stay in watch a movie and I'll cook? Kiss a little?" She grinned.

"Or if that's not to your fancy, we could paint something together. I don't know. Did I mention kissing as an option? Because that's definitely a possibility." Avery was now close enough to brush her nose against Kadence's.

Kadence chuckled, pressing a chaste kiss to her lips. "You're such a dork. I can't believe that's how you got girls to fall for you." She rolled her eyes, but indulged Avery's pursed lips, peppering feather-light kisses on them.

"To be fair they didn't fall for me." Avery shrugged, rolling onto her elbows so she was lying with her chest on Kadence's, the comforting weight blanketing her with warmth. "They just...fell into bed with me."

Kadence snorted. "Fell into bed with you." She rolled her eyes as she raised a brow incredulously between their almost naked bodies.

Avery laughed. "Okay. I see your point."

Kadence loved the way her husky breath beat against her skin. "For the record, I fell in both ways."

"Both ways?" Avery asked teasingly. "You're bi now. I'll have to update my records."

Kadence poked her side in retaliation. Avery squeaked, squirming on top of her. Kadence took advantage of the moment, quickly reversing their positions.

"You know what I meant." She pinned Avery under her.

"Yeah." Avery spoke playfully before lowering her voice. "I was just hoping to hear you say it."

Kadence softened. She dipped her head down, fingers pressed into Avery's waist. "I'm falling for you,

Avery Bennett." Her heart thrummed as the words left her lips. In their tightly pressed position, she could feel Avery's heart beating just as quickly.

"I'm falling for you, too."

Chapter Thirty

KADENCE'S HEART WAS RACING. Logically, she knew it shouldn't be and she had no real reason to be this anxious. She saw Avery all the time. But this was their first official date as a couple, and she had no idea what to expect. Avery had done an irritatingly great job of remaining tight-lipped about the entire plan for the evening. The only tip Kadence managed to weasel out was that she should dress comfortably, which wasn't much to go by.

She decided on a simple skater skirt, tucking a soft pastel top into the waistline. She fastened a loose, thin belt around her middle before flipping her hair once more. Just as she was satisfied with her appearance, a knock resounded on the apartment door.

She smiled, heart skipping as she answered. Avery was wearing a pair of black leather shorts and white tank top. It was not her usual attire, but Kadence could definitely appreciate the change, eyes trailing down Avery's smooth legs until they fell to her black sneakers, laces undone. She giggled, enjoying the small sense of familiarity as she kneeled, slender fingers working quickly to tie the strands back into place. When she stood, meeting her girlfriend's gaze, she noticed Avery's amber eyes had darkened.

"Sorry," Avery said with a bashful pink in her cheeks. "I'm a mess." She shook her head to ward off what Kadence could only assume was a lustful thought.

"Yeah." Kadence smiled. "But I like it."

The red deepened. "You look really nice," Avery complimented her with a bite of her lip as she shamelessly scanned Kadence's figure.

"So, do you." Kadence invited herself into Avery's personal space, catching her bottom lip between her own.

Avery groaned. "Nooo. If we start, I'm not going to be able to focus."

Kadence chuckled, wrapping her hands around Avery's waist, pecking her nose. "Okay, okay. I'm sorry. What's the plan?"

"Well, I was thinking we could take a little walk to dinner. I have a nice little reservation set up."

"Do you?" Kadence raised a brow suspiciously. "And where might that be?"

"Not far."

"But aren't you gonna tell me where?" She leaned in again, batting her eyes with an innocent jut of her bottom lip.

A flash of Avery's resolve wavered in her eyes. Avery whined. "Kadence!"

"Okay, okay. Lead the way."

Avery took her by the hand, not letting go of her gentle grip until they arrived at their destination.

***

"Hello. I'm Ryan and I'll be your server tonight. And may I just say that you are the most..." He paused to glance into the pocket of the apron that was tied around his neck.

"I mean...you are the most beautiful and

breathtaking person in the world. Avery is very lucky to have you as her date this evening," the boy recited, shooting Avery a grin as he poured them each a glass of sparkling cider from a picnic basket.

Avery must have already dropped it off before she picked up Kadence. She gave him a thumbs up. Kadence nudged Avery with a kick under the table.

The swing set had been redecorated with battery powered fairy lights, hanging from the top beam and woven around the handles of the swings they were now sitting on. Avery had also managed to set up a collapsible table for their dining experience, complete with cutlery and glasses.

"For tonight's main course, we have a lovely rosemary and garlic chicken, seasoned with extra virgin olive oil, lemon zest, wine, and the chef's secret ingredient."

Kadence pretended to listen to the recitation with rapt attention. But she found her eyes drifting toward the woman sitting across from her.

"So how much are you paying him?" she asked when Ryan skittered off to bring them their meal from wherever the picnic supplies were hidden.

"Psh, what? Ryan is doing this because he adores me and would do absolutely anything for me."

"Mmhmm." Kadence rolled her eyes. "Hey, Ryan," she called out to the bushes. A few moments later, a freckled face emerged.

"Yes, Miss Cooper?"

"How much is Avery paying you to do this?"

"Uhh." He looked hesitant between the couple, finally catching something in Avery's eye that decided his answer. "Nothing. I'm doing this because...you deserve the best?"

Kadence snorted as Avery beamed.

"What if I told you I'd double it?"

His jaw dropped. He looked to Avery, eyes pleading for some sort of out.

"When you double zero, you still get zero," Ryan replied eventually.

Kadence threw her head back in laughter.

"Well played, kid," Avery complimented, hitting Kadence with a smug smile.

Kadence shook her head, allowing him to finish his tasks, but not before subtly slipping a ten-dollar bill into his front apron pocket.

After delivering their food, Avery sent him off with a ruffle to his hair and a quick hug. She whispered something into his ear, and he grinned with nod. She also caught Avery sliding a twenty-dollar bill of her own into his apron. Kadence didn't mention it, offering a farewell wave to the youngster as he departed.

The meal itself, starting from the appetizer all the way to dessert, was phenomenal, which still somehow came as a surprise to Kadence. She knew Avery was an exceptional cook, but her own dietary habits suggested otherwise.

***

They concluded dinner with an easy stroll across cobbled streets. Rainbows dancing in the water fountain in the square reflected the dusk of the sunset. They sat on the ledge, Kadence's head resting on Avery's shoulder as she traced patterns on her arm as they watched the sky fill with stars.

"I know I'm not good at doing fancy things, but I hope you had a good time," Avery said when they returned to Kadence's apartment.

"I didn't have a good time."

Avery's shoulders fell.

Kadence took a step forward, hand cupping Avery's cheek. "I had a wonderful time."

Avery grinned from ear to ear, slithering her hands around Kadence's waist. One kiss led to a second. And the second led to a third. And a third led to a question.

"Do you want to spend the night?"

"I don't put out on the first date," Avery said. "But a few kisses won't hurt." Avery brushed the hair from her neck, placing a chaste kiss at the base of her skull.

"Sure, just kissing," Kadence purred.

By some miracle, they managed to find their way to the bedroom without injury or separating from one another's grasp. Lost in the feeling of fingers combing through hair, breathy sounds escaped their lips.

"What are we doing?" Avery panted as they fell onto the bed in a tangle of limbs. Her lips were swollen, pupils dilated, and her hips were starting to roll against Kadence's thigh.

"I don't know." All Kadence knew was that Avery was under her and it felt really, really good. "Do you wanna stop?" Avery's hips rose against Kadence's thigh involuntarily causing both of them to moan.

"God, no." Kadence pressed down. "Tell me what you like," she whispered in Avery's ear.

"I like you," Avery said earnestly causing Kadence to chuckle. She nibbled Avery's collarbone, eliciting a low groan and a jolt of her hips.

"Biting." Kadence nodded. "Noted."

Before taking off their clothes, Avery halted her

hands. "Kadence, wait…"

Kadence froze after propping herself on her hands. "Are you okay?"

"Yeah. I'm great. Just…if anything doesn't feel right, or you're uncomfortable, just tell me, okay? We can stop if…"

"Avery Bennett." Kadence cut her off with a lighthearted roll of her eyes. "If you don't kiss me right now, I swear…"

Avery grinned and pressed her lips against Kadence's with willing obligation.

***

"You, Kadence Cooper, are ridiculously sexy," Avery said, rolling onto her back to lie next to her girlfriend atop the ruffled sheets.

"You're not too bad yourself." Kadence smiled, before surprising Avery by finding a second wind, pinning Avery's hands above her head. She gazed hungrily at Avery's figure— creamy skin, wild hair, and glowing cheeks. She hovered micrometers above her mouth.

"Fuck me," Avery gasped, turned on yet again.

"I mean, I just did." Kadence captured her lips in a heady kiss. "But I'd gladly do it again."

Avery shook her head. "I'm happy just doing this." She opened her arms for Kadence, the mood easily transitioning between lustful to domestic.

"Okay." Kadence placed a kiss atop her breast, right above her beating heart.

Avery's finger drew lazy patterns on her back as she yawned, body spent and heart satiated. "That was better than any sex I've ever had."

"Yeah?" Kiss-bruised lips tilted to the side in her signature smirk.

"Don't get cocky." Avery arched to give her chest a jerk causing Kadence to wobble.

"I'm not." Kadence laughed, waiting for Avery to settle before resituating herself into the previous position. Her fingers skimmed along Avery's jaw.

"Hmm." Avery threaded her fingers through Kadence's waves, combing the wild sex hair. "Do you know why it was better than sex?"

A sparkle danced in Avery's eyes as she nodded. She placed a kiss to Kadence's knuckles, palm, and finally her wrist.

"Because it wasn't just sex." Avery's eyes filled with enough affection for Kadence to drown in time after time. "We..." She giggled, burying her face in the sheets.

"We made love," Kadence finished for her.

"Yes, we did," Avery agreed. "I love you, Kadence Cooper."

Her heart soared. "I love you, too, Avery Bennett."

"Wanna make love to me again?"

Kadence grinned as she moved to straddle her waist. "Gladly."

***

Kadence woke up to Avery gone and a terrible wave of anxiety washed across her. She frowned, throwing the sheets off her body before scurrying around the room to pick up the discarded articles of clothing from the night before. Just as she was about to grab her T-shirt dangling precariously from the desk chair, she caught a glimpse of a bright sticky note.

> *Kae,*
> *Didn't want to wake you. I'm in the living room.*
> *Avery* ♥

She sighed in relief, slipping on a T-shirt before retrieving the fallen snapback she had knocked off Avery's curls in her eagerness. She smiled to herself, placing it on her head for safekeeping. Her heart fluttered at the sight of Avery sitting cross legged on the floor, bedhead tied into a messy bun. She had one of Kadence's button-ups draped across her shoulders, buttons undone. Kadence's stomach somersaulted.

"I hope you don't mind." Avery looked up from her makeshift workspace. "I may have gotten some paint on it." She looked down at herself. Sure enough, a small drop of acrylic paint made its mark on the left breast pocket.

Kadence chuckled, shaking her head before approaching. She pointed her finger in the small spot, smearing it into a sad excuse for a finger-painted heart. Avery didn't seem bothered by her subpar artistry. "I don't mind," Kadence said, kissing soft golden curls as she settled beside her. "What are you working on?"

Avery had managed to drag some supplies from the bedroom without waking Kadence from her slumber. The blank canvases that were normally stashed against her dresser were now propped against the coffee table, streaming with lively colors.

"Another painting for the new gallery exhibit," Avery said cryptically as she gestured to the stockpile around them. "It's more of a series though, I guess."

Kadence took a moment to observe them. One by

one, she recognized them. Her eyes welled with tears she was met with reflections of herself, her profile, various angles of her form, and her wrist with flecks of gold and intricate patterns shaded into her skin.

She gasped. "Is that...are these all of me?"

Avery nodded, handing her a small index card where she had written the title of the collection.

Making _____

Kadence cocked a brow, confused by the blank space. "Am I supposed to...?"

"Turn it over."

Kadence read the subheading with a bit of difficultly, tears clouding her vision.

There are two things in this world that I want to do endlessly, make love and make art. And with you, they are one and the same.

She surged forward, only to be stopped by the rim of the snapback bumping into Avery's forehead. "Sorry." She giggled.

Avery looked back at her with adoration, removing the cap and setting it on the table. "Now, where were we?"

Kadence tugged her by the collar, properly connecting their lips.

"Good morning, Avery."

"Good morning, Masterpiece."

"You're such a sap," Kadence accused, though her cheeks were now aflame.

"Only for you." Avery placed the cap back on Kadence's head. "Don't tell anyone else though."

"I don't think I have to." Kadence tilted her chin at the paintings scattered around them.

"Touché." Avery chuckled. "I guess I'll bend the rules for you."

"Care to bend for me in other ways?"

"What?"

Kadence burst into laughter, mischievous demeanor falling away. "Yoga, Avery. I'm talking about yoga."

"You did that on purpose."

"I did. But for the record, you're my exception, too. And I'd bend for you," she said with a wink before sauntering into the kitchen to make breakfast.

She only managed to crack one egg before a pair of paint stained hands snaked around her waist.

"Breakfast can wait," Avery whispered in her ear. "Let's work on my flexibility."

Kadence laughed, following her girlfriend back into the bedroom.

Truth be told, they did a lot of bending after that.

Author's Note

To those who know the inspiration for the novel, may these two lovers continue to live on.

And to those who do not, I hope this new story brought a smile to your face. No matter where you're going, or where you're coming from, remember that your experiences should shape who you are, not hinder who you want to be.

May each and every one of you find that person that makes you bend over backwards, question everything you thought you knew, laugh until you cry and cry until you start to laugh. But most of all, I hope that person is so special that you realize you could never live without them. And that they cannot live without you.

About Jessica Yeh

As a little girl, Jessica Yeh had always expressed her thoughts was through pencil and paper. Jessica attended the Pennsylvania State University, graduating as a Dean's List Scholar with a Bachelor of Arts in Advertising. Two years later, she began writing her debut novel, *Something Tragic*. Shortly after completing the manuscript in 2017, she was signed under Desert Palm Press. She now resides in California where she works in as a creative marketing specialist. When she's not working, she spends her free time immersing herself in any and all creative outlets including drawing, painting, music, and more.

Contact info

Email: heyjayjay@gmail.com

Facebook: jessicayehwrites

Note to Readers:

Thank you for reading a book from Desert Palm Press. We have made every effort to edit this book. However, typos do slip in. If you find an error in the text, please email lee@desertpalmpress.com so the issue can be corrected.

We appreciate you as a reader and want to ensure you enjoy the reading process. We would like you to consider posting a review on your preferred media sites and/or your blog or website.

For more information on upcoming releases, author interviews, contest, giveaways and more, please sign up for our newsletter and visit us as at Desert Palm Press: www.desertpalmpress.com and "Like" us on Facebook: Desert Palm Press.

Bright Blessings

www.ingramcontent.com/pod-product-compliance
Lightning Source LLC
Chambersburg PA
CBHW07084326062
47170CB00007B/2485